Advance Praise

Imagine a soft-boiled twist on detective Sam Spade as a liberal alcoholic female social worker and you'll begin to get a sense of the originality of Sylvia Jensen, the dysfunctionally unstoppable protagonist of Dorothy Van Soest's new novel *At the Center*. With moments of heart-pounding tension and others of heart-breaking poignancy, the tale follows Jensen's guilt-ridden mission to expose and right the terrible injustices of a child-welfare system more concerned with self-protection than protecting the children under its care—who are turning up dead. The fast-moving plot and sharply drawn political and moral conflicts grabbed me by the heart and dragged me through to its surprising conclusion.

> —Shawn Lawrence Otto, award-winning author of *Sins of Our Fathers*

The violent death of a small child and plight of innocents enmeshed in a broken foster care system set the stage for this bold page-turner. Through rich, complex characters and compelling storyline, the author binds us in themes that raise our hackles, break our hearts and has us cheering for the flawed heroine whose search for hope and justice crisscrosses five generations. If you're a reader who demands substance and depth with great storytelling, don't miss this one. It kept me awake for three nights so plan your days accordingly.

—Hal Zina Bennett, bestselling author of *Write From the Heart: Unleashing the Power of Your Creativity*

At the Center is an engaging read that had me guessing until the end. Dorothy Van Soest has managed to take a very complex and emotionally charged set of issues and weave them into a story that honors the real lives of people touched, and sometimes mauled, by the child welfare system.

—Terry Cross, Director, National Indian Child Welfare Association

At the Center is a mystery novel that completely engages you as it weaves and resolves a set of facts and intertwining stories. As a lifetime social worker, I know that foster care is a mystery to nearly everyone outside the system. Dorothy Van Soest does a beautiful job of illuminating policy and practice issues that effect abused and neglected children and their families. Readers will come to understand some of the complex factors in child protection as the mystery unfolds.

—Janis Avery, CEO, Treehouse

At the Center grabs your heart early as it leads you on the neverending cultural clash that exists in our country. You will not want to set this book down until you have read it to the end.

—Roy I. Rochon Wilson, Honorary Chief and Spiritual
Leader, Cowlitz Indian Tribe

No stranger to the child welfare system, Van Soest has written
a page-turner that weaves many important themes into a novel
that sometimes reads like an expose. The system is flawed, but
the author manages to capture different points of view in an
engaging and interesting saga.

—Pamela Lowell, LICSW, Author, *Returnable Girl* and
Spotting for Nellie

Van Soest's experience as a writer, social worker, political activist and university professor come together in *At the Center* to
plunge you into the underpinnings of a broken system. Her
familiarity with the complex system of child protection, foster
care and adoption, as well as the legal issues involved in the
Indian Child Welfare Act (ICWA), is apparent in the way she
has crafted a mystery that will keep you guessing until the very
end. For me, as a social worker who has worked in child protection and trained staff on the legal requirements of ICWA, *At the
Center* was a heartbreaking read. As an avid fan of mysteries, I
could not put the book down until I had finished the very last
page!

—Yvonne Chase, PhD, LCSW, University of Alaska
Anchorage

At the Center, a bold and courageous novel that tackles the difficult issues confronting the child welfare system, speaks in considerable depth to the question of 'what is in the best interest of
a child' and how that plays out in the context of a native child.
It is told through the voice of a tired social worker that carries

considerable trauma from her years of social work practice. She joins an investigative journalist to expose the facts of a child's death and in the process finds inner peace and purpose. In the telling of the story, Dorothy Van Soest brings to life characters that have depth, compassion, human failings and values, in a masterful way. This is a very good read.

—Uma Ahluwalia, Child Welfare Professional

At The Center is a compelling and multi-layered page-turner. Through her story revolving around a Native American child caught in the foster care system, Van Soest manages to entertain as she enlightens on how culture, history, identity and institutions interact in often-tragic ways.

—Robin DiAngelo, author, *What Does it Mean to Be White: Developing White Racial Literacy*

At the Center provides valuable insights into an important area of child welfare practice-American Indian child welfare (ICWA). This mystery novel illuminates some of the influences that impact worker's decisions and relays the complex, multi-layered effects of removing Indian children from their families and communities. While not providing any answers, the engrossing stories of two American Indian boys will get you thinking.

—Priscilla Day, Department Chair, Social Work and Director, Center for Regional and Tribal Child Welfare Studies, and Anne Tellett, Assistant Professor, Department of Social Work, University of Minnesota Duluth

At the Center is a mystery novel filled with drama and surprises that make it impossible to put down. The interconnected stories of two American Indian boys provide one of the most powerful portrayals of the intricacies of the child welfare system that I have ever seen. This is a must read book for child welfare practitioners, students, educators, and just anyone interested in a powerful story of family relationships.

> —Ruth McRoy, Professor, Boston College School of Social Work

At The Center

...come now? If so could I blame her but happened so long ago shape a life as profoundly as they helped mine?

J. B. returned with a pitcher of ice water and started to pour some into my glass. I glanced over his shoulder at the twinkling lights in the buildings across the street.

"Maybe there are some things you can never get over," I said, still looking out the window. "Maybe some things you never should get over, like what happened to Anthony Hightower. Maybe the only thing any of us can do is try to make up in the future for what we got wrong in the past. But do you think that's enough? Can anything ever be enough?"

I turned my face away from the window and toward J. B. He appeared to be lost in thought as he refilled his glass.

"We do some good," I continued. "We protect a lot of kids, but we make mistakes, too, sometimes deadly ones, and there's just no way to make up for those."

"I guess life's contradictions have a way of balancing out, other ones over time," he said wistfully.

"Do you have any regrets?" I asked toward the end. "Of anything you've done?"

I expected him to give me his usual "don't-pry" look, but instead he walked over to his desk and came back carrying a framed photo. He opened it so it was facing me and pointed to a black and white picture.

"Cute. How old were you?"

I hear back, being in love...

At The Center

Dorothy Van Soest

Apprentice House
Loyola University Maryland
Baltimore, Maryland

First Edition

Printed in the United States of America

Paperback ISBN: 978-1-62720-063-9
E-book ISBN: 978-1-62720-064-6

Design by Rory Nachbar

Published by Apprentice House

Apprentice House
Loyola University Maryland
4501 N. Charles Street
Baltimore, MD 21210
410.617.5265 • 410.617.2198 (fax)
www.ApprenticeHouse.com
info@ApprenticeHouse.com

"Humankind has not woven the web of life. We are but one thread within it. Whatever we do to the web, we do to ourselves. All things are bound together. All things connect." - Chief Seattle

PROLOGUE

The boy had no idea he was about to die. He sat on the floor next to the train set he was told to play with until dinnertime, moving the little metal engine, the passenger cars, and the yellow caboose back and forth on the track and digging his bare toes into the brown carpet to feel how soft and thick it was. He reached for two police cars in the box off to the side and put them in the middle of the round train track, had them start to chase each other. Then he glanced up at the books, games, and puzzles on the bookshelf along the playroom wall, and he dropped the cars back into the box. He hadn't been told to play with them, or if he could touch them even. He didn't know if the police would come back if he did.

No one had told him yet what he'd done wrong, but it must have been something really bad for the police to come and take him away. He'd never stolen anything. He was sure about that. Except for the one time he brought his friend Kenny's baseball home, but that was by mistake and he gave it back the next day. Even Kenny knew he didn't steal it, he said so himself.

"You okay up there, Tony?"

"Yes," he said in barely a whisper. His name wasn't Tony, it was Anthony, but if he didn't answer the lady would come upstairs to check on him. The lady had told him to call her Mom. The other lady, who brought him here, had told him her real name. But he couldn't remember, so he didn't call her anything.

"Tony?"

"Yes," he said, a little louder.

It didn't bother Anthony that the lady's brown hair was so thin he could see through it down to her scalp, or that her pale skin was so transparent he could see the veins underneath. What did bother him was that sometimes he didn't know what she was saying. Like when she said "You'll be safe now" when he first got here. And the way she watched him, always watched him. She kept asking him if he was having fun and she jumped up at meals to give him more food before his plate was empty, and whenever he nodded she smiled so big all her teeth showed.

He looked through the glass doors that went out to a small balcony outside the playroom. The sun was hiding behind the top of the tallest pine tree in the backyard. He'd been here three days now, long enough to know that meant in a little while the lady would start rattling pans down in the kitchen. He pushed the train off the track so it made a little noise but not too much.

Then he heard heavy footsteps above his head. That's how he knew the man was still upstairs. That morning before breakfast, Anthony was sitting on his bed waiting for the lady to call him down to eat when the man stopped outside his door and looked in on him. The girl with a room at the end of the hall stood behind him, watching.

"Mornin', Anthony," the man said, all friendly-like.

Anthony kept his eyes down and picked at the tufts of the blue cover on his bed.

"I see the cat's still got your tongue," the man said with the smile that didn't match his eyes. Then he looked down at the cell phone in his hand and went upstairs.

Every morning the man went upstairs, and he stayed there until dinnertime, so quiet no one would know he was in the house except for the floorboards creaking every now and then. He was a big man with muscles on his upper arms that bulged out under the long-sleeved white shirt he wore every day. Like he was going to someplace fancy. Anthony didn't know what the man did upstairs all day, but at dinner he talked a lot about houses and buildings and stuff that no one else acted interested in. When he yelled sometimes his sharp voice hurt Anthony's ears, but he didn't dare cover them when the man was looking.

"Cindy," the lady called up the stairs, "time to help with dinner."

Anthony looked out into the hall, hoping to catch a glimpse of the girl. She had curly brown hair and skin that reminded him of milk. He liked her. She smiled at him a lot but she didn't talk to him, at least not yet. What he liked most about her was the way she curled her lips down in a pout and made her face go crooked, like that morning at breakfast.

———

"Tony, honey," the lady said, like she did every morning, "how about some bacon and eggs this morning? We've got to put some fat on those bones of yours."

Anthony nodded without thinking.

"Mom," the girl said, "Deedee's having a party on Saturday night."

"Do you like your eggs scrambled like they're all mixed

together, Tony?"

"I'm going. To Deedee's party."

"Scrambled then, okay?"

"*Mom*, I'm talking to you." The girl banged her spoon on the side of her glass and the orange juice jiggled and some of it spilled onto the table.

"I know, Cindy. I already told you that fourteen is too young for boy-girl parties. We'll talk about it later."

That's when the girl curled her lips down into that pout and tapped her feet on the floor.

"I'm going," she said.

Anthony looked at her long legs and wondered if he would ever get that tall. He counted on his fingers from seven up to fourteen to see how many years it was before he would be as old as her. When the girl noticed him counting she smiled at him in that way of hers that made him wriggle in his seat, and he didn't know whether he should smile back or not so he looked down at the table.

——

Anthony pushed his shoulder-length black hair behind his ears and watched for the girl now, hoping she would stop and say hi to him on her way downstairs.

"Cindy! Now!"

Her door opened at the end of the hall and slammed shut with a loud bang. The girl did stop outside the door to the play-room, just as Anthony had hoped she would. She smiled at him, only for a second, and he looked up at the cat's tail ticking back and forth on the clock on the wall that looked like it had been there forever.

——

The next time Anthony looked out the glass doors he saw
that the sun was gone and the balcony was in the shade. It would
be dinnertime soon. He stood up, went out onto the balcony,
and looked at the neighboring houses, all of them even taller and
fancier than this one. After dinner the lady would take a walk
with him and they would look at the green grass and flowers and
the curlycue fences around the other houses. But there was no
corner market where the people hung out. Maybe it was too far
to walk. He never saw any men walking home from work looking tired and greasy and smelling bad, either, so he guessed they
must work at home like the man did.

He leaned over the short railing, careful not to push against
the wood posts. They were wobbly and could give him slivers.
He peered down at the concrete patio below, at the barbeque
grill in the corner, the round glass table with its closed umbrella
in the middle off to the side, the padded lounge chairs next to
pots filled with red and yellow flowers. Then he felt hands on his
back. Warm hands. Like his mama's hands. His heart skipped a
beat, then two. *You're a good boy, Anthony.* She had come to get
him. He should have known she would. He hadn't brought any
of his things with him, so he was ready. They could leave right
away.

But when he tried to turn around, the hands on his back
burned like coals through his shirt and into his skin. He tried to
push back, but the hands were too strong. His chest tightened
and he got a sick feeling in his stomach as the hands pushed
him forward, into the railing. His feet slipped out from under
him. He heard the wood posts crack. He went over the edge, his
mouth turning into a scream that had no sound. He was in a
tunnel that pointed straight down and inside the tunnel a rum-
bling, a rushing, plunging him down and sucking the concrete

up. He wanted to shut his eyes but they were frozen and then finally there was no space between him and the ground.

ONE

It was Wednesday morning. Five days ago, Anthony Little Eagle had been placed in foster care. Two days ago, he died. I could still see him, walking by my office last Friday with the uniformed police officer's hand on his bony shoulder, his dark brown eyes wide with fear, holes in both knees of his jeans, his T-shirt dirty and thin from wear.

Now I heard the knock on the door that I'd been waiting for. I let out the breath I had been unaware of holding in and fingered the beads on the necklace I always wore.

"Come in," I said.

"Your ten o'clock appointment is here, Sylvia." Mabel's voice was uncharacteristically subdued and cracked ever so slightly when she said my name. "Should I see him to the conference room?"

"No," I said, "here in my office, please."

"Coffee?"

"No."

My secretary stood to the side of the door to make way for

the reporter from the *Monrow City Tribune*.

J. B. Harrell strode into my office like he knew exactly what he was after. Everyone said he was the best investigative reporter our city had ever known, and after reading his exposés about bank fraud and the heroin trafficking in some of our upscale communities, I had to agree. I'd never seen him in person before. In his perfectly tailored three-piece gray suit with a blue and maroon striped tie, and his chiseled cheekbones set off by an expensive salon hairstyle, he looked more like a corporate business executive than a journalist.

Something about his appearance caught me off guard, something vaguely familiar. Maybe it was the unusually deep lines in his face, for someone I guessed to be only in his early forties.

I stood and extended my hand but instead of shaking it he glanced around my office. A confusing sense of dread made its way from my abdomen up into my windpipe and got stuck in my throat.

"Please, have a seat," I managed to say.

I was prepared for him to ask the questions that our agency attorney, Brion Kacey, had instructed me not to answer. I was well-versed in issues of family privacy and client confidentiality. But now I found myself thinking only of what I *shouldn't* say—that I felt responsible for Anthony Little Eagle's death, though I didn't know what I could have done to stop it. That I'd had trouble sleeping since I heard the news. That I was sorry. I was so, so sorry. The deep sadness I'd experienced up to now was joined by a sense of guilt that was all too familiar to me.

With a noticeable hint of impatience around his lips, J. B. Harrell lowered himself onto the edge of the chair on the other side of my desk. His back was long and straight as his eyes moved from the weaving of the Navajo tree of life on the wall to the collection of Navajo, Hopi, and Pueblo pottery on my book-shelf to the wicker, birch bark, and coiled baskets on the long table under the window, to the gourd-shaped earthenware water bottle in the middle of my conference table. He settled on a group photograph taken in the 1970s, in the months before the Wounded Knee protests, with my face way in the back, circled in black marker. He made a harsh sound, forcing the air through his nose. Memories of the role I'd played in the movement back then—cooking and doing the dishes while the protesters planned their strategy, sleeping with a couple of them—brought a blush to my cheeks.

I ran my fingers one by one over my beaded necklace and saw myself as I imagined Harrell saw me—a sixty-year-old white woman with a gray ponytail wearing a peasant blouse and a long denim skirt that was simple and inexpensive in a too-obvious way. A do-gooder with crinkly age lines radiating out from the corners of perpetually earnest blue-gray eyes in an expression of fake sympathy. Someone not to be trusted.

"Would you care for some coffee?" I asked. "Mabel can run down to the café for some sweet rolls if you'd like. They have delicious croissants."

Harrell reached into his expensive-looking leather briefcase and pulled out a yellow legal pad and a designer fountain pen. The Edward Curtis print of the *Mohave Water Carrier* hanging on the wall adjacent to my desk caught his attention. I stared at it with him. It was frustrating to me how most white people saw Curtis's image of the mother balancing a little boy on her hip and a water jug on her head as a symbol of strength and inspiration. Like they were blind to the harsh terrain and the rocky bluff under the mother's bare feet, which screamed out the unspeakable circumstances she should not have to endure. That no one should have to endure.

"A seven-year-old boy is dead." J. B. Harrell's first words since he walked into my office were an indictment. His eyebrows came together in a momentary flash of anger and then his face went blank. He wrote something on his legal pad. He still hadn't looked directly at me.

"Yes," I said, close to tears. "Anthony Little Eagle."

The silence between us was disrupted by the sound of Harrell flipping the page of his legal pad. He wrote the dead boy's name on the pad in capital letters and underlined it twice with quick, staccato movements. I held my breath and thought about our attorney's instructions.

"Of course you should show compassion, Sylvia," Brion had said, "but in a professional way. What's important is not to say anything while a police investigation is under way. I'm usually the one to speak to the media at a time like this, but I'm sure you'll be careful not to say anything that could be misinterpreted or that might reflect negatively on our agency."

"When was Anthony Little Eagle placed in your care?" I heard the reporter ask.

In my care, I said to myself. The boy had died under my watch. That made me responsible. What happened was my fault. I had failed to protect him.

"Less than a week ago," I managed to answer.

"When?"

"You mean the exact date?"

He looked up at the ceiling.

"Anthony Little Eagle was placed in foster care on June 17, 2005." My voice sounded surprisingly professional considering the self-doubt that was threatening to devour me. I'd made a vow, when I became supervisor of the foster care unit, to do everything within my power to make sure nothing like this would ever happen, and I'd worked hard to keep that promise. So what went wrong? Where did I go wrong?

Harrell wrote the date on his legal pad. "A white foster home, I presume?" he asked in a flat voice, without looking up.

"I'm afraid so," I said. "We make every effort to locate American Indian families who are able and willing to take foster children. I believe that it's critically important for children to be placed in homes that share their culture. That's why we try so hard."

"Why?" he asked, his voice still flat.

"Why was he placed in a foster home or why was he placed in a white foster home?"

Harrell made a snorting sound. I bristled. I knew the damage done to children who'd been placed in white homes or sent away to boarding schools.

"We only place children when it's necessary for their own safety," I said.

"Why, exactly?"

"I can't share confidential client information with you, Mr. Harrell. I'm sure you understand."

The reporter stiffened. "I suppose this is when you're going to tell me that you only remove children from their homes when they're in danger."

"That *is* our policy," I said.

"And yet it seems that the greater danger for Anthony Little Eagle was in one of your licensed white foster homes rather than in his own home."

I cringed. Would Anthony Little Eagle still be alive if he hadn't been removed from his home? Was there any way to have been certain where the greater danger lay? Following approved policies and procedures only went so far. In the end, ensuring child safety boiled down to professional judgment, which I knew from experience was subjective and not without bias.

"Mr. Harrell," I spoke slowly and deliberately. "Our job is to protect children, and we try to do our best. I can assure you that our agency takes a child's death very seriously."

"Murder," he said. "A child's murder." He turned his head and fixed his brown eyes on the Hopi Kachina doll on my desk.

I picked the doll up and moved it to the other side of my desk. "We will cooperate in every way we can with the police investigation," I said. Why was I resorting to legal jargon? Why did I feel such a desperate need to defend myself?

"Every way you *can*?"

"Every way possible. I assure you."

J. B. Harrell put his pen down and scooted back in the chair. He let out his breath with a whistle. "Ms. Jensen," he said.

"Please, call me Sylvia." I knew my smile was obsequious but I couldn't seem to help it.

Harrell flipped back to the previous page of his legal pad. "The foster parents are Paul and Linda Mellon, right? So, was Anthony Little Eagle the first foster child ever placed in their home, Ms. Jensen?"

"No."

"How many other children have been placed with them?"

"The Mellons have been foster parents for quite some time."

"How long, exactly? How many children?"

"Since the late 1990s, I think. I don't know how many children they've fostered. I'd have to look that up."

"And do you know if any other children have been injured or died while in their care?"

I clenched my fists. Now he had gone too far. Yes, I felt

responsible. Yes, I felt guilty. Yes, I was asking myself if there was something I could have done to prevent Anthony's death. But to insinuate that other children had been injured, let alone died, in the same home? That was plain unfair. And was he actually accusing the Mellons of murder? I sat up in my chair and looked straight at him, daring him to look at me, to just this once for God's sake look at me. But he didn't. I was beginning to suspect that the man wasn't as principled as I'd thought. That he might in fact just be full of himself, like so many men I'd known in my life.

"I can assure you, Mr. Harrell, that if any child had been harmed while in the Mellon home before, our agency would not have placed any other children with them."

"I see." He flipped through the pages of his legal pad until he found what he was looking for. "Then perhaps you can explain," he said, running his finger down the page, "the incident that occurred in that home in 2000."

A bead of sweat was making its way down my left temple. What incident was he referring to? Was it possible he already knew I'd been on leave in 2000, that I'd been arrested for driving with a blood alcohol level of .2 and would have lost my job if I hadn't checked myself into a treatment center? Surely he didn't know about the mornings I'd come to work late and hungover, about the bottle of wine I'd kept in the bottom left-hand drawer of my desk. I reached for a tissue, blew my nose, and wiped the perspiration from my upper lip. Harrell was studying his notes. I wondered if he was going to use my history against the agency, if he planned to make my drinking part of a series about the failings of the foster care system. Well, it wasn't too late to stop him. I looked at the clock on my desk and feigned surprise.

"I have another appointment," I said, with a smile I

intended to appear apologetic. "I'm afraid our time is up."

"Here it is," he said. "A foster child, a five-year-old girl, was injured and taken by the Mellons to the hospital on June 8, 2000."

"I'm sorry," I said, no longer able to keep my voice from trembling. "I wasn't here then, but if there was any suspicion that foster parents were responsible for a child's injury, I can assure you that there would have been an investigation."

"So you *assure* me that no child ever came to any harm at the hands of Mr. or Mrs. Mellon in the past but you provide me with no evidence, is that what you're saying, Ms. Jensen?"

"I can assure you...I mean, I'm not aware of any other accident."

"*Incident*," he said. "Any other *incident*."

"Mr. Harrell, I want to find out what happened to Anthony Little Eagle as much as you do, believe me." I found myself experiencing a disturbing need for him to understand that I wasn't the enemy, that I wasn't your typical bureaucrat who didn't understand issues of privilege and oppression. Couldn't he tell that I was different?

"And you, of course, can assure me of that, too." He tore a page from his legal pad and scribbled something, crumpled it up, and dropped it on the floor. Then he put his pen and legal pad away and closed his briefcase with a loud click.

His quiet hostility left a bitter taste on my tongue. I watched him glance around my office one more time. My head grew heavy. I rested my elbows on the desk and held my chin in the palms of my hands. Then I saw him looking at the picture on my desk of me sitting on a big rock.

"That was taken in Machu Picchu in the 1980s," I said, glad to have something to say. "It was an incredible experience to be there and imagine the beauty of the city built on those rocks."

"The city where they sacrificed small, perfect children to gain the favor of the gods," he said.

His words jolted me back to my trip to Peru. I heard the voice of the Spanish tour guide describing the beauty of a ten-year-old child whose father had offered her to the Inca emperor as a Capacocha sacrifice, telling us that there were skull fractures on the backs of the heads of most of the sacrificial mummies.

I looked at Harrell. "I'm devastated about what happened," I said. "I'll do everything I can to find out what happened."

"I'm glad to hear it, Ms. Jensen," he said, standing. Then he turned and walked out of my office.

I slammed the photograph facedown on my desk, and all I could see was Anthony Little Eagle, his skull fractured, lying dead on the concrete patio below the balcony of his room.

TWO

I stared at the crumpled-up piece of paper on the floor. I was strangely off-balance, so much so that I had to face the truth: after five years of recovery, right now I wanted to pick up a drink more than ever before. My legs were shaky as I crouched down, my fingers tingly as I picked the paper up by its edges. I was about to throw it into the wastebasket but something stopped me. I unfolded the note. "If you're serious about wanting to help, give me a call. 819-050-2301."

The message was obviously intended for me, so why didn't he just say it? And what did he mean if I was *serious about wanting to help*? Hadn't I already told him I was?

"Well, Mr. Harrell," I said out loud, as if he were still there, "if you need proof that I care, then I guess I'll just have to give it to you."

I sat down at my computer and typed in the password to access the electronic case files for all the foster homes that were my social workers' responsibility. I typed in *Paul and Linda Mellon* and the words Record Unavailable came up on the screen. I figured their case record must be among those not yet converted to an e-file. But when I went to the records room for the hard copy, it had already been signed out to our agency attorney. I went back to my office and called Brion Kacey.

"I have to see you," I said. "I'll be right up."

"I'm sorry, Sylvia," he said. "I'm about to leave for a meeting, but I can see you first thing tomorrow morning."

"It'll only take a minute, Brion."

I hung up and rushed out the door, holding up the hem of my skirt as I took the steps two at a time up to the third-floor administrative suite. I had to see for myself that all agency procedures had been followed with the Mellon case. A life or death need to disprove J. B. Harrell's allegation that Anthony Little Eagle's death might not have been an accident threatened to overwhelm me. It was irrational, out of proportion, and somehow out of my control.

The door to Brion Kacey's huge corner office was open. I leaned against the doorframe to catch my breath. He was huddled at the far end of his highly polished mahogany conference table with Betsy Chambers, the agency administrator and my supervisor. Today, as usual, Brion was wearing a black suit, fresh white shirt, and red bow tie, always at the ready to appear in court. He sat up straight when he saw me. I thought it might just be my imagination until I strode over to the table and saw his eyebrows draw together. He closed the folder he and Betsy had been looking at and crossed his arms on top of it.

"Are you okay, Sylvia?" Betsy asked.

"Is that the Mellon case file?" I asked.

"It's a terrible thing," Brion said. "A tragic accident."

"I want to read it," I said.

"Your diligence is much appreciated," he said, "as always."

I winced. It wasn't like Brion to patronize me. I decided to ignore it and held my hand out for the folder. He moved it to the side and tapped his index finger on top of it.

"I won't keep it for long," I said, leaning toward him and reaching for it again.

Betsy placed her hand on my arm to hold me back, with a sympathetic wince. She was an attractive woman, the lines in her face framed by soft gray curls and her trim figure presented to its best advantage today in a tailored royal blue suit set off by a golden scarf. I liked her and had always admired her. Over the years she'd taken a dozen foster children into her own home, and adopted half of them. She'd never lost her ability to care, in spite of having risen through the ranks of an institution in which colleagues at each level conspired more ferociously than at the previous level to subordinate subjective human relationships to data-driven objectivity.

"With an investigation under way," Brion said, "I know you appreciate more than anyone the importance of following agency policies and procedures."

I was well aware of my reputation as a stickler for details. If any of my social workers were to ask for a case file under similar circumstances, I would tell them the same thing.

"Of course," I said. "I have no intention of interfering with the investigation."

"I knew you'd want to read it," Betsy said. "And I understand why."

"It's for my own peace of mind, that's all."

"I know this has been awfully hard for you," Betsy went on. "But you have to know that Anthony Little Eagle's death was not your fault."

I bit my bottom lip.

"There can be no doubt, Sylvia," Brion said, "that you made sure everything was done properly with this case."

He looked out the window at the green turrets on top of the Gothic stone courthouse across the street. Then he turned back to me with a benevolent smile. "Here," he said as he pulled a thin folder out from under the Mellon file. "You can have a copy of Lynn Winters's statement. I think your social worker's report of what she did when she placed the boy will put your mind at ease." He waved his hand in a gesture that I took as a dismissal, that as far as he was concerned the meeting was over.

I took Lynn's statement from him and said, "But I'd like the case file, too, please. Just for a few minutes."

"We need to follow protocol," Betsy said.

"You know I can't hold people accountable for their actions if I'm not fully informed, Betsy." I didn't mean to sound whiny, but I couldn't seem to help it.

"After you read Ms. Winters's statement," Brion said, "you can talk to her yourself. You have my permission to do that."

A flame rushed up my neck and burned into my jaw. Brion had just pulled rank on me, as if I needed his permission to talk to one of my own social workers. I didn't understand what was going on. I knew they considered me to be one of the most highly respected supervisors in the agency. This was the first time they had ever questioned my competence.

"You don't really care what happened to that boy, do you?"

"Now, Sylvia," Betsy said. "It's not Brion's fault. He's just doing his job."

"I see. So since when is it his job to tell me whether I can talk to my own social workers or not?"

"The best way to get to the truth of what happened," Betsy said, "is to follow our child death protocols." She paused. "I know you are not responsible for Anthony Little Eagle's death."

I fought off the tears unexpectedly filling my eyes. "I wish I did."

"That boy's death was no one's fault." Brion said. "It was an accident."

"The reporter from the *Monrow City Tribune* doesn't think so," I shot back at him.

Brion pulled a crisp white handkerchief from the pocket of his suit jacket and wiped his forehead with it. "You are not to meet with him again," he said.

I couldn't believe my ears. How dare he? I looked at my supervisor. "Betsy?"

Her shoulders moved up and stayed there like they were stuck. It wasn't the first time I wondered if caution had become second nature to her after twenty-five years of directing the agency, or if she had been put in charge because that was the way she already was. But then, what difference did it make? What mattered was that Betsy and Brion, for some reason I couldn't understand, were treating me not like a colleague but rather like someone they didn't trust.

"Mr. Harrell said another child was injured in the Mellon home," I said.

Brion and Betsy exchanged quick glances.

"If he contacts you again," Brion said, "refer him to my office."

"He said it happened on June 8, 2000," I said.

Brion's face turned beet red. He wagged his finger in the air. "This is what the media does. They lead you to think they know something as a way to get more information out of you. Now tell me, if you will, exactly what you told this Mr. Harrell."

"I told him the truth."

"Which was?" He sounded like he knew it was already too late, that whatever I had said to the reporter had already been said, and there was nothing he could do about it.

"I told him I wasn't aware of any incident in 2000." I stopped there. I knew better than to mention that I had been on leave that year. The less Brion knew about my history the better. I pointed to the folder on the table. "It should be in the case file."

Brion looked at me for a long time. I glared back at him.

"What else did you say?" he finally asked.

"That we would cooperate with the police."

"Good," he said. "Are we clear now that you are not to talk with anyone about this case?"

I weighed my chances of striking a bargain. Maybe if I promised not to talk to J. B. Harrell or anyone else he'd let me read the Mellon file in exchange.

"Well? Are we clear?"

"I don't understand what's going on here," I said. "Come on, Brion, we've worked together a long time. You know I take my job just as seriously as you take yours." I heard the desperation in my voice but I didn't care; I would have done anything, gotten down on my knees if I had to.

"This is the way it has to be," he said. "Until the police conclude their investigation, no one can be allowed access to the evidence, and that includes the case file."

"It wouldn't be responsible of me to not even..."

"The way to be responsible is to stay out of it."

"We have to do this by the book, Sylvia," Betsy said with an apologetic smile.

I stood there, unable to move, clenching and unclenching my fists in rapid succession. I didn't understand what was going on or what was happening to me.

"You're covering something up, aren't you? Something that might make our agency look bad. We most certainly wouldn't want anything negative about us to appear in the newspaper, now would we?"

"Sylvia," Betsy said. "I care just as much as you do about finding out what happened so we can make sure it never happens again. We'll get to the truth."

"I know your first commitment is to the children, Betsy," I said. I turned to Brion. "And I'd like to think that your first commitment is to the children placed under our care, too, and not to the agency."

"I don't think there's anything else to discuss here." Brion's voice was low and thicker with authority than before.

"Oh, right," I said, "I guess you have to run off to that supposed meeting you said you had to get to so fast." I made no attempt to disguise my sarcasm.

Then I walked away from the administrative office suite and down the hall. Was Betsy really putting children first or was she, perhaps inadvertently due to her cautiousness, aligned with Brion in making the agency's image the priority? Maybe I was overreacting. I knew I was prone to bouts of self-righteousness at times—it was a character defect I'd worked hard to change— but right now I didn't care. What was worse, I didn't care that I didn't care. Something bigger than me, something I didn't understand, had consumed me. I ducked into the women's restroom and locked the door behind me.

THREE

May 1972

Jamie's sinewy arms and lanky legs sliced through the air. He bounced across the deck and skidded to halt, and his best friend Tommy slammed into his back.

"Mom, guess what?" Jamie said.

Mary Williams had just finished washing down the picnic table. She put the bucket of soapy water and the wet sponge down. "What, sweetie?" She folded her son in her arms, taking in the smell of him.

"If you cut a worm in half you have two worms and you can cut it in threes or fours or even more. A man at camp showed us how to dissect them and Melissa almost fainted but I didn't."

"Wow, that's really something. How about you go wash your hands now. There's a treat for you in the kitchen. Soon it'll be time to get ready for the parade." Mary puckered her lips and Jamie giggled, gave her a little kiss.

"Race you to the door," Jamie said as he and Tommy took off like lightning.

Mary picked up her bucket and followed the boys into the

house. Memorial Day, for most people in the small town of Basko, signified the end of another long midwestern winter and the beginning of summer, when the air would once again be filled with the smells of charcoal grills and freshly cut grass. But for Mary, today marked the nearing of Jamie's seventh year as her son. It was a celebration of the emergence of a life as flawlessly designed as the backyard tapestry of regal pines and brilliant white birch, a life with hopes and dreams as bright as the daffodils and tulips blooming next to the garage.

Jamie and Tommy, their hands still wet, sat in their usual places at the kitchen table, where Mary had placed pastry crisps, still warm from the oven, and two glasses of milk.

"I wish my mom knew how to make these." Tommy took a noisy gulp of milk from his favorite glass.

"I know how, don't I, Mom?" Jamie puffed up his little chest, as proud of himself for sprinkling sugar and cinnamon on top of the pastries as if he had landed a rocket on the moon.

"You sure do, sweetie."

The cinnamon crisps, made with leftover dough from the meat pies that were still in the oven, were Jamie's favorite snack—just as they had been Mary's when she was a child. That made her think about her own mother, how having only one child had been, at times, too heavy a burden for her, although she'd tried hard to be a good mother in between the dark spells. Whenever Mary found herself wishing she'd been able to bring her mother the same kind of joy Jamie brought her, she'd tell herself it was best not to think too much about some things. Then she'd redouble her efforts to create the childhood for Jamie that her own mother had been unable to create for her.

Just then the door leading to the garage opened and Wayne walked into the kitchen, wiping his dirty hands on his jeans.

"Hey, boys," he said. He grabbed one of the pastries and shoved it into his mouth. He glanced at Mary with a sheepish smile and reached for another one.

"Get your greasy mitts off," she said, slapping at his hand. "It's about time you stopped tinkering with that old truck of yours and got cleaned up. Your folks will be here any minute."

Wayne curled his lips into a pout. She laughed, handed him another cinnamon crisp. At times like this, she nearly forgot what it had been like before Jamie. Before Jamie, when shame ruled her life, like an unrelenting dictator in a desert of barrenness. All the medical procedures she and Wayne had undergone back then, all their attempts to find the right moment and the right way to conceive, had led to the truth that she would never feel a baby, a new life, growing inside her, and that it was her fault.

———

Mary's descent into a state of sadness and hopelessness back then was subtle at first. She couldn't decide what to have for breakfast. She couldn't concentrate enough to read the newspaper. She began to wonder if she was incapable of doing anything right. Sunny days seemed cloudy and dreary. She was often irritated with Wayne, suffocated by his attempts to help. Their marriage lost its meaning for her, now that they would never realize the dream they'd shared since junior high school of creating a home filled with children.

She questioned whether she loved Wayne anymore. She'd burst into tears over nothing. Some days she found it hard to get out of bed.

She thought more and more about what a welcome relief it must have been for her mother when she committed suicide ten years ago.

One morning when she lay in bed, once more unable to face the day, Wayne brought her breakfast.

"I talked to a social worker." He put the tray down and placed his hand on hers. "About taking in a foster child."

She didn't say anything.

"Just to see how it goes. Maybe later we can think about adopting. Please, Mary. We can't go on like this."

The love in Wayne's eyes reached Mary's heart and cut through her pain. "Okay, I'll talk to a social worker," she'd said, "but that's all, just talk."

In the end, she agreed to give foster parenting a try. There was no way she could have known then how that decision would change everything. The moment Jamie was placed in her arms and she saw his scrunched-up three-day-old face peeking out from the fluffy blue blanket, she fell utterly, hopelessly, in love with him. She wondered if this was what other mothers felt, if it was possible that she might be experiencing the same kind of joy, the same kind of pure love they reported feeling after giving birth. Maybe the price she had paid for this gift of life had simply been a different kind of pain than the physical pain they experienced. With Jamie's arrival, life became a carnival of laughter and discovery and love. How wrong it seemed now to consider that it had been born in such desperation.

———

"Knock, knock!"

The cheery voice of Wayne's mother came through the back door. Rose Williams, a petite woman with a stoop to her back and the perpetual smell of roses about her, stood on her tiptoes and hugged her son.

"And you, my dear," she said, planting a kiss on Mary's cheek, "are as gorgeous as ever."

Mary smiled indulgently. Her mother-in-law had a propensity to be fast and loose with the compliments. Like the time she told the pastor's wife her new hairstyle looked ravishing when any fool could see what a botched job it was. But she meant well, and Mary loved her.

"Where's Dad?" Wayne asked.

"Checking his new Cadillac for scratches before he comes in," Rose said. "You know how he is."

A few minutes later Harold Williams roared into the kitchen and slammed a six-pack of Coke down on the counter. He patted Mary on the back and with an exaggerated sniff tipped his head toward the oven.

"Now those meat pies are something even *I* couldn't make," he said. "Course, I've never tried." He chuckled.

Mary ignored him. Wayne's father could be a challenge sometimes, but he was devoted to his family—unlike her own father, who'd moved to Florida after her mother died and dropped off the face of the earth.

"Hi, Grandpa Harold." Jamie's brown eyes lit up with excitement.

"*Uncle* Harold." Wayne's father tousled Jamie's hair.

Mary gritted her teeth. No matter how many excuses Wayne made for his father and no matter how often he and his mother joked that the man had simply been born stubborn, she wasn't going to let him off the hook on this one. Jamie was her son, and that made Harold his grandfather, and that was that, end of discussion.

"I bet Grandpa would like to dig worms with you," she said.

"Wanna, Grandpa Harold? Please?" Jamie grabbed his grandfather's hand and pulled him toward the door. Tommy tagged along behind, his freckled nose twitching on his goofy-looking face.

—

Half an hour later, Mary called them in to get ready for the parade. She instructed Jamie to wash the mud from his hands and then change his clothes. She laid out his new red, white, and blue T-shirt and his clean jean shorts on his bed. Harold hurriedly changed into his old World War II army uniform. Since he always marched with the Veterans of Foreign Wars on Memorial Day, he had to leave early.

"I'll be right behind the American Legion Band," he told Jamie before he went. "Don't forget to wave to me."

It was only a two-block walk to Main Street, but by the time they reached it, everyone in town was already there. Wayne lifted Jamie up on his broad football shoulders so he could see over all the heads. When the veterans came into view Jamie waved his arms so hard he nearly fell from his perch. Mary gasped and Wayne increased his grip on his son's ankles.

"Here I am, Grandpa! Over here! Here!"

"He can't hear you, sweetie," Mary shouted up to him. "The band's too loud."

Couldn't he at least nod to his grandson? she thought. Doesn't he know we always watch the parade from in front of the five-and-dime store? She glanced down at her mother-in-law, sitting on a lawn chair by the curb and watching her husband with a face blank with restraint—or was it simply a lack of awareness—that was as remarkable to Mary as it was irritating. But then Rose looked up at her with a warm smile that melted her frustration.

The parade, which made up in passion for what it lacked in size, seemed to be over as soon as it started. The town cop rode by on his motorcycle and people started to fold up their lawn chairs and head toward picnic lunches with their families.

Back home, Mary, Wayne, and Rose carried the food out to the deck while Harold—still in his army uniform—regaled Jamie with war stories. Tommy showed up like he always did when it was time to eat. Jamie reached for one of the meat pies—stuffed with ground pork and beef, potatoes, rutabagas, carrots, and onions and displayed on a platter like spokes on a wheel—and smothered the crust with ketchup.

"Hey, chief, don't you have a birthday coming soon?" Harold said with a wink.

"I'm going to be seven," Jamie said with his mouth full.

"What kind of party you having this year?" Grandma Rose asked.

Jamie jumped up from the bench with both hands raised in the air. "Pirates!" he yelled. "Mom's gonna make a sign for across the driveway that says Landlubbers Beware, and we're gonna cover the picnic table with black and make it into a ship with a skull and crossbones flag on a mast in the middle. We're gonna have a treasure hunt and play games like walk the plank and pin the eye-patch on the pirate and everything."

"Don't forget movie time," Wayne said.

Mary saw Jamie shrug. She wondered if he might be embarrassed to have his father show films from all his previous parties and point out how much the boys grew from year to year. She would have to talk to Wayne about it.

"The invitation is a treasure chest," Jamie said. "There's a map inside. Can I go get one, Mom?"

"Of course, sweetie."

"My, my," Grandma Rose said after Jamie and Tommy had disappeared into the house. "He was so tiny when you first took him in. Just as if he were your own."

Mary bit her tongue. She thought of all the times she cooed and sang to the rhythm of the rocking chair while Jamie sucked on the bottle until his little belly was round and his eyes closed in contentment. All those times she obsessed about ear infections, sniffles, and fevers. How she celebrated his first smile, first laugh, first word—*Mama*—first steps.

"He's a cute kid all right," her father-in-law said. "But you could be in for trouble if he's still with you when he's older."

Mary sucked in her breath.

Rose winced. "Now, Harold, dear..."

"Dad doesn't mean that the way it sounds." Wayne put his hand on Mary's arm. She shrugged it off.

"I'm just saying," Harold muttered under his breath.

Mary leaned forward, her eyes flashing. "You're just saying what, Dad? You're just saying *what* about my son?"

"Here it is!"

Jamie rushed over to his grandpa, waving a party invitation in the air. His face glowed. Mary smiled, but inside she was shaking. She had steadfastly refused from the start and always would refuse to consider the possibility that this beautiful child could ever not be her son. She hated the way Wayne worried that if he were taken from them, she'd be devastated and go back to the way she was before. Things had been agonizingly tense between them the two times Jamie's birth parents came to visit, but fortunately, after Jamie turned one, John and Josephine Buckley disappeared. On Jamie's second birthday, Mary had announced that from then on his name would be Jamie Buckley Williams, and after that Wayne stopped saying anything to her about being worried and she stopped noticing that he still was.

"Jamie Buckley Williams."

"What? What's wrong, Mom?"

Alarmed to realize she'd said Jamie's name out loud, Mary pulled him into her arms. "Nothing's wrong, sweetie," she said. "Absolutely nothing."

FOUR

I stayed in the women's bathroom until I was able to regain my composure. Then I speculated about why Brion Kacey and Betsy Chambers would refuse to let me read the Mellon case file. I couldn't rule out the possibility that there was something in the record they were afraid might damage the agency's reputation. That could have explained why Brion got so upset when I told him about J. B. Harrell's allegation that a five-year-old foster girl had been hurt in the Mellon home.

But then why, once Brion and Betsy knew that I was already aware of the incident, did they still refuse to let me read the file? The more I thought about it, the more I wondered if they knew more about Anthony Little Eagle's death than they'd let on. I pressed my back against the wall and told myself to slow down, be careful not to jump to conclusions.

Brion's voice kept echoing in my head. *No one...no one will be allowed access to the case file.* I thought about how he had given me "permission" (so to speak) to talk to the social worker who had placed Anthony Little Eagle in the Mellon home.

"Thank you, Brion," I said into the mirror as if speaking directly to him. "That is exactly what I am going to do. Lynn knows what's in the case file, and she will tell me what it is since you won't. And don't worry about Mr. J. B. Harrell, because I am about to prove him wrong."

With my confidence somewhat restored, I headed down the stairs to the second floor to see Lynn Winters. If she had seen anything in the case file about a suspicious injury to a child in the Mellon home, I was sure she never would have placed Anthony Little Eagle there.

When I walked into the foster care suite, I was surprised to find myself comparing its brightness, from the afternoon sun shining through the floor-to-ceiling windows, to the smoke-filled stench and fog of the courthouse basement up north where I had worked before. The soft voices of social workers talking on their phones was a stark contrast to the cacophony of ringing phones, loud voices, and hiss of steam rushing through the ceiling pipes back then. I hurried between the rows of white cubicles that formed a passageway that led to my office at the end.

I stopped at Lynn's cubicle and peered over the waist-high wall, but she wasn't there. Her workspace, unlike those of my other staff, was not yet decorated with family pictures and other personal items. No pictures on the walls, only a computer, a telephone, and a neat stack of papers on her desk.

"She's in the field." I turned toward the sound of Melanie's voice, from the adjacent cubicle. "She was here earlier but she left a few minutes ago."

"Thanks," I said. I didn't know how to respond to the unspoken concern in my worker's voice. "I'll leave her a note, but if you see her, could you let her know I want to see her right away when she gets back?"

"Sure, Sylvia."

I left the note propped up on Lynn's phone and then went back to my desk to do paperwork. As the day dragged by, every time someone knocked on my office door, I looked up expectantly, and each time I was disappointed to see that it wasn't Lynn Winters. At five thirty I finally gave up and headed home.

———

My Suzuki Sidekick, fifteen years old and with 180,000 miles on it, wasn't the only beater car in the lot behind my apartment building, but it had to be the most reliable one there. In the drab lobby I checked my mailbox before getting on the elevator. The man-boy with spiky blond hair and perpetual sleep in his eyes who lived on the second floor and yet never came up with enough energy to walk up one flight of stairs got on with me.

"Hey, Miss Jensen." He smiled, showing his perfect white teeth. Like he was following his mother's admonition to be respectful to the resident spinster.

"Good evening," I said. I didn't know his name. He, like all the other college students and young professionals who lived in the building, would move out as soon as he was able to improve his circumstances. I stared at the holes in the knees of his jeans.

"Have a nice evening, Miss Jensen," he said when the elevator stopped and he got off.

I pushed the button for the fifth floor, wondering how I might manage to have a nice evening when all I wanted was for tomorrow to come. When the elevator door opened on my floor, the smells of pizza and Chinese takeout made my stomach growl. I was hungry, and glad I'd made enough tuna casserole on Sunday night to last through the week.

I dropped my keys onto the round table that divided the

kitchen from the living room in my tiny apartment. I found myself speculating about what my naighbor would think if he knew I chose to live this simply not out of necessity but based on principle. What would he say about my dated gold and orange shag area rug? The drab off-white walls that hadn't been painted in all the years I'd lived here, the black imitation-leather couch I'd bought at the Salvation Army, the array of candles and pottery on the windowsills? My old political posters? I imagined telling him that I'd won custody of the antique pulpit chair with its high, hand-carved walnut back and burgundy velvet upholstery as part of my divorce. But I didn't expect that he would make any connection between my life and the privileges he probably thought he deserved and the luxuries with which he aspired to surround himself.

Speculating about what the man-boy might think of me, while a welcome diversion, soon led me to wondering if J. B. Harrell might be more inclined to trust my sincerity if he saw the way I chose to live. I read a magazine while I ate. I swept then mopped the kitchen floor. I sorted through the papers and magazines that had been piling up for months on top of my old scratched desk in the corner of my otherwise neat living room. But the sadness in the pit of my stomach was still there and soon I found myself ruminating again, about Brion, Betsy, Lynn. I went to bed thinking about who knew or didn't know what and lay there counting the hours until I would be able to talk to Lynn Winters.

—

I woke up the next morning with my stomach twisted into a pretzel of anticipation after having dreamed that I called J. B. Harrell to tell him he was wrong. With a cup of coffee and a plain bagel I'd picked up from the café on the first floor of the

Health Services Building on the way to my office, I sat down at my desk. Eating the bagel made my stomach relax, so I decided to give the coffee a try. I was just lifting the cup to my lips when a timid knock on the frame of my open door startled me. The coffee splashed over the rim and I watched a brown circle spread over the flowery print on my skirt.

"Are you ready for me?" Lynn Winters stood in the doorway. Her eyes, which were usually a luminescent green, were cloudy and red-rimmed, and her cheeks were puffy. She was wearing a shirtwaist dress that hung loosely off her shoulders like she'd recently lost weight and hadn't had time to buy new clothes.

I motioned for her to come in. She sat in the chair on the other side of my desk with her shoulders hunched over, the stringy tips of her long hair brushing the tops of her thighs. I thought about seeing her for the first time just a few months ago, an eager, compassionate, and idealistic twenty-four-year-old with a master's degree in social work. Her hair had been a thick and fluffy blond; by everyone's estimation she had been the most fashionable and beautiful woman ever to work in our agency. It made her disheveled appearance now all the more alarming.

"Are you okay?" I asked.

She nodded.

"I know this must be terribly hard for you," I said.

She nodded again.

"Do you feel up to talking about it?"

"Do you want me to tell you what's in my statement?" she asked.

I pressed my hand on the folder lying on the desk in front of me. "I already read the statement you gave to Brion Kacey," I said. "But I'd like to hear more about what happened the day you placed Anthony Little Eagle."

"I'm sorry...uh...you mean...?" Lynn's voice was a barely audible whisper.

"Take your time. Just anything you remember."

Lynn started to speak but then stopped and looked around uncertainly. I empathized with her, remembering what it was like to be young and new on the job.

"It's okay if you want to start with what's in your statement," I said. "I'm also interested in anything that isn't in your statement, anything you thought of later or maybe something you weren't asked."

A piece of paper slipped off Lynn's lap and fell to the floor. She moved to the edge of her chair, looking a little shaky as she scrambled to pick the paper up. I thought back to the times I'd gotten into trouble as a new social worker. Only unlike Lynn Winters, I didn't think I'd done anything wrong. I'd firmly believed I was in the right when I licensed a foster home with only one exit in the house (after all, there wasn't a single house on the reservation that had the required two exits), and when I gave out birth control information against agency policy. How ironic it was that now, as a supervisor, I had a reputation for demanding that my social workers adhere to all agency procedures, when most of my own offenses had involved skirting bureaucratic red tape.

"I'm sorry...I don't know what you want me to say." Lynn's voice wavered.

I cleared my throat and picked up my pen. "Maybe if you start with the day you placed Anthony Little Eagle, it will help us work through what happened, see what we can learn from it."

"It was late on Friday afternoon," Lynn said with a tremor in her voice. "A child welfare worker named Ted Pound called just before our office closed saying he needed an emergency placement. He said the police found Anthony Little Eagle's parents passed out in an apartment in the public housing complex and a drunken uncle was screaming and waving a gun around. They arrested the uncle and brought the boy here."

"And how did you decide to place him in the Mellon home?"

"They were on our list of emergency foster homes and we'd used them before, so I figured..." She sniffled and wiped away a tear. "I didn't want to send the boy to a shelter for the weekend. Most of the kids there are tough teenagers. He was so little and so scared."

I pushed a box of tissues on my desk closer to her. I sympathized with her, but at the same time, there was something missing. Something wasn't making sense.

"I understand that a child might have been injured in that foster home in the past. Tell me what you know about that."

"What? I...I didn't..." Lynn's green eyes widened.

I began to wonder if the girl was hiding something, if maybe she was in collusion with Brion and Betsy. If maybe she'd been told what to say and what not to say. Or maybe, it was possible that Lynn, in her eagerness to protect the boy by keeping him out of the shelter, had ignored a red flag about the foster home. Was that why she looked so guilty?

Lynn twisted a piece of tissue into a pile of little white scraps on her lap. "I guess I didn't...I didn't think..."

I tried to put myself in her shoes. It had been late on a Friday afternoon. Maybe Lynn had been so anxious about protecting Anthony Little Eagle from the dangers that might await him in an emergency shelter that she simply didn't think, didn't see any warning signs. I wanted to believe that she had operated with the best interests of the boy in mind, that she had followed agency procedures.

"We can come back to that," I said. "So you brought Anthony Little Eagle to the Mellon foster home. Then what?"

"I went home."

"Actually, I was thinking about what you did to follow up. The training manual says that workers are required to check on children four hours after they're placed in a home."

Lynn leaned forward. "Oh yes," she said with an eager nod of her head. "I called the foster home first thing the next morning. I was worried about him. He was so scared and confused when I left him there. I had to make sure he was okay."

"It was good that you called right away. Who did you talk to?"

"Mrs. Mellon. She said everything was fine. She said Tony, that's what she called him, she said he ate a good dinner but that she would have to fatten him up, that he was too skinny. She said he was quiet but that was to be expected and he did respond when she asked him questions. She said he wanted his eggs scrambled that morning. Everything was okay."

"Did you talk to Anthony?"

"No, but I called again the next day," she said, looking at me as if seeking my approval. "Mr. Mellon said Anthony was taking a walk with his wife and that he thought the boy was adjusting as well as could be expected."

"Did you visit the home on Monday then," I asked, "so you could see Anthony yourself?"

"I...was planning to...but...all my other cases...it was so busy that day...I thought he was okay."

Okay, I thought. I might have assumed the same thing myself after calling the Mellon home twice to check on him.

"Tell me," I said, "about your consultation with the Indian Child Welfare Act compliance officer. It seems to have been left out of your statement."

"Who?"

"We're required to confer with Peter Minter, the Indian Child Welfare compliance officer, before removing or placing American Indian children in non–American Indian homes."

"I'm sorry, I...I guess I..."

I bit my tongue and waited for her to say more. We'd spent a whole day during orientation discussing the ICWA requirements, but my social workers didn't always absorb it or understand how important it was to follow all the proper procedures. I worried about the unacceptably high number of American Indian kids that were still being removed and placed in white foster homes.

"I guess...," Lynn went on. "The poor boy just looked so scared...I'm sorry. I guess I was too anxious about that to think about anything else."

A rush of heat radiated up into my chest. The image of Anthony Little Eagle's fear-filled eyes rose before me once again, the uniformed police officer's gigantic hand crushing his bony shoulder.

"I saw him that day," I said. "I saw how frightened the boy looked."

I wondered if I expected too much of Lynn. She was so young and fresh, one of those social workers who had gone directly from a bachelor's degree program into an advanced standing graduate program without any work experience in between. And then, after only two weeks of training, I had given her too many cases. I knew it was essential because of our agency's heavy workload, but I should have monitored her more closely. Maybe she was so intimidated by my emphasis on policy and procedure, by my high standards, that she'd been afraid to ask any questions. Maybe she'd been unable to exercise common sense out of fear of making a mistake. Maybe she'd been so anxious to protect Anthony Little Eagle that she convinced herself she was keeping him safe. Yet the question remained: had she ignored the warning signs, had she not seen them, or hadn't there been any?

"Let's go back to the other child who was injured in the Mellon home. I understand it was about five years ago." I said. "Tell me what you know about that."

Lynn's shoulders sagged and she stared at her lap for a long time. She finally raised her head and I saw a shadow—was it fear? guilt?—cross her face.

"I'm sorry. I know...I know..."

"What is it? What do you know?"

I leaned forward and my chair squeaked. Lynn jumped. She looked as guilty as if she herself had killed Anthony Little Eagle. I knew then that she was hiding something. Did she know a child had been hurt in the Mellon home before? Did she know and place another child there anyway?

Lynn choked on a sob and started crying loud enough to be heard by the other social workers in the row of cubicles outside my door. She said something, but her words came out garbled.

"What?" I asked. "I didn't understand what you said."

"I...it's just that...well...I don't know why the Mellon home was on our emergency list...if...if...It's just that...that...I think someone should have known if that home was safe or not."

"That's true. Did you see anything in the case file about the five-year-old girl that was injured in that home?"

"I'm sorry, Sylvia. I'm so sorry, but...I didn't...I didn't..."

"You didn't what?" I heard the impatience in my voice.

"I didn't...read the case file."

I sat back in my chair and pushed my hands into my stomach. I was stunned. *So that's it. That's her secret.* It was one thing for her to make a conscious decision to do what was best to protect the child by keeping him out of the emergency shelter, but it was quite another thing to not think things through—and Lynn Winters clearly did not think things through. The more I thought about it, the angrier I got. It was unacceptable to not read about a foster home before placing a vulnerable child there.

I looked down at my hands, clasped tightly in my lap, and tried to talk myself down. *Calm down. Be professional. The poor girl is devastated.*

When I was finally able to look at Lynn, she jumped up and ran out of my office. I didn't try to stop her. Maybe I was being too hard on her, but damn it, there had to be consequences for not following procedures, and especially for not even bothering to read the case file.

I rested my head on the back of my chair. I hadn't gotten the reassurance that I'd hoped for from talking to Lynn. I still didn't know if a girl had been injured in the Mellon home, as J. B. Harrell had said, and not only that, I was left with more questions than before. Was it possible that the Mellons had lost their license to be foster parents but their home had not been removed from the emergency list, through some administrative error? Was that why Brion and Betsy had glanced at each other when I mentioned the injured girl? Or did they know something else? I was sure something was going on that I was not being told about, and I didn't know how to find out what that was. I leaned forward and reached for my cup of coffee. It was cold and tasted bitter on my tongue and when I swallowed it my stomach howled in protest.

FIVE

I gave the Budai statue at the entrance to the Laughing Buddha Lounge a wide berth. Its gold belly was all shiny from being rubbed by innumerable patrons seeking protection for their children. Inside the lounge my senses were assaulted by the smell of booze and the tantalizing glow of liquor bottles reflecting the yellow and red paper lanterns on the ceiling. I considered leaving. *Just because someone recommends meeting somewhere doesn't mean it's mandatory.* But I hadn't suggested somewhere else, had I, and so here I was, for better or for worse.

I hurried through the bar to the restaurant area and made my way to the back. As I walked between booths with Formica tabletops and cranberry-red suede benches a forty-something couple glanced up at me with illicit-affair guilt in their eyes. On the back wall, the soft glow cast by five rows of glass-enclosed candles barely punctuated the darkness. I sank into a soft red crushed-velvet sofa, propped my feet up on a gold vinyl footstool, and closed my eyes. I wondered what Brion Kacey would say or do if he knew who I was meeting here.

Then I sensed J. B. Harrell's tall, slender frame looming over me and opened my eyes. The glow of the candles accentuated the sharp angles of his square jaw and high cheekbones, the whiteness of his pressed shirt inside a smart gray vest and suit jacket. I had the impression that he was all too aware of how suavely handsome he looked. He tipped his chin down and brought it back up in a perfunctory greeting. He sat next to me on the sofa, a safe distance away.

"So, Ms. Jensen. What do you have to tell me?"

"Nothing, I'm afraid."

"And yet you called."

"It's not that I didn't try," I said. "I did. I tried to find evidence that would refute your suspicions about Anthony Little Eagle's death. I tried to prove that another child hadn't been injured in the Mellon foster home."

"So you're here to confirm my allegations?"

"I can't confirm or refute them."

We were interrupted by the appearance of a silver-haired waiter with facial features that made him look perpetually amused.

"Want a drink?" J. B. Harrell asked.

"No."

"I didn't think so." He smiled ever so slightly and told the waiter he'd like a glass of their most expensive pinot grigio.

"I'll have a Diet Coke," I said.

J. B. Harrell sat back, stretched out his long legs in a relaxed position incongruent with the look on his face, and waited. Finally, I couldn't stand the silence any longer.

"I'm sorry," I said.

"So much for promises," he said with a shrug.

So much for white people's promises is what he might as well have said. I turned toward him, weighing the lack of trust between us. The edge of antagonism in his body language came off as arrogance but something told me it was something else entirely.

"I guess I shouldn't have come," I said.

He opened his mouth and I assumed he was going to agree, but just then the waiter returned and placed our drinks on the round glass table. My eyes were immediately drawn into the pale, straw-yellow blush of the pinot grigio; my nostrils sucked in its bright, flowery fragrance. J. B. Harrell tipped his head ever so slightly and reached for the glass. I felt myself blush.

He took a sip of wine, placed the glass back on the table, and then sat back on the sofa. "I actually believed you," he said, staring over my shoulder at the candles on the wall behind me. "I believed you when you said you would do everything you could to find out what happened to Anthony Little Eagle and the other child."

I tasted his hostility on my tongue and spat it back at him. "You have no idea what I did."

"So enlighten me," he said.

I glanced at his wineglass, then down at the table. "It was a mistake for me to call you."

"And yet you did," he said.

"I'm suspicious," I said. "Something is going on but I don't know what."

He looked surprised and started to say something but then seemed to think better of it. He reached into his jacket pocket, pulled out a pen and a small notebook.

"The agency attorney told me I should stay out of it."

"Brion Kacey," he mumbled and then scribbled something in the notebook.

"And my supervisor backed him up."

"Betsy Chambers."

The man had obviously done his homework. He looked at me, his eyebrows raised, his hand poised.

"Brion got really upset when I told him you claimed another child had been hurt in the Mellon home. He ordered me not to talk to you again."

His lips curled up into a hint of a smirk. "Yet here you are," he said. "Talking to me."

"They wouldn't let me see the case record."

"There you have it." He slapped the sofa with the palm of his hand. "They know Anthony Little Eagle's death wasn't an accident."

"Or maybe they're just trying to protect the agency's reputation," I said.

"Which begs the question, does it not," he said, "what it is they're covering up. What is it exactly that they are afraid might tarnish the agency's image?"

"Maybe they don't want it to get out that another child was injured in the Mellon home...*if* that actually did happen. What makes you so sure?" I said. "Who said it happened on June 8, 2000? Where did you get the information?"

"My sources are confidential," he said. "All I can tell you is that the girl was five years old."

I stared at him. How could I dispute him when I knew nothing? "But...but why did you say there were others?"

"Well," he said, "the girl and Anthony Little Eagle make two, right?"

"So you're just guessing there might have been more."

"Why wouldn't there be?"

"You have no evidence."

"Neither do you."

"But to insinuate that the Mellons are murderers is outrageous. In fact, quite frankly, I find all your allegations offensive."

"Yet how can you know what happened to that little girl or to any other child when you weren't around in 2000?"

I lowered my head and looked down at my lap. Thoughts, fears, and ideas about what I might say swirled around in my head. *It was a mistake to come. What did I think it would accomplish anyway?* Harrell was staring at me. His face was so strong, hard, determined, so strangely unsettling.

"You don't know," I said through gritted teeth. "You don't know what I did to try to get information. You don't know how hard I tried."

"Pray tell."

"Brion and Betsy wouldn't let me read the case record, so today I talked to the worker who placed Anthony Little Eagle. I asked her to tell me what was in it."

"Now we're getting somewhere," he said.

"But she didn't know anything." I looked down again, embarrassed about mentioning my meeting with Lynn Winters at all. I'd only done it because I was defensive.

J. B. Harrell put his pen down. "Your social worker put a child in a home...that she knew nothing about?" His words, slow and drawn out, oozed with a judgment I recognized as my own.

"She...she screwed up. She never read the case record."

A sneer formed on his lips. "And you're her supervisor?"

It wasn't his accusation itself that startled me most. It was the scope of its implications. I caught myself tearing up. No, I didn't know that Lynn hadn't read the case record. No, I didn't know that the girl hadn't followed other agency procedures either. And yes, I should have known. I was the supervisor. Lynn was new. She needed my guidance and coaching. I should have intervened when I saw the police bring Anthony Little Eagle into the agency that day. I should have left my office and asked Lynn if she had any questions, should have given her instructions whether she asked for them or not. I had been so busy pointing my finger at Lynn Winters that I hadn't noticed the three fingers of blame pointing back at me.

"Yes," I said in a voice laden with both defiance and humiliation. "I am her supervisor, and I didn't know."

Two horizontal lines cut into Harrell's forehead. "What else?"

"She didn't comply with the Indian Child Welfare Act."

There it was. I'd told the truth.

Harrell nodded as if to say so what else is new. "So now what? What are you going to do?"

"What are *you* going to do?" I shot back at him. Hadn't he listened to anything I'd said? Hadn't I just told him I'd tried and failed? What else could I do?

"Fair enough," he said. "I'll tell you what I've done so far. I went to the police and told them what I knew. I told them they should subpoena the case record as part of their investigation."

My eyes widened. This I hadn't expected. "What happened?"

"They blew me off," he said with a shrug. "To them, Anthony Little Eagle is just another Indian kid. Indian kids die. That's what happens. They've already decided it was an accident."

"What makes you so sure it wasn't?" I asked.

"What makes you so sure it was?" he retorted.

"I'm not," I said. "I'm not sure about anything."

We sat for while in silence. *Walk away while you can,* I told myself. *You don't know what you're getting yourself into.* But then a shiver went through me and I saw myself standing on the edge of a cliff looking down at the truth of what I would become if I did nothing.

"Looks like we'll just have to use the information you've given me," I heard J. B. Harrell say.

I bristled. "What? What information? How could I have given you any information when I don't have any?"

"Well, for starters, it's pretty clear there is a cover-up when the supervisor isn't allowed access to the file. And I know that the social worker didn't bother to read about the Mellon home before placing a child there. Oh yes, and there's that matter of noncompliance with the Indian Child Welfare Act. If these allegations were made public, maybe that would get the police to subpoena the file and read it for themselves. But then again, they still might not care."

"I told you those things in confidence," I said.

He looked at me for what felt like a long time. Then he muttered under his breath, "Just another dead Indian kid."

"You don't think I know what happens to Indian kids?" I said. "You don't think I know that Anthony Little Eagle's death was my fault? Well, I have news for you, Mr. Harrell. I know and I care and I feel responsible. But if you don't believe me, then go ahead and use what I told you today against me. Just know that if you do, you will lose the only person who cares as much about the boy as you do."

J. B. Harrell's face was expressionless as he stood up and placed a ten-dollar bill on the table. He turned to leave, then looked at me over his shoulder. "Was Hazelden the treatment center you went to?" he said. "I hear it's nice there this time of year."

And then he was gone. I stared at his glass of pinot grigio, still three-quarters full, on the table in front of me, feeling as vulnerable and exposed as if I were sitting there naked.

SIX

September 1972

Mary Williams hoped the colorful fish on the umbrella under which she and Jamie were huddled would help to brighten his mood. They warded off the morning chill as best they could by half walking and half running past the red-, yellow-, and brown-splattered lawns to the bus stop on the corner. When the school bus pulled up, Jamie got on, looking back at her with trust in his eyes and a brave smile on his lips. She waved until the bus was out of sight, each wave a promise to him that everything was going to be all right. And then she rushed home to get her car.

"No one's going to get away with hurting my son," she muttered as she drove to the school. "No one!"

—

"Sean keeps calling me a dirty injun, Mom," Jamie had sobbed. "Is there something wrong with me?"

"There is *nothing* wrong with you, sweetie," she said, squeezing him tight. "That boy is a bully and I'm going to make sure he doesn't bother you ever again."

She'd wept inside to see the devastation on Jamie's face and hear the confusion in his voice. But it was Wayne who had crushed her, later that night when they got into bed and she told him she was going to see the principal.

"I'll teach Jamie how to fight," he said. "Boys get like that if they think someone's a sissy."

"What? You're worried your son is a sissy?"

"I worry about making things worse by talking to the principal."

"I guess I'll have to go to the school alone," she'd said, as tears flooded her eyes. "But don't worry, I'll be sure to tell the principal that you're going to teach Jamie how to fight and be a man."

"Be fair, Mary. Don't you think it would be better to help him solve his own problems rather than solving them for him?"

"He's only seven, Wayne."

———

Mary pulled the car to a halt in the first available space in the school parking lot. She marched to the front entrance, gripping the front of her jacket.

"I'm here to see the principal," she announced in the front office.

"Mr. Nelson isn't in yet," the receptionist said.

"I'll wait."

She sat on a metal folding chair facing the principal's office door. She tapped her foot. *If only Wayne were here with me. If only I'd known what to say to Jamie. If only I could get my hands on the bully myself.* Then the door to the hallway opened and a stocky man in a rumpled suit strolled in.

"Good morning, Mr. Nelson," the receptionist said. "Mrs. Williams is waiting to see you."

The principal swiveled his beer belly in Mary's direction. She noted the whiteness of his teeth inside his pasted-on smile and the chubbiness of his outstretched hand and decided he was no match for her.

"What can I do for you today, Mrs. Williams...may I call you Mary?"

"Certainly. I'd like to speak with you in private, *Ray*," she said. "It's about a serious matter."

The spurious smile on the principal's face showed her he was annoyed at having to deal with an irate mother first thing in the morning. She sat across from his desk in an overstuffed chair that was big enough for two of her, even with her being a bit on the plump side. With all the aplomb she could muster, she plunged in.

"Jamie is in tears. He can't sleep. Sean, a boy in his class, is calling him names. Pushing him. He was so excited about being in second grade this year, he couldn't wait to go to school. Now he makes up excuses not to go. Twice this week he pretended to be sick. He didn't tell me until last night what was going on. I think he was ashamed." She gripped the arms of the chair and bent her upper body toward him. "I'm sure you don't want bullying in your school any more than I do, Ray. I know you'll make sure that boy is punished."

The principal scratched his chin and glanced out the window. "It's good you came in," he lied. "Tell me, how is Jamie doing in school otherwise?"

"He's being bullied. He's being called a dirty injun. How do you think he's doing?"

"I'm not suggesting..." He paused. "It's just that sometimes when children like Jamie reach second grade, they start to have problems. Especially, you know, given his background...

environmental risks and other factors."

"Excuse me?" Mary glared at the principal. She didn't know which infuriated her more, what he'd just said or the obscure language he'd used to cover up what he really meant.

"We're here to help. It's important that children get the services they need early. You know what they say, Mary: an ounce of prevention is worth a pound of cure."

The soft cushion under her started to suck her down and she fought it off, extricated herself to the edge of the chair. "I would think Jamie's teacher would have called me if he was having trouble," she said. "I'm surprised she didn't notice that he was being bullied."

Mr. Nelson picked up the phone. "Please ask Miss Withersteen to come to my office," he said to the receptionist. "Great, tell her Jamie Buckley's mother is here."

"Williams," Mary said. "His name is Jamie Williams."

She looked at her watch. Only a few minutes left before school started. She shot a fierce look at the principal. There was nothing wrong with Jamie. He was reading at grade level. He was a happy, well-adjusted boy. Jamie was not the problem. The bully was the problem.

"Good morning, Miss Withersteen," the principal said. "I'm sure you remember Mary, Jamie Buckley's foster mother?"

"Jamie's been with us since birth," Mary said, her hand sweating as she shook the teacher's much slimmer hand.

"Mary and I were just wondering if Jamie might be having any learning difficulties...or any other problems," the principal said.

"Ray here is the only one wondering that." Mary curled her fists into the soft folds of the chair cushion.

"Is there something *you're* concerned about?" the teacher

asked.

What a cleverly disguised accusation, Mary thought, from a teacher who looked too young to have graduated from high school much less have children of her own. What could she possibly know about Jamie? She took a deep breath and looked directly into Miss Withersteen's eyes.

"A boy in your class named Sean is pushing my son around. I want him punished and I want the bullying to stop."

"Jamie is the sweetest little boy," Miss Withersteen said, "but he doesn't like to read out loud. I was going to mention that to you at parent-teacher night. It's not unusual for these children to have problems like that."

"What do you mean *these* children? Jamie is just like any other little boy."

"Of course he is," the principal said. "I'm sure Miss Withersteen didn't mean to imply otherwise."

"I certainly did not," the teacher said. "What I am suggesting, though, is that it might not hurt to get him tested."

"What kind of testing?" Mary started to feel shaky. She'd noticed that Jamie wasn't interested lately in reading his favorite Archie comic books to her. Was that because he was too upset about the bullying to read or because he was having some kind of trouble reading? Could it be possible that he didn't want to go to school because of some learning difficulty? Could he have made up the story about the bully because he didn't want to tell her what was really going on?

"There's a whole battery of tests," Miss Withersteen said. "I don't usually recommend all of them because they're expensive, but in Jamie's case the Bureau of Indian Affairs will absorb the cost. He's enrolled with his tribe, isn't he?"

"I...I...I think so," Mary stuttered, not because she wasn't sure whether Jamie was enrolled but because one too many seeds of doubt had now been planted for her to ignore. She was floundering. Should she insist that Sean be punished and refuse to have Jamie tested? Was Jamie really having difficulty learning or did the teacher think she saw symptoms of learning disabilities, probably fetal alcohol syndrome, too, because she expected to see them?

"Well, then," the principal said. "It seems that the next step is for you to make sure Jamie is enrolled with his tribe, okay?"

"He is," she muttered.

Miss Withersteen and the principal glanced at each other, eyebrows raised, then looked back at her.

"Jamie is enrolled."

"Good." Mr. Nelson smiled. "Then our school psychologist can take it from here." He sat back in his chair, obviously pleased with himself.

"It's wonderful that people like you are willing to help children like Jamie," Miss Withersteen said with a sympathetic smile. "He's such a lucky little boy. So sorry, there goes the bell."

Miss Withersteen rushed out the door then, leaving Mary clutching at her self-confidence like a timid mouse trying to keep it from trailing behind an imposingly large and self-possessed cat.

"Rest assured." The principal stood up. "We'll do everything we can to help Jamie."

Mary suddenly felt slow and heavy. It took all her energy to pull herself up and release herself from the chair. She stood as erect as she could and looked the principal in the eye. "What about Sean," she said. "What about the bullying?"

"This kind of thing happens all the time with boys. They usually work it out on the playground...if you know what I mean," he said with a chuckle and a wink.

Mary clenched her fists, then realized she didn't have enough strength left right then to fight both Mr. Nelson and Wayne. The principal reached out to shake her hand and she turned away from him. At least she could do that.

"We'll be in touch," he said with a wave.

She dragged herself from the building, her steps weighed down by doubts now nibbling at the edges of the truth that had been so clear to her just an hour before. She sucked in the crisp fall air and spit out a wild fury of invectives through her clenched teeth. Wayne was right; she never should have come. She'd only made things worse.

SEVEN

J. B. Harrell glares at me and I glare back. His face shifts and changes into a man I knew on the reservation up north. I cringe. George's long black hair flaps over his rage-filled eyes like crow's wings and he screams at me, just like he did years ago. "We don't need any fucking welfare bitches in our business. Get the hell outta here, white girl." He vanishes. I'm back in the Laughing Buddha Lounge. I'm alone. My fingers shake as I curl them around J. B. Harrell's glass and pick it up from the table. I gulp down what is left of his pinot grigio and call for the waiter. I order another glass of wine and then another and another until I pass out on the red velvet sofa.

I woke with a start, relieved to feel the soft cotton of my sheets and threadbare nightgown on my skin. Everything on the bed stand was in its proper place—my reading glasses on top of my book, the beige doily my grandmother crocheted for me when I was a toddler, my black gooseneck reading lamp, my alarm clock showing three o'clock in the morning. I took a sip of water from the glass I fill nightly to ward off bad dreams, obviously nothing but a silly superstition, and thought about my meeting with J. B. Harrell.

I got out of bed and made my way to the bathroom. I looked hungover even though, in fact, I hadn't touched the glass of pinot grigio that J.B. Harrell left behind last night when he walked out on me, except in the dream. But I had wanted to and right now I craved that glass of wine more than anything else in the world

You know what to do, I told myself as I pulled on the faded pink cotton bathrobe that I inherited from my mother. My bare toes gripped the parquet flooring in the hall, then sank into the long thick pile of the shag rug in the living room. I sat down at my oversized desk in the corner, turned on my computer, and signed into NAICS, the North American Indian Clean and Sober recovery website. I typed in my chat room screen name, Numees, which was an Algonquin name for sister that I chose because it had a nice ring to it. My online recovery sponsor was Hehewuti, a Hopi from somewhere in Arizona. She was always online. Sometimes I wondered if she was a real person, because she never slept. But real or not, over the years of our relationship, there hadn't been a nook or cranny of my inner psyche, of my soul, that I hadn't laid bare before Hehewuti. Well, almost none.

"Hehewuti," I typed. "Are you there?"

An instantaneous reply popped up on the screen. "Hey, Numees. Can't sleep, huh?"

"I had a drinking dream."

"Did you wake up before or after you got wasted?"

"I passed out."

"Okay...so?"

"I want a glass of wine in the worst way."

"Lie number one."

"Okay, okay. I want a whole bottle of wine."

"Better get it out, Numees. Nothing you say can shock me, girl."

I wasn't sure about that. Hehewuti might be plenty shocked if she knew I was a white woman from the Midwest and not an Ojibwe from Canada. I justified my lie by telling myself it was okay to identify myself as an Ojibwe from Canada as long as I sincerely felt like an Ojibwe from Canada when I was in the chat room and as long as I was scrupulously honest with Hehewuti about what I was feeling about drinking.

"I know the dream was a warning," I said. "I want to escape into a state of complete and total oblivion where there are no demands, no guilt, no consciousness, no conscience...no nothing."

"Why?"

"Something terrible happened," I said. "And this guy's breathing down my neck to get me to do something about it. But I don't know what to do. I have this need to show that I care, and I really do care, but I don't know why I feel so desperate to prove it to this guy, or to anyone for that matter."

"What happened?"

"That's the problem. I don't know. I don't know what the truth is." I knew I was being vague, but if I told Hehewuti the details and then later she heard about Anthony Little Eagle on the news, she might put two and two together and realize I lived in Monrow City. I couldn't risk her finding out that I'd lied to her.

"What are you most afraid of, Numees?"

"I don't know."

"Stop and think."

"I guess I'm scared that I'll find out what's going on," I said, "but no one will believe me."

"And then what?"

"I could lose my job."

"And then what?"

"I wouldn't be any good to anyone anymore."

"And then what?"

"I don't want to do this. I want a drink."

"Walk it through, Numees. If the worst thing that could happen happened and you got fired, then what?"

"It's not," I typed.

"What?"

"Losing my job isn't the worst thing that could happen."

"What would be?"

"Losing myself."

"Which is what happens when you get drunk, right?"

"How do you do that?" I typed.

"What are you going to do now?"

"The next right thing. Whatever I have to do."

"What's that?"

"I don't know yet."

"What about that drink?"

"I don't need it anymore."

I thanked Hehewuti and signed out of the chat room. I went back to bed, and although my compulsion to drink had been lifted, I still expected to lie awake trying to figure out what to do next. But as soon as I rolled onto my side and covered my head with a pillow I drifted off to sleep.

———

At seven o'clock my alarm rang and I jumped out of bed. I knew what to do, as if the next right thing had seeped into my unconscious as I slept and popped out as soon as I opened my eyes. I also knew that what I was about to do could alter my life forever. I splashed cold water on my face, brushed my teeth, and combed my hair back into a ponytail. I grabbed my yellow peasant blouse from the closet but then realized it would be too bright and threw it onto my unmade bed. I pulled out my navy blue blouse and a pair of dark blue slacks. Perfect.

Outside, the air was muggy and still, the sky filled with the threat of thunderstorms on the horizon, as I started walking north along Center Avenue. I usually drove to work, but the forty-five-minute walk gave me time to work out the final details of my plan. I carefully weighed and compared the risks of one action over another, and each time I chose what I considered to be the better alternative I experienced a surge of relief. I'd never been able to understand people who couldn't make the smallest decision because they couldn't bear to eliminate other options. For me there was nothing worse than the ambivalence of indecision.

When I got to my office I told Mabel that I had a lot of paperwork to do and asked her to hold my calls. Then I closed the door and reviewed my plan for getting my hands on the Mellon case record. I tried to prepare for every contingency. The possibility that there might be some things that couldn't be definitively figured out in advance made my mouth go dry. I knew myself well, both the searing anxiety I experienced up until a decision was made, and then, once made, how I pursued it like a dog chewing on a bone. *Better be careful,* I warned myself. *If something goes wrong today, you'll have to be flexible. Be ready to switch to a different strategy, maybe one you'd already discarded. At any point.*

My anxiety grew as the day wore on. One minute I was sure I'd covered all the bases and that I would emerge triumphant.

The next minute I imagined all kinds of unknowns and missteps that would guarantee my downfall. By five o'clock my surroundings had become distorted, as if everything I saw was corrupted by what I was about to do. By five thirty the only thing I was aware of was my breathing, the movements of my body, the butterflies under my ribs.

When I was sure everyone else had left for the day I opened my office door. Then I sat down at my desk and shuffled some files, doodled on a pad of paper, pinched my arm, blew my nose. But no matter what I did I couldn't chase away the hovering sense that a devious creature had taken up residence inside me and was about to devour me.

"Working late, huh?" Craig, the night janitor, poked his head in the door.

I jumped.

"Sorry," he said. "Didn't mean to freak you out."

I glanced at my watch and saw that it was five forty-five. "I didn't expect you yet is all," I said. "You're early tonight."

"It's Friday," he said, with a shy smile at odds with his handsome, frat-boy appearance.

"Ah, yes, party night." I was relieved to hear how normal my voice sounded.

Craig vacuumed the carpet around my desk with the efficiency of a boy eager to finish his work so he could start the weekend partying with his college buddies. I kicked myself for miscalculating the time of his arrival. It wasn't a fatal error but it wasn't an auspicious way to set my plan in motion either. I couldn't afford any other missteps.

I hoped I was right about Craig. My plan depended on him having no loyalty to his part-time job or to the agency. It also depended on him being as innocent and naive as he looked, with his baby-pink cheeks, butch haircut, floppy T-shirt and jeans.

"That's it, then," he said. He emptied the contents of my garbage can into a large bin and started to wheel it toward the door.

"Have a good one," I said. I paused, and when he was just about out the door, made my first move.

"Oh, by the way, Craig, before you leave tonight. I may need to borrow your master key. I forgot to get it from Mabel and I think I may need to get into the mail room to make some photocopies."

"Sure thing, Miss Jensen," he said. "Just give a whistle when you need me. I work my way up the floors and finish on the third."

"Thanks. I'll let you know."

He left, and a bolt like an electric current shot through me. Risky actions I'd taken in the past, noble things like placing welfare rights literature in the waiting room against agency policy and silly things like speeding in the county car, were child's play compared with what I was about to do. And the reprimands I'd endured when I got in trouble at work when I was young were nothing compared to the consequences I would face if I got caught tonight. So why was I doing this? What was driving me?

Pay attention, pay attention, the clip-clop of the garbage bin wheels called out to me as I heard Craig pull the bin from office to office. The elevator door opened and I took off my watch. I laid it on the desk and stared at it. My blood pressure was rising with each passing half hour, each fifteen minutes, and then each five minutes. Finally the time came when, based on my best estimation, Craig would be close to finishing his work for the night. I took the elevator up to the third floor. When I stepped off I saw that Craig was pulling the vacuum cleaner and the large bin, now overflowing, down the hall. I hurried to catch up with him.

"Hey," I said. "About ready to call it a night?"

"Yup," he said, "just these two bathrooms left."

"I guess I caught you just in time then. Looks like I will have to get into the mail room."

"No problem. I'll unlock the door for you before I leave. It'll only take me about fifteen minutes to finish up here."

Before I could think fast enough, Craig disappeared into the men's restroom. I didn't want him to unlock the mail room for me. My plan was to borrow his keys, open the door myself, and then slip the master key off the ring before bringing it back to him. I hesitated, not sure what to do. I was afraid if I followed him into the restroom I might give myself away by appearing too eager. I heard him whistling, the whooshing sound of water, the rhythmic slapping of the mop on the floor. If I went in there now I might startle him. I finally decided the best thing to do was to go back to my office and figure out another way to get my hands on the master key.

But as I walked past the garbage bin that Craig had left in the hall, I spotted the janitor's key ring hanging on its handle. At least a dozen keys dangled like teeth from the ring's metallic smile.

I glanced over my shoulder at the restroom door. Then I looked the other way. The administrative office suite was no more than fifteen feet down the hall.

Go for it. Be quick.

I slid the key ring up and off the handle. I pressed the keys against my waist to keep them from jangling and ran on my tiptoes down the hall. I stopped at the outer door to the office suite, my hands trembling as I inserted one key after another into the lock.

Finally, with only two keys left to try, one of them slipped in and turned with a click. I opened the door and slipped through, closing it silently behind me. I darted past the receptionist's desk and slipped the master key into the lock on Brion Kacey's office door, leaving the door closed so no one would suspect that it was unlocked. Betsy Chambers's office was right next to his, so as an afterthought, I unlocked her door, too. Then I hurried back to the outer door and slipped out into the hall, checking to make sure the door to the suite was still unlocked behind me.

I heard Craig whistling in the men's restroom as I slipped the key ring back onto the handle of the bin. Then he stopped whistling. I ducked into the women's restroom, fell into one of the stalls, and pressed my back against the door. I closed my eyes and waited a few minutes then flushed the toilet. I went over to the sink and ran the water to the count of thirty. Then, with feigned casualness, I walked out of the restroom just as Craig was coming in with the mop in his hand.

"I'll be down in a few minutes to open the mailroom for you," he said.

"Perfect," I said with a smile.

———

What I'd done didn't hit me until after Craig had unlocked the mail room door and said good-night. He never suspected a thing. I patted myself on the back for thinking fast and being flexible enough to change my plan. Unlocking the doors, it turned out, was the better plan anyway, because now I didn't have to worry about how to return the master key later. It was smart of me to unlock Betsy's door, too, although it would quite likely prove unnecessary. Brion Kacey wasn't about to let the Mellon case record out of his sight. I'd be willing to bet my last dollar that that he kept it locked up in his office.

I sat down on a chair in the mail room as if I were waiting for the photocopy machine to warm up. Thirty minutes should be plenty of time for Craig to put his things away and sign out for the night. But the glow of my good fortune so far didn't last. It wasn't long before with each tick of the clock a new worry would pop into my mind. What if I couldn't find the file? What would I discover if I did find it? What if Craig came back for something and saw me on the third floor? What if he found me in the agency attorney's office?

Finally, when I found myself worrying that if I waited one minute longer and worried about one more thing I'd lose my nerve and not carry out the rest of my plan at all, I couldn't stand it any longer. It was time to act.

I went back to my office, retrieved a small flashlight from my desk drawer, and slipped it into one pocket of my slacks. I put my wallet and office keys into the other pocket. The cubicles outside were empty, yet I found myself tiptoeing past them. Then I ran down the hall and up the stairs to the third floor, leaving the stainless steel railing slippery from the sweat on the palms of my hands.

At the door to the administrative office suite, I stopped and looked up and down the hall. I pushed the door open just wide enough to slip through, then slowly and silently closed it behind me. I wiped my sweaty hands on my slacks, reached into my pocket for the flashlight. My knees went cold and I thought my chest was going to explode as I turned the knob on the door to Brion Kacey's office. I slipped inside. I pressed my back against the closed door and crossed my hands over my chest. I heard Brion's voice in my head, ordering me to stay out of it, to leave things alone. I knit his words together into a pulsing defiance and anger that, to my surprise, created within me a beautiful feeling of courage and heightened awareness. It made my skin tingle. I was ready. I was more than ready.

Brion's desk was tidy to the point of fastidious, the top cleared of everything but a telephone and a computer, nothing remotely personal. One by one I opened his desk drawers and rummaged inside. The deepest ones were filled with reams of paper, mostly legal documents, none of them related to Anthony Little Eagle, the Mellon foster home, or the police investigation. Inside the shallow drawers I found paper clips, a stapler and box of staples, pens and pencils, legal pads, and other uninteresting office supplies. Using the flashlight I looked around the room— at the mahogany conference table and ten matching chairs, at Brion's obsessively organized collection of legal journals and other official-looking documents on floor-to-ceiling bookshelves, at two brown upholstered chairs with a dark mahogany end table in between. The beam of light landed on a black six-drawer file cabinet in the corner. I rushed over to it, caught the toe of my shoe on the corner of an area rug and lurched forward, somehow managing not to fall.

"Damn it," I whispered under my breath.

I could feel the blood rushing to my head as I closed my fingers around the handle of the top cabinet drawer. I couldn't believe it. It was actually unlocked. But just as I started to pull it open I heard footsteps. My fingers were like ice frozen on the metal handle. I held my breath. The footsteps stopped outside the door. Then there was a click, a quick flash of light on the wall, the shadow of a man in the doorway. He was wearing a uniform.

"What the hell?" The security guard took a step into the room.

My fingers flew off the handle and onto my lips to smother

a gasp. It felt like my throat was in my mouth. I dove into the corner without, to my amazement, making a sound. I crouched down behind the cabinet with the still-lit flashlight facedown on the floor. I clenched my teeth. Since when did the agency hire a security guard to check the building at night? How could I not have known that?

A beam of light made its way slowly along the wall. I squeezed my body farther into the corner. My pulse was pounding so loud I was sure the guard could hear it. I tucked my head between my knees, squeezed my eyes shut. When the light reached the file cabinet my life was going to be sucked into it. I pictured myself standing up, hands in the air, ready to be tried, found guilty, and punished. After an excruciatingly long wait I heard a click, the doorknob jiggling, the guard's footsteps receding outside the door. I opened my eyes. There was nothing but darkness. No sounds. I rested my head against the side of the metal cabinet. It was cool on my temple. Betsy's door slammed against the wall next door and I gasped. My hand flew up to cover my mouth.

"Young people these days," I heard the security guard shout. "Too lazy to do their damn jobs."

Poor Craig. He'd be blamed for leaving the doors unlocked. I hoped he wouldn't lose his job because of it. I stared at the door, waited for the guard to come back. My eyes started to burn but I didn't dare blink. Several minutes passed. I didn't hear anything else but still I was afraid to move. I waited. Then waited some more. Finally, when I was absolutely sure the guard was gone, I scooted away from the wall. I slowly began to unfold my legs, my thighs numb from being in one position for so long. Pulling myself up was like hauling a piece of wood into an upright position. I moved my shoulders up to my ears and down again. I raised my feet up onto my toes, lowered them back onto my heels, up and down, up and down. I reached my arms behind my back, interlocked my fingers so my palms were facing each other and lifted my arms behind me until I felt the stretch across my chest and shoulders.

Once my blood was pumping again, I was able to think. And worry. What if the guard had locked me in? I tiptoed over to the door and turned the knob. *Thank God.* Just like my office door, Brion's door opened from the inside even when it was locked on the outside. I opened the door a crack and peeked out, then quickly closed it again. I had to stay here and see this thing through. With the security guard walking around the building checking all the other doors, this was probably the safest place for me to be right now anyway.

I tiptoed back to the file cabinet. I opened the top drawer and aimed the beam of the flashlight inside. There was the Mellon case record, right in front, hidden in plain sight. I couldn't believe my good fortune. I wondered if it meant I was doing the right thing or if it was just a sign of Brion Kacey's carelessness...or arrogance.

I pulled the folder out and closed the drawer, careful not to make a sound. I slowly lowered myself onto the floor and sat cross-legged with my back against the cabinet. I placed the file on my lap, opened it, aimed the flashlight onto the page. I took in, then let out a deep breath and started to read.

EIGHT

It was past midnight when I staggered out of the Health Services Building. I got into a cab and handed the driver the piece of paper on which I'd jotted J. B. Harrell's address. I sat back in the seat and rested the side of my head against the window. I tightened my grip on the briefcase on my lap. The photocopies of the Mellon case record were inside.

"Here we are." The driver came to an abrupt stop at the curb in front of a red-brick building.

"Thanks," I mumbled as I got out and started to walk away.

"Ma'am?"

I turned and saw the driver leaning out the window with his hand out. "Oh, sorry," I said, and I gave him the wadded-up twenty-dollar bill that I'd been clutching in my hand.

I stood at the curb with my briefcase securely tucked under my arm and stared up at the geometric windows and open-air balconies. I'd read that some of the old industrial buildings near the riverfront had been converted into upscale loft condos but I'd never seen one before. I went inside and took the elevator up to the fourth floor.

"Over here."

J. B. Harrell stood in an open doorway to my left. In a white T-shirt and sweat pants with no shoes or socks, there was still a studied refinement about him. He stepped to the side and with a slight motion of his hand invited me in.

I was taken aback at the spaciousness of his penthouse, with its exposed timber beams and brick walls, polished hardwood floors, floor-to-ceiling windows framing skyline views, and designer furniture. Could anyone who lived in a place like this, and wore three-piece Calvin Klein suits and Van Heusen shirts, really care about a boy like Anthony Little Eagle?

"Must be important," J. B. Harrell said, running his fingers through his hair, "to wake someone up at this hour."

I held up my briefcase, and he raised his eyebrows and led me to a brown leather couch in the middle of the open living area.

"Can I get you some water?" he asked.

I nodded, then my eyes followed him to the kitchen. It was immaculate, its stainless steel appliances and black granite countertops uncluttered. No smells, a place for show and not for living. I wondered why he chose to live in such luxury. Why I chose to live simply. For that matter, why were so many people deprived of any choice at all about how they lived?

Harrell placed a glass of sparkling water with ice and a slice of lemon in it on the marble-topped coffee table in front of me. Then he sat down in the adjacent matching leather chair. Behind him, on a sleek black bookshelf, there was a framed photograph of him arm in arm with an attractive blond woman, the two of them smiling at each other. Harrell caught me staring at the picture and frowned.

"Why don't you want to be an Indian?" The force of my

inappropriate outburst propelled me back against the couch.

"Why do you want to be one?" he shot back at me.

"I'm sorry," I said. "I was out of line. It's just that...it's just that I admire Native culture. I hate how your people are treated." I chewed at the skin around my thumbnail and looked away. A wave of heat rushed up my neck and onto my cheeks.

"You and I make about the same amount of money," he said.

I squinted at him. "What?" I asked.

"You're wondering how I can afford this place," he said.

"So you're a mind reader?" I said.

"I inherited some money from my grandfather."

He sat back in his chair with a closed expression on his face and crossed his arms over his chest. I opened my briefcase, pulled out the stack of photocopies and placed it on the coffee table.

"Here," I said. "The Mellon case record."

J. B. Harrell leaned forward and pushed the air out through his nose so it sounded like an aborted sneeze. He stared wide-eyed at the copies, with his mouth open. Then his lips curled into a little smile.

"How?"

"Don't ask," I said.

"I'm afraid I misjudged you, Ms. Jensen."

"Sylvia. Call me Sylvia."

"Sylvia," he said.

"Thank you," I said. Then I put my hands up against my neck, covering the skin in case red blotches sprang up as they were prone to do when I got emotional. Harrell shook his head and looked at the papers on the table for a few minutes.

"I didn't have time to read it all," I said.

He scooted to the edge of his chair, leaned over the pile, and shuffled through the copies. "Here it is," he said. He pulled out a page and started reading it. "Uh-huh, uh-huh, uh-huh." He slapped the page down on top of the stack of copies and sat back in his chair.

"What?" I asked.

"It's all in there," he said. "Ellie Moon was the name of the five-year-old girl. She was taken to the emergency room on June 8, 2000. Her arm was broken. Mr. Mellon said she was running down the stairs and fell. The report says it was an accident."

"Yeah," I said. "I read that part. So you're still not going to tell me how you knew about that?"

"Like I said, my sources are confidential."

"Well, if you can't trust me..." I laid the palms of my hands on the stack of copies.

"I know someone who works in the ER at HarbourPointe Hospital," he said. "When Anthony Little Eagle died, I asked her to run a check on the Mellons. That's how I found out about the girl."

"What about the others? You said there were others." I braced myself. I really didn't want to know the answer.

"There's never just one," he said. "That's what my source said when she found out about the girl."

"So that's it? That's all the evidence you have that other children were hurt in the Mellon home?"

He shrugged his shoulders and pointed to the copies on the table. "It looks like we're about to find out if there were or not."

I set about dividing the copies into two equal piles. I handed half of the pages to him and he sat back on the chair and started to read. I bent over the table with my stack.

"Do you have some paper?" I asked.

J. B. handed me a yellow legal pad and I tore off a sheet.

I placed the paper sideways on the first copy in my stack and moved it slowly down from line to line on the page, my eyes moving from left to right, searching for trigger words, like *accident, incident, injury, hospital, doctor.* I skimmed each page in the same way, and when I didn't find any evidence of another injured child, I turned the page upside down on the table. Every once in a while I heard a scratching sound and a mumble coming from J. B. I'd lift my head and watch him write something down in his notebook. We'd glance at each other, then lower our heads and get back to work.

"Ellie Moon," I mumbled at one point.

"What?" J. B. placed the page he was reading onto his lap.

"It says here that she'd been in the Mellon home for less than a month at the time of the accident."

J. B. raised one eyebrow and frowned. "Yeah," he said.

"But it doesn't say whether anyone ever talked to the girl alone to ask her what happened. Damn it, they're supposed to do that."

I dog-eared the page and flipped through the rest of the still unread copies in my stack, stopping whenever I saw Ellie Moon's name. "After she broke her arm," I said, "it looks like she continued to live with the Mellons. There are some reports here of regular home visits, routine stuff, nothing out of the ordinary, no more injuries." I kept turning the pages as I talked. "Whoa. This is strange. Just a few months ago, the Mellons asked that Ellie be removed from their home."

J. B. placed the palms of his hands on top of his copies and cocked his head. "Why?"

"It says here that Linda Mellon wasn't able to handle her any more," I said. "Hmm." I flipped back to some of the previous entries. "There's nothing in here about her being any trouble at all. That means she lived with the Mellons for about five years after she broke her arm, without any problems. Or at least none that were reported. It says here that after Ellie was removed, Mr. and Mrs. Mellon requested that their foster home be used for temporary, emergency placements until further notice. This is strange."

J. B. Harrell started flipping through the pages on his lap as if he were looking for something in particular.

"What are you looking for?" I asked.

"I'll know when I see it. Wait a minute. This is odd."

"What?"

"Are you sure you made copies of all the pages in the file?"

"I thought I did."

"Let's see," he said, and he spread several pages out on the coffee table. "The first entry in the file was in October 1999, when Mr. and Mrs. Mellon applied to be foster parents. Then there are all the application materials. Does it look to you like everything's here?"

I shuffled through the copies one by one. "Here's the home study," I said, "and the home safety inspection report. Yup, here's the criminal background check, then the foster home worker's recommendation, the certificates showing they completed all the required orientation and training workshops. It looks like it's all here."

"So when were they qualified to start getting foster children?" he asked.

"Looks like the end of April, 2000," I said.

"So Ellie Moon must have been the first child placed in their home," he said. "She broke her arm on June 8, 2000, after living with them...wait, I don't see any record of her being placed with them. No date."

"Let me see," I said. "I know what to look for."

J. B. sat back and crossed his arms as I studied the copies.

"Maybe I got some pages out of order." I went through them a second and then a third time. Finally I gave up. "It looks like some pages aren't here," I said with a shake of my head.

"About how many are missing, do you think?"

"Ten or so, I'd say. Maybe some pages were stuck together and didn't get copied."

"Two pages might get stuck, maybe three, but not ten in row."

"What are you saying?"

"It seems to me that some pages were removed from the file." He puckered his lips and sat back in his leather chair.

"But that doesn't make any sense. Don't you think if someone wanted to hide something it would be Ellie Moon falling down the stairs and breaking her arm? Why hide information about when she was first placed in the Mellon home? It has to be in the file. I was in a hurry when I made the copies. I must have screwed up. That's the most logical explanation."

"It's one explanation," J. B. said.

"But who would mess with the file?" I said. "Who would do such a thing? And why?"

"Brion and Betsy?" He shrugged.

"No, they wouldn't do that. No. That would be illegal." I lowered my chin and pressed the palms of my hands on the back of my head. "No." I moved my hands to the sides of my neck and then to my cheeks.

"Maybe what's missing isn't about Ellie Moon," J. B. Harrell said. "Maybe there's something else they don't want you to know."

I raised my head and looked at him. "You still think there

were other children injured."

He tipped his head to the side and shrugged his shoulders. Our eyes locked.

"I'll find the missing pages," I said.

The look on J. B.'s face suggested that he knew what I didn't say out loud: that nothing was going to stop me until there was justice for Anthony Little Eagle.

NINE

December 1972

Mary Williams couldn't shake the feeling that something wasn't right but she couldn't put her finger on what it was. The dining room table was meticulously arranged with the five candles on the red Scandinavian-style candelabra ready for Jamie to light. The pine-green tablecloth, holly-decorated plates, red Christmas goblets, and gold-plated silverware looked as beautiful as they did every year. She could smell the savory aroma of the pot roast in the oven and the sugary sweetness of deep-dish apple pie cooling on the kitchen counter. Boxes of decorations and strings of multicolored lights crisscrossed the living room floor, ready to be hung on the tree. Everything she could see was perfect.

Just as she told herself there was nothing to worry about, the holiday scene sprang to life. Wayne and Jamie pushed through the kitchen door carrying the Christmas tree they'd cut down in the woods out back.

"See, Mom, we got the long needles, the kind you like."

Jamie's face was flushed from the cold and excitement. After the rough start to the school year, he was back to his normal self. He clamored to read out loud to her at night before bed. He danced to *I'll Be There* by the Jackson Five every chance he got. His teacher finally conceded that there didn't seem to be any need for testing, especially after he'd told his second-grade class jaw-dropping details about the last Apollo manned mission to the moon earlier this month.

Mary had spared no words; she let the principal know that she thought people at school had been confused because Jamie's brilliance didn't match their expectations of him. She also made sure the bullying had stopped for good. She grilled Jamie every day after school. She even admitted, after Wayne bought boxing gloves and a book about wrestling, that the way he taught Jamie how to fight looked like harmless father-son horseplay.

"This is the best tree ever." Jamie managed to hold the white pine steady with his small hands while Wayne adjusted the stand and positioned the tree. Then he ran to the kitchen to get water. Ever since he was big enough to carry the pitcher, it had been his job to keep the tree from drying out.

It wasn't long before Wayne's parents came through the back door, their faces as flushed as Jamie's with holiday excitement. They were all ready to set about decorating the tree before dinner. Wayne and his father followed their tried-and-true system for putting on the lights. Then everyone dug into the boxes in search of their favorite ornaments. Jamie pulled out the seven ornaments that had his picture on them and laid them out on the floor, organized by age.

"Me as a baby." He held up the first ornament and walked around the tree in search of the perfect place to hang it. "Now, let's see, where should I hang this one of me on my first birthday." Everyone laughed. Watching Jamie was Mary's favorite part of the tree-decorating tradition.

Soon the boxes were empty and the ornaments were all hung. Silver tinsel icicles dripped from each branch. Mary turned all the lights off except for the ones on the tree. Everyone clapped. Then they held hands and said what they were grateful for this year.

"I'm thankful for the puppy I'm getting for Christmas." Jamie gave his parents a shy sideways look.

Mary and Wayne laughed and rolled their eyes. Jamie was determined that this year, the one special present they got him every Christmas would be a dog.

"You're going to have to hang in there until tomorrow morning," Wayne said.

"And now it's time to eat," Mary announced.

Christmas dinner—pot roast and mashed potatoes, gravy, green beans, and molded Jell-O with cranberries, apples, and walnuts, topped off by apple pie à la mode and coffee—was as delicious as ever. After dinner it was time to open presents. Jamie was left giddy and breathless by the profusion of gifts, most of them toys, that Wayne's parents, as always, showered on him. After they were gone and it was time for bed, he was still bouncing off the walls.

"Morning will come faster if you go to sleep," Mary said when she tucked him in. He sprang up from the bed to hug her.

"This is the best Christmas ever, Mom. I'm too excited to sleep." He kissed her, then threw his body down on the bed and closed his eyes. Within seconds he was snoring.

Mary smiled and closed his bedroom door. She was glad she hadn't told Wayne about the sense of doom that had followed her all evening. If she had, he would have watched her like a hawk for signs of depression, which would have made her more anxious and him more worried. She'd just had a case of the holiday jitters and she was proud of herself for not letting her premonition spoil the festivities.

———

Wayne got up before dawn to drive sixty miles to pick up the dog they'd found through an ad posted on the bulletin board at his work. When Mary got up a few hours later, Jamie was already in the living room. She found him rummaging under the tree, pulling tissue paper out of boxes and tossing it off to the side, digging through the coat closet in the hall.

"I can't find my puppy, Mom."

"Dad went to get him, sweetie. How about I make you some blueberry pancakes and you play with your new toys while we wait?"

She looked at her watch. Wayne should be back by now. She looked out the window and saw that it was snowing. The roads were probably getting icy. She wondered if it had been a mistake to arrange to get the dog on Christmas morning instead of picking him up earlier in the week. But then, they'd wanted to surprise Jamie—she smiled about that now—and the man they went to see about the dog had said he was happy to keep the pup for one more week. Wayne was probably having coffee with the man and his wife now, basking in the heat radiating from the wood-burning stove in the middle of their charming one-room cabin. In her head she could see their round antique table with claw feet, the dog with his chin resting on Wayne's foot, the assortment of candles, pottery, macramé, and political posters. She could understand how Wayne might have settled in and lost track of time.

All of a sudden Jamie squealed. "Dad's truck is here," he shouted. "He's home."

Wayne walked into the kitchen with a big smile on his face,

a small white ball of fur tucked inside his parka. Jamie shrieked with delight. The dog wriggled free, jumped down onto the floor and up into his arms. It was love at first sight. Mary and Wayne doubled over with laughter. They watched Jamie kiss the dog's nose and the top of his head, the dog's tongue slobbering Jamie's nose, cheeks, eyes, and neck in return.

"What should I name him?" Jamie said.

"The people we got him from called him Tick," Wayne said.

Jamie laughed. "Why?"

Wayne started to answer, but Mary cut him off with a jerk of her head. "Maybe because ticks are attracted to white fur," she said with a smile. The puppy was healthy and happy now, so what would be the point in telling Jamie that when the man's wife found Tick he'd been nothing but skin and bones, filthy and with swollen ticks hanging all over him. Why would her son need to know that?

Jamie took off for his bedroom, with Tick running behind. The two of them were inseparable from that point on. All day, every day, wherever Jamie was, Tick was there. Whenever Jamie sat down, even at the dinner table, Tick was in his lap. And at bedtime the dog crawled under the covers and wriggled down to Jamie's feet as if that was where he'd slept all his life.

—

Three days after Christmas Mary was doing the dishes when the phone rang.

"Hello, is this Mrs. Williams?"

"Yes?"

"My name is Karon Pate. I'm a new foster home social worker with the county. How are you? Did you folks have a good holiday?"

"Yes...yes, we had a good Christmas...thank you."

"That's good. I'm just calling to schedule a home visit."

"Uh, sure...is there something...um...about something in particular?"

"Just to see how Jamie's doing and how things are going," the social worker said. "It will be good to meet you. We can talk more when I get there."

Mary sank into a kitchen chair and began to shake. What could there be to talk about? She wondered if maybe the school had decided Jamie should be tested after all. Could it be that they had reported her to the county for being uncooperative, or worse yet, neglectful?

"Mrs. Williams?"

"Yes, I'm here." Why now, after years with no contact, do you suddenly want to know how Jamie is doing? she wanted to ask.

"I could come right after the new year," Karon said. "Can you believe it's almost 1973? Let's see, how about..."

The social worker's cheery voice grated on Mary's ears. If she had been able to, she would have told the woman that a home visit wasn't at all necessary, that they were all doing just fine. But she was barely able to breathe, much less say anything. All she could do was write down the date and time of the home visit and say good-bye. After Karon hung up, Mary kept a tight grip on the phone for so long her knuckles turned white. She couldn't move, couldn't do anything, because now she knew it hadn't been her imagination. Something was wrong.

TEN

After sneaking into Brion Kacey's office on Friday night, making photocopies of the Mellon case record, and then studying them with J. B. until three o'clock in the morning, I was drained. I slept until midafternoon on Saturday and then spent the rest of the weekend trying to figure out how to get my hands on the file again and find the missing pages without breaking into Brion's office. Once had been enough. There had to be another way.

Monday morning at work, I turned on my computer and read my emails, which, as usual, took most of the morning. Then the last message from the administration caught my attention. "Congratulations everyone," it said, "on the successful conversion of all paper case records to our new electronic system. Thank you to everyone in advance for your cooperation and patience as we deal with any residual computer glitches."

That was it. When I'd tried to open the Mellon e-file before, and was denied access, it must not have been converted yet. And now it was. That was the answer. This was going to be much easier than I thought.

I closed my email and typed in my password to get access to the case files. Once in, I typed Paul and Linda Mellon's names. I sat back and waited. But instead of their e-file opening on the screen, the words Access Denied, Incorrect Password emerged. Strange. That was a different message than before. Thinking it might be a glitch in the new system, I logged out, re-entered my password, and tried again. Access Denied. Incorrect Password. I picked up the phone and called our technology manager, who everyone called the wizard because he'd never met a computer problem he couldn't fix.

"Ross Seibert. Technology records department."

"Hey, Ross, how are you? This is Sylvia Jensen. I need your help. I can't open an electronic file for one of our foster homes. My password doesn't work."

"Sure thing, Sylvia. What's the name?"

"Mellon. Paul and Linda Mellon. I don't have their case number handy."

"No problem. Give me a sec."

"It says 'Access Denied' when I try to open it," I said. "Last time I tried, it said the file was unavailable."

"Hmm. I think I see what the problem is, Sylvia."

If only I'd called Ross before breaking into Brion's office. I could have saved myself a whole lot of trouble. "So can you get me in?"

"You aren't authorized," he said.

"That can't be right."

"The electronic files are password-protected," he said. "Only those people classified to have access are allowed to open them."

"Ross, I was on the committee that developed the policies and guidelines for the new system, remember? Supervisors are authorized to open all the files in their workers' caseloads. My password has always worked before."

"Hmm, of course. Oh, now I see what's going on," he said after a pause. "There's a litigation hold on that one. Brion Kacey is the only person authorized to open it until further notice."

"I guess you can't help me, then," I said through the sourness filling my mouth.

"Sure I can. I can't give you the password but I can get you in. All you have to do is talk to Brion first."

When hell freezes over, I said to myself. I thanked Ross and hung up the phone. Damn! Why was Brion Kacey so hell-bent on hiding something in that file? And how was I going to find out what it was? Ross would take my word for it if I went back and told him that Brion had authorized me to read the file. But I didn't want to lie to him like that, nor did I want to get him into trouble like I probably got poor Craig into trouble. There had to be some way to get the password without implicating anyone else. I massaged my temples with the tips of my fingers. What do people usually do in case they forget their passwords? I asked myself. Do they hide them in the same place I hide mine?

There was only one way to find out. I glanced at my watch and saw that it was noon. Most people in the building would be away from their desks now, either out for lunch or down at the first-floor coffee shop. I grabbed a three-by-five card and a pen and hurried out the door. The records department was on the same floor as the foster care unit but at the opposite end of the building. When I got to the large, open room filled with desks and computers, everyone was gone, just as I'd hoped. Ross had his own private office back in the corner. On my way to it I was stopped by a voice that came out of nowhere.

"Can I help you with something?"

I turned around. A young woman—young enough I

thought she could pass as a high school student—stood behind me with eager-to-help eyes tempered by a tentative half smile.

"You must be new here," I said.

She nodded. "Yes, ma'am. My name's Janice. Today's my first day."

"Nice to meet you," I said. "I was just on my way to see Ross."

"Mr. Seibert left for lunch," Janice said. "Can I give him a message...or tell him...something?"

"I thought I might have missed him," I said with a shrug. "It's okay. I'll just leave a note on his desk and call him later."

I glanced from side to side as I hurried down the aisle between the rows of desks. The door to Ross's office was open. Before going in I turned around and saw the young woman sitting at a desk at the far end of the spacious room, with her back to me. I sauntered over to the desk as if it were mine. Then I kept one eye on the door as I slid open the top left-hand drawer. I rummaged through pads of paper and sticky notes, pencils, pens, boxes of paper clips. Then I pulled the drawer out as far as it would go. I spotted a sticky note attached to the side, way in the back. I detached it and took it out. There was a list of numbers on it, written in pencil. I quickly copied the numbers onto my card and slipped it into the pocket of my skirt. I reattached the note where I found it, closed the drawer, and got out of Ross's office as fast as I could.

"I'll catch up with Ross later," I said with a wave of my hand as I passed the young woman at her desk.

I hurried back to my office and closed the door. I pulled the card from my pocket and placed it on my desk, then sat down at my computer and logged into the system. I typed in my own password first, followed by the Mellon name, and, as expected, was denied access. I entered the first number that I'd copied from Ross's sticky note and the message Access Denied. Incorrect Password popped up. I tried the next number and then the next and the next. I typed in the last number on the list, and the Mellon e-file opened on the screen. "Yes!" I punched the air with both fists.

I leaned closer to the computer screen and scrolled through the pages I'd already read. I slowed down after the application materials and searched for information about the first child that was placed in the Mellon home. *This is strange,* I said to myself. There were no entries in the record between the date in April of 2000 when the Mellon home was licensed as a foster home and June 8 of the same year. Had the social worker failed to record the placement of Ellie Moon? That didn't make any sense. Could it be J. B. Harrell was right and someone had tampered with the file?

I backtracked to look again. That's when I spotted something I'd missed the first time, something I'd neither seen nor made a copy of. Nothing made sense, and at the same time, I began to think that everything was beginning to fall into place. I called J. B. He picked up on the first ring.

"Harrell here."

"Anthony Little Eagle's death wasn't an accident." As soon as I blurted out the words I was sure they were true.

I heard newsroom sounds on the other end of the line. I thought I heard J. B. say something but I couldn't be sure.

"I said it was *not* an accident."

"You found the missing pages?"

"Not all of them. I mean, I don't know. I found something."

"I'm listening."

"I don't know what to think. Well, maybe I do know what

to think, but this doesn't make sense. Or does it?"

"Slow down, Sylvia. What did you find?"

I pointed at the computer screen. "There's an incident report here. It's signed by a police officer. But here's the thing. It doesn't say what the incident was about. And I don't see any dictation from the social worker about what happened either. Maybe what happened to Ellie Moon wasn't an accident. Maybe that's what the secret is. And if that's true, then we can be sure what happened to Anthony Little Eagle wasn't an accident either."

"Wait a minute. What's the date on the report?" J. B. asked.

"Oh," I said. "I didn't look at that. Let me see. The signature at the bottom is dated May 1, 2000."

"That was more than a month before the girl was injured," he said.

"Right." I paused, confused and embarrassed. "What was I thinking? I assumed the incident report had something to do with Ellie Moon, but of course it didn't, unless the officer wrote the wrong date down." I studied the words on the computer screen. "There's no record...at least none that I see here...of the placement of Ellie Moon or any other child in their home before the incident, whatever it was."

"Could have been a domestic violence situation," J. B. said. "Maybe Mrs. Mellon called the police and then backed off once they got there and no charges were filed. Happens all the time."

"But if there was no foster child in their home yet...I mean, if it had nothing to do with them being foster parents, why would a report like that be in the file?"

"What was the name of the officer?"

"Bradley Finch."

"Did you find anything else?"

"I don't know yet. I...I...I called you as soon as I saw the incident report. I'll keep looking for information about when the first child was placed. It was probably Ellie Moon, but without documentation we can't know that for sure."

"Uh, Sylvia?"

"I'm sorry. I guess I overreacted."

"You never told me how you got your hands on the case file Friday night."

"My sources are confidential," I said.

He laughed. I hadn't heard him laugh before.

"Right," he said. "I'll see what I can find out about Bradley Finch."

We said good-bye and I sat back in my chair and tried to focus. The police were called to the Mellon home because of some kind of incident. That was five years ago, but before Ellie Moon's arm was broken, and it was definitely not related to Anthony Little Eagle's death. I might have jumped to conclusions, but still, wasn't this a sign that something wasn't right? And why hadn't I seen that incident report before? Maybe I'd slipped up and failed to copy it, but there was another explanation that I was now willing to consider. Someone could have removed the incident report from the paper case record on purpose but then forgotten to remove it from the e-file. The question remained: Did the incident report have anything to do with Ellie Moon?

And then there was another question: Why was there nothing in the e-file about when Ellie Moon was placed with the Mellons?

I went back to searching the record, and this time the information practically jumped off the screen and hit me in the face. There was a short entry, only a few sentences long, on a page I had somehow missed before. The date of the entry, May 5, 2000, answered one of our questions; that was the day Ellie Moon was placed in the Mellon home. Then I saw the name of the social worker who had signed it.

"Not Inez," I moaned, and I held my head in my hands. "Of all people."

ELEVEN

I stared at the entry in the Mellon e-file for a long time. I couldn't make sense of it and the harder I tried the more questions it raised. It was short, just three sentences long, and the only entry on a page. Easy to overlook.

> *Paul and Linda Mellon were licensed as a foster home on April 26, 2000. Mrs. Mellon called on May 4th to say she was still distressed about what happened. She wanted to know if we would be placing any more children with them. I assured her that we would. Five-year-old Ellie Moon was placed in the Mellon home today, May 5, 2000. Signed: Inez Koreskovsky*

I closed the e-file and turned off my computer. Inez Koreskovsky had been the bane of my existence for years. The list of grievances against her by other social workers was legion. She was rude both to her colleagues and her clients. She told a teenage girl she could find her own damn way back to the foster home from which she'd run away. She warned colleagues not to be fools and not to listen to foster children, because they all lied. She bragged about not answering the phone at the end of the day to avoid having to work late. She was the last person I wanted to deal with about this.

I left my office and hurried past the cubicles beyond. My social workers watched me pass with curious glances on their faces, both fascinated by my frenzied state and fearing it. Later they would talk about it behind my back.

Inez had managed to claim the cubicle that was the farthest distance possible from my office. It was tucked away in a corner where, undetected, she could while away the days until retirement rescued her from having to help people. Secure in her forty years of seniority, the complicated maze of bureaucratic procedures and union protections, and a deep-seated administrative fear of lawsuits, Inez clearly thought she could do whatever she wanted to do these days. I tensed at the sight of her now, sitting at her desk and staring off into space. If it were winter her mink coat would be draped over the back of her chair so no one could steal it. I'd heard more than one social worker wish out loud that someone would.

"I need to talk to you, Inez," I said. "Now."

She rolled her eyes and followed me back to my office like she was doing me a favor. I closed the door and sat down behind my desk. Inez lowered herself stiffly onto the chair facing me. Blood-red lipstick oozed into the deep wrinkles above and below her mouth. Her dyed-black hair was plastered with gel into an old-fashioned bun at the back of her head.

"Do you remember Mr. and Mrs. Mellon?" I asked.

"Who?"

"The Mellon foster home. You dictated an entry into the case file on May 5, 2000." I tapped my fingers on the armrests of my chair.

"Hmm. You remember me having that case, do you?" Inez said.

I knew only too well what she was implying. "Not directly," I said. "As you know, I was on leave then." I tried to ignore the judgment-laced disapproval oozing from her pores. If cornered, she wouldn't hesitate for a minute to use my history of addiction against me.

"You placed a five-year-old girl in the Mellon home," I continued. "Ellie Moon."

Inez's face was blank.

"The Mellons." I spoke slowly and in the most reasonable tone I could muster. "Where Anthony Little Eagle just died."

"Oh yes...that poor woman."

I clenched my fists under the desk. "You wrote in the file that Mrs. Mellon called you to ask if they would be getting any more foster children after what happened."

"What does any of this have to do with that Indian kid?"

I let my breath out in a slow stream before speaking. "There wasn't anything in the record about what happened, what Mrs. Mellon was referring to," I eventually said. "Do you remember what she talked to you about? I'm sure you do."

"The poor woman couldn't have any more kids of her own. Since she already had the one daughter before she got married, I figured it was the husband's fault," Inez said. "But that's beside the point. It was really important to her to be a good foster mom, and then to have such bad luck with that baby. Poor thing."

An old image from the past came into my head. When I was a research assistant in graduate school, one of my co-workers, who always expected the worst to happen, had taped a picture of an axe on the wall above her desk. Funny thing, she was fired a week later and no one ever told us why. It made the rest of us wonder if we would be next. I looked at Inez, waited for the axe to fall.

"Bad luck?" I asked.

"To have a newborn die on her like that."

I felt like my head had just been split in two. I stared at Inez, my mouth open.

"Sudden infant death syndrome isn't anybody's fault." Her bony back was ramrod straight as she spoke.

A newborn? SIDS? Is that what's missing from the record? The empty hole that had been inside me since Anthony Little Eagle died opened into a massive cavern filled with gigantic boulders, all of them lumbering in the same direction, all of them headed for Inez.

"First night in their home," Inez went on. "Mrs. Mellon blamed herself for laying the baby on her stomach."

I pressed the palms of my hands down on my desk and tried to appear calm.

"What do you remember about what happened?" I asked.

"Nothing. Mrs. Mellon didn't seem to want to talk about what happened so I never asked," Inez said with a shrug.

"Was Mr. Mellon there? Who found the baby dead? Were the police called? Tell me everything you remember."

"Only thing I knew was that Mrs. Mellon was upset. She thought it was all her fault."

"Why isn't any of this in the case record? A child mortality review is required when there's a SIDS death. Where's that report?"

"Beats me." Inez caressed the bright red polish on one of her fingernails.

"Do you really think it's of no consequence," I said, no

longer able to hold back, "that a baby dies and there's no mention of it in the case file?"

"Don't point your finger at me," Inez said. "Alexandria's the one that up and quit on us. I was assigned her caseload on top of mine. Even *you* couldn't handle that many cases."

I squeezed my temples between the palms of my hands. I wanted to scream but instead I spoke slowly and with precision. "Were you supervising the Mellon home when the baby died?"

"Nope." Inez crossed her bony arms and legs. She jutted her pointy chin forward and up.

"Then who was?"

"Alexandria."

"But you were the one who placed another child in that home right after the baby died."

"Nothing wrong with placing another kid there to help Mrs. Mellon get over it," she said. "What happened to that baby wasn't her fault. I was sorry for the woman. I would think you of all people would approve of that."

I gritted my teeth. "So you were more concerned about protecting Mrs. Mellon than you were about protecting children."

"Are we done here?" Inez stood up and glared down at me.

That's when I lost it. I jumped up and gripped the back of my chair. My knuckles went white. "Why isn't any of this information in the file, Inez? Why are some of the pages missing?"

"I have nothing to hide," Inez huffed. "Unlike you, Sylvia."

With an exaggerated clicking of her heels, she turned and headed for the exit. She grabbed the doorknob and threw the door open with such force it slammed against the wall. And then she was gone.

TWELVE

At six o'clock J. B. Harrell and I met to compare notes about what each of us had learned that day. We sat at a small round table in a back corner of the Higher Ground and Spirits Café and Pub. Bradley Finch worked at the Monrow City Police Department's Second Precinct, which was only a few blocks away. J. B. had learned that Finch started his shift at seven o'clock tonight, so we planned to walk over to the precinct then and ask him about the mysterious report he had signed about an incident at the Mellon home.

"I used to hang out here when I was in grad school," I said as I soaked in the café's surroundings—the chartreuse and purple art deco color scheme, the antique furniture and jungle of live green plants. "Nothing's changed."

J. B. crinkled his nose. "Only thing missing is a black velvet painting next to that moose head on the wall."

"I like the funkiness of this place," I said. "I always did."

Suddenly serious, he leaned forward. "Did you find any of the other missing pages from the case file?"

"I found one short entry that I'd missed before. And that led to more information," I said with a shake of my head. "It's not good."

He pulled out his notebook and pen, poised to write.

"The first child placed in the Mellon foster home wasn't Ellie Moon. It was a baby girl, a newborn." I paused. "She died her first night there."

J. B.'s eyebrows went up. "That's why they didn't want you to see the file. That's what they're covering up."

"I don't think so," I said. "There was nothing in the file about the baby's death. *Nothing.*"

He sucked air into his cheeks and then released it. "A baby dies," he said, "and no one bothers to put it in the record. How did you find out about it?"

"From one of my workers. Inez Koreskovsky." He saw my face when I said her name and gave me a curious look. "Inez supervised the Mellon home temporarily after their social worker left the agency. Apparently the worker quit in a hurry and didn't finish her dictation. At least that's what I surmise. The one short entry in the case file was written by Inez, but she didn't mention the baby. So I talked to her, asked her a lot of questions."

"And this Inez," he said, "she knew how the baby died?"

"She said it was SIDS but that Mrs. Mellon thought it was her fault. Inez felt sorry for her so she placed another foster child, a little girl, with them right after the baby died."

"Ellie Moon," he said.

I nodded. "I felt like slapping her." The words flew unbidden from my mouth.

J. B.'s eyes widened. He looked confused.

"Inez. When she told me. I wanted to slap her. I wanted to slap her so bad my hand hurt."

"Damn." His head jerked back.

"She knew the baby's death wasn't recorded in the case file," I said, "yet she never bothered to correct it."

"Or maybe it was recorded in the case file and someone removed it," he said.

"I pretty much accused Inez of doing just that," I said.

J. B. saluted me.

I bit my bottom lip and looked down at my lap. "I shouldn't have."

"Yes," he said, laughing. "You should have. You should have slapped her, too."

I caught myself feeling warm toward him and rubbed the back of my neck. "I figure the incident report signed by Bradley Finch must be connected to that baby's death," I said. "But why did he just sign and date the report and not fill in any other information?"

"Maybe that has something to do with the reason Finch left his job," J. B. said. "He moved away not too long after that. Maybe he was suspended for not completing the incident report."

"Wait a minute. He moved? I thought we were going to see him tonight."

"He was only gone for a few years. He came back home to Monrow City and got his old job back. Probably got tired of working part-time as a security guard and making archery bows from Osage orange trees down there in small-town Texas."

"How do you know all that?"

"I'm an investigative reporter, remember," he said. "It's my job to know things."

"What else do you know?"

"Well, for starters, Paul Mellon is a pretty shady character, or at least he was in the past," he said. "Looks like there may be a lot more missing from the case file than we thought."

"What do you mean?"

"He was heavy into drugs when he was young and there was some criminal involvement. He served six months in jail for dealing crystal meth. Some cocaine, too."

My mouth dropped open. "Didn't we see in the case file that a criminal background check had been done and it had turned up nothing? Who gave you this information?"

"Let's just say someone owed me a favor," he said.

"You're sure?"

"Pretty sure. My source is reliable. And he had details. Down to Paul's nickname back then. Mellonhead. How original is that?"

"There must be someone else named Paul Mellon. It's not an unusual name, you know."

"There's more," J. B. said. "Good old Paul was married before, too, when he was eighteen. And get this, when he and his first wife divorced, he was not only denied custody of their two children, who were two and four at the time, he didn't have *any* contact with them at all."

"I don't believe this," I said.

"It's all right here," he said.

He slid some official-looking documents toward me. I looked at his fingernails, like little manicured baseball caps at the ends of his long slender fingers, and tucked my crooked arthritic fingers and chewed nails under the table.

"You can read it for yourself," he said.

I stared at the papers on the table. In my gut I knew what happened. Everything was clear to me now. "Mr. Mellon killed that baby. He broke Ellie Moon's arm. He pushed Anthony

Little Eagle to his death. We have to tell the police." I stopped, out of breath. The artery in my neck expanded and contracted to accommodate the blood gushing up from my heart and invading my head.

"Hold on. There's nothing here that will convince the MCPD of any of that," J. B. said. "We need more evidence. Do you suppose you could find a way to confirm this information?" He tapped his fingers on the documents.

"I don't know," I said. "Don't you see? I don't know anything except the truth. I don't know why none of that information is in the case file. But I'll tell you what I do know. There's no way the Mellons could have met our stringent licensure requirements..." I paused. "Unless something went wrong...terribly wrong. But we saw that a criminal background check was done, so what happened?"

"Maybe it was altered."

"But who would do that? And why? Do you think Mr. and Mrs. Mellon lied on the application form? You know, just failed to provide some information? Maybe the intake worker didn't double-check the information like she was supposed to. Maybe it was just sloppy work."

"It wouldn't be the first time," J. B. said. "It seems Mr. and Mrs. Mellon were honest about some things, though. My source told me Linda Mellon had a daughter out of wedlock that Paul adopted, but it sounds like your Inez already knew that. Then again, it would make sense for them to tell the truth about the things they thought would make Paul look good."

What he said about it not being the first time knocked the air out of me. My throat tightened up. "Not again," I whispered.

"Again?" J. B. asked.

I looked at him in silence for a minute or two. "I know only too well how a mistake, intentional or not, can wreak havoc on a child's life," I finally said. "And when something goes wrong, I know how it can go undetected, because it's hard to trace or it's covered up or because no one cares enough to find out what happened."

We sat in silence for another minute, the air heavy between us.

"Well, you can mark my words," I announced. "If Anthony Little Eagle is dead because one of my workers made a mistake or did something wrong, it will *not* go undetected or unpunished. Not under my watch. Not this time."

"Then best we get on with it," J. B. said. "Time to go see what Officer Bradley Finch has to say for himself."

THIRTEEN

I was in a daze during our walk to the Second Precinct. There was so much new information swirling around in my head. When we reached the precinct J. B. asked to see Bradley Finch and the receptionist led us to the back and pointed him out to us. He was the only officer in the room, a burly man with a thick chest, a beer belly, and a shaved head that put me on wary alert. We walked over to the desk where he was sitting and introduced ourselves.

"Please sit down," Finch said in a loud, friendly voice. "What can I do for you folks? Must be important."

I reached into my briefcase, pulled out a copy of the incident report, and placed it on the desk in front of him.

"You signed this, Officer Finch," J. B. said. "Can you tell us what happened that day?"

Finch glanced at the report, his face blank. "Sorry." He pushed the paper back toward J. B.

"Sorry, you can't tell us?" J. B. asked.

"Sorry, it's not ringing a bell for me."

"A baby died in that foster home around the same time you signed this report," J. B. said. "Does that ring a bell?"

Finch blanched and looked down at his desk. He squeezed his forehead between his fingers.

"Well?" I looked at him, hard.

"Sudden infant death syndrome," he said with a shake of his head. "There was no foul play."

"You didn't write a report because there was no foul play?" J. B. asked.

A flush crept across Finch's face. He coughed into his hand.

"Well?" I sat on the edge of my chair. "Well?"

An uneasy silence followed.

"I felt sorry for the mother," Finch finally said. His voice cracked. "She was crying and carrying on something fierce. Had it in her head that it was her fault."

I crossed my arms over my chest. I'd about had enough. What was it with Mrs. Mellon that made both a burly guy like Finch and a coldhearted person like Inez Koreskovsky care more about her than about a baby who had just died?

"Did you believe her," J. B. said. "Was it her fault?"

"It was a SIDS death. I'm sure that's documented in the archived file." There was a defensive edge in his voice.

"A baby died." I drew out each syllable, carefully studying Finch's reaction to each enunciated word. He flinched. His eyes flitted off to the side. "And yet," I went on with deliberate slowness, "there is no record of it. Why is that?"

Finch's upper body shifted ever so slightly away from us. "The...the mother," he stammered. "She was so upset, crying and all, carrying on like a crazy person and getting all the more hysterical by the minute. She kept pleading with me not to write anything that would hurt their chances of getting more foster children. Finally I put my pad and pencil in my pocket and she calmed down a little. I didn't want her starting up again, so instead of writing up the report I just signed the form and left."

"You remember quite a bit about that day," I said.

It was J. B.'s turn to move to the edge of his chair. "So," he said, "whenever a woman gets upset, you can't do your job?"

Finch shot him an angry look. "It wasn't like that," he said. "I planned to go back and fill in the report later."

J. B. raised his eyebrows. Bradley Finch ran his hand over the stubbles of hair on his shaved head. His eyes darted from J. B. to me and back to J. B. again. Finally he lowered his head and looked down at his hands.

"It wasn't my best call," he mumbled.

J. B.'s lips vibrated as he blew the air out through them. He sat back in his chair with his hands up in the air.

"But you never finished the report, did you?" I said. "Did you forget?"

"It was an accident," Finch said. I saw his right eye twitch. "It was SIDS. No one was to blame. No crime was committed."

"And you're sure about that?" J. B. asked.

"Look," Finch said, "it was a mistake, a harmless mistake."

"Maybe not so harmless," I said. "Did you know another child died recently in that same foster home? His name was Anthony Little Eagle. He was seven years old."

The tendons on Finch's neck visibly pulsed. "Look," he said, lowering his voice. "I admit it was a bad judgment call not to write up the report on-site, and it was a lousy mistake to forget to do it later. But that isn't a crime. I'm due to retire in a few years, you know what I mean?"

J. B. rubbed his chin and nodded. "Yeah, I do." He sat back with a smile on his face. "So, tell us what you remember about

Paul Mellon that day."

"What do you mean? He was worried about his wife."

"How did he sound? Was he angry? Upset? Did he seem threatening in any way?"

Finch's eyebrows drew together. He looked annoyed. "All he cared about was protecting his wife. He kept telling her everything would be all right, that he'd make sure it was."

All of a sudden J. B. scraped back his chair and stood up. "Thank you for your time." He handed Bradley Finch one of his business cards. "If you decide there's something else you want to tell us, anything at all, please call me."

"Wait a minute," I said. "I still want to know why you didn't finish the report."

"I told you," Finch said, exhaling noisily. "I forgot. I made a stupid mistake. No harm done, okay?"

My head hurt. Short of clawing our way through Bradley Finch's insides and searching for a conscience in there from which we could wring the truth, there was no way we were going to get him to say anything else. J. B. motioned to me with a tip of his head that it was time to leave, then walked several steps ahead of me out of the room.

"What the hell was that about?" I said once we were outside the building. "The man practically says his pension is more important than the deaths of two children and all you do is thank him for his time?"

"He was lying."

"So we just up and leave?"

"He's too afraid to tell us anything else. I started to realize that this thing is bigger than him."

"What made you think that?"

"When Finch said Paul Mellon kept telling his wife that

everything would be all right, that he would make sure it was."

I nodded. I always knew social workers were pretty good at reading people but I'd never considered the idea that investigative reporters might be equally good.

"I don't know what Mellon might be capable of," J. B. went on, "but I bet his ex-wife has some ideas. Maybe it's time to pay Blanche Mellon a visit. She lives one state over. It's not far from here, just across the river."

"I'm going with you," I said.

[...] I couldn't [...] into [...] slammed [...] door behind. Linked his with the still fly light darkened the floor. I clenched my teeth. Since when did I the agency hire a security guard to check the building at night? How could I not have known that?

A beam of flashlight made its way toward the cabinet shelf. I dropped to my back. Getting into the corner. My pulse was pounding so hard I was sure they'd hear it. I lowered my head between my knees, a pace of nervous fear. When they'd reached the file cabinet my life was going to be sucked into it. I pictured myself standing up, hands in the air, ready to be tried, found guilty, and punished. After an excruciatingly long wait I heard a click, the doorknob jingling, the guard's footsteps receding out of the door. I got to the door. I got to listen. There was nothing but darkness. Slowly I lowered my head against the side of the metal cabinet. It was cool on my cheek. Linda Berry's door slammed against the wall next door and I jumped. I clapped both my hands to cover my mouth.

"Young people these days," I heard the security guard sigh. "Too lazy to do their damn jobs."

Poor Craig. He'd be blamed for leaving the doors unlocked. I hoped he wouldn't lose his job because of it. I stared at the door, waited for the guard to come back. My eyes started to burn but I didn't dare blink. Several minutes passed. I didn't hear anything else but still I was afraid to move. I waited. Then waited some more. Finally, when I was absolutely sure the coast was clear, I stepped away from the closet. I had left one room full [...]

FOURTEEN

January 1973

It was still dark outside when Mary Williams turned back the covers and got out of bed. Today was the day she'd been dreading. Only a few more hours of fighting off her demons and Wayne's solicitous attention, and the foster home worker would be here. And then she'd know. Or would she? She slipped on her pink chenille robe and stepped into her fuzzy slippers, careful not to wake Wayne.

In the kitchen, she waited for the fingers of dawn to drive away her night tremors. She lit a candle. Its reflection flickered in the window and cast layers of light onto the ceiling. Karon Pate would come this afternoon. When Jamie was home from school, of course, otherwise how would she be able to assess how he was doing. *Make no mistake*, Mary said to herself. *The only reason for a home visit is to assess, to evaluate, and to judge.*

"You're up early."

At the sound of Wayne's voice, she jumped. She blew out the candle as if she'd been caught doing something wrong.

"I'm sure it's just a routine home visit," he said. He stood behind her and started to massage her neck.

"Want coffee?" She pushed his hands away and stood up, walked over to the stove.

"She's new," he said. "She's probably going around meeting everyone in her caseload."

Mary pulled her bathrobe tight around her breasts. She leaned with her back against the counter, her arms crossed like she was trying to ward off Wayne's penetrating assurances. "What do we tell Jamie?" she asked. "How do we explain who Karon Pate is?"

"If it's like the other times," he said, "Jamie will think we're having coffee with a friend."

"I'm sorry, but what other times are you referring to? The last time anyone from the county was here, Jamie was only a year old."

"I'm sure it'll work out." She glared at him and he paused. "So... ," he went on, "we agreed that I'll take Jamie to school this morning and bring him home at three, right?"

"I'll make cinnamon rolls," she said.

———

Mary spent the morning getting the house ready—dusting, vacuuming, polishing. At eleven o'clock she considered scrubbing the kitchen floor with a toothbrush to get into the corners. But then the image of her mother on her hands and knees doing just that before one of her spells stopped her. She started making the cinnamon rolls instead.

While the dough was rising, she ran downtown to the florist. She came back with a bouquet of yellow roses, which she arranged in a white vase. She placed the flowers in the middle of the dining room table on a lime-green linen tablecloth that had never been used before. Then she made a final spot check of the house. She lined up magazines on the coffee table. She straightened all the family pictures that were already straight. She fluffed the pillows on the couch one more time.

She went into the kitchen to take the cinnamon rolls out of the oven. Her insides were already straining to jump out of her skin when Tick zoomed across the linoleum floor. He jumped up and down with his tail wagging so fast it was a blur. Then the door opened and he leaped up into Jamie's arms as if he hadn't seen him in years. Mary braced herself. It was time.

"Put your backpack away, sweetie," she said with a forced smile. "We're expecting company."

Wayne followed Jamie into the kitchen. He put his hands on Mary's shoulders, gave them a firm squeeze.

"Everything looks perfect," he said.

Just then the doorbell rang. Mary thought about how cheerful Karon Pate sounded on the phone.

"The worker sounded nice when she called," she said as she and Wayne walked to the front door. "Maybe she won't be so bad."

"Just coffee with a friend," he said.

But when they opened the door, there were taken aback to see two women standing on the porch. One was close to six feet tall and as muscular as Mary was short and round. The other one was considerably shorter and a bit on the thin side. The taller woman stepped forward with her hand outstretched.

"Mrs. Williams? Mr. Williams? I'm Karon—Karon Pate—your new social worker. It's so nice to meet you. And this is Mrs. Waters. She's with Child Protective Services."

Mary took a step back. Her fingers covered her mouth. "Is this about us not getting Jamie tested?" she said. "Because if it is..."

"No, no, nothing like that," the social worker said.

Wayne stood there with his mouth open. "Well, I'll be," he finally said, shaking his head.

"This *is* a surprise," Mrs. Waters reached out to shake Wayne's hand.

"Remember the man at the cabin when we went to see about the dog?" Wayne explained. "Well, this is his wife. She's the one who found Tick wandering around the reservation. She was there when I went to get Tick on Christmas morning. Can you believe this?"

Mary was momentarily stunned by the coincidence. Something else she didn't want to think about.

"I'm Mr. and Mrs. Buckley's social worker," Mrs. Waters said. She shook Mary's hand, squeezing it too tight and holding it a few seconds too long. Mary pulled her hand away, unsettled by Mrs. Waters's intensity. The sincere look on her face bordered on distress. And did she smell alcohol on Mrs. Waters's breath? Surely she was mistaken.

"Please come in," Wayne said.

He led the two women into the living room. Just then Jamie flew across the rug with Tick at his heels. When he saw the two women, he skidded to a halt. Tick whimpered, then leaped up into Mrs. Waters's arms and slobbered wet kisses on her face and neck. Jamie stood frozen in place, glowering.

"This is Mrs. Waters," Wayne said, putting his arm around Jamie's shoulders. "She's the nice lady who gave Tick to us. And this is Miss Pate. These ladies work for the county like I do."

Jamie snatched Tick from Mrs. Waters's arms. He held the puppy close, running his fingers through Tick's white fur and whispering in his ear. "He's *mine*," Jamie muttered.

"Yes, and I'm so glad he is," Mrs. Waters said.

"He sleeps in my bed. On my feet, under the covers."

"That's wonderful, Jamie. Tick is very lucky."

Jamie snuggled his nose into Tick's neck.

"Those two have been inseparable right from the start," Wayne said with a laugh.

He motioned for Karon and Mrs. Waters to sit on the couch. He and Mary sat in chairs facing them.

"Wanna see the tricks I taught my dog?" Jamie said.

"Absolutely," Mrs. Waters said with a smile.

Jamie ordered Tick to sit up, shake hands, and roll over. He had him fetch a chewed-up tennis ball over and over again and Mrs. Waters clapped and cheered each time. Mary studied her. The woman was friendly enough, but what was with the formality of her name? Why introduce herself as "Mrs." instead of with her first name? Maybe she thought it made her appear professional. But there wasn't anything professional about the miniskirt she wore or the way her hair hung down in two long braids over her shoulders. She looked like a hippie named Rainbow or Spring, certainly not like a married woman.

Jamie finally grew tired of giving Tick commands and asked if he could go to Tommy's house. Mary nodded her permission. Surely Karon and Mrs. Waters had seen enough of Jamie to know he was a happy, well-adjusted boy, she thought.

After a few minutes Karon leaned forward with an apologetic look on her face. "I know you were only expecting me," she said. "I tried calling earlier to let you know Mrs. Waters was coming along, but there was no answer."

"That must have been when I was out," Mary said. She regarded the foster home worker more positively than she did Mrs. Waters but she didn't trust either of them. They were too young to have much experience. Karon looked more professional than Mrs. Waters. Still, her brown tweed suit and two-inch heels were strangely at odds with her informal, eager-to-please, call-me-by-my-first-name demeanor.

"So why are both of you here?" Wayne said.

Karon opened her mouth to answer but Mrs. Waters cut her off. "Jamie's mother asked me to find out how he was doing."

Little hairs sprang up on the back of Mary's neck. She leaned forward so fast she came close to slipping off the chair. "After six years of silence," she said, "why is she all of a sudden asking about him now?"

"That *is* a long time," Karon said.

"Yes. It is," Mary said. "I hope they haven't decided they want to visit him now. It wouldn't be fair to Jamie. He doesn't even know them."

"Mrs. Buckley isn't asking for a visit," Mrs. Waters said. "She wants to know if he's doing all right."

"Well, I guess you've seen for yourself that he is," Mary said. "But of course Mrs. Buckley would have known that if she didn't care more about drinking than coming to see him."

Mrs. Waters furrowed her brow. "Actually, Mr. and Mrs. Buckley haven't had a problem with alcohol for several years now."

Mary squinted at her. Why is she being so defensive? She has to be lying.

"Then why haven't they come to see Jamie?" Wayne asked.

"They thought..." Mrs. Waters hesitated, looked down at her hands. "They were told he was dead."

"What?" Mary was incredulous.

"Whoever gave them that idea?" Wayne asked.

"There seems to have been an unfortunate misunderstanding," Karon interjected.

Mrs. Waters frowned. "I'm afraid that's not exactly true," she said. "Apparently one of our social workers misled Mrs. Buckley."

"I'm sure it wasn't intentional," Karon mumbled.

"The reality is that Mr. and Mrs. Buckley were led to believe their son was dead when he wasn't." Mrs. Waters's voice sounded heavy, like her tongue was too thick for her mouth. "And now we have to deal with the reality that they haven't seen Jamie since he was a year old and he doesn't know them."

"Why is this not making sense?" Wayne said. "If Mrs. Buckley thinks Jamie is dead, why is she asking about how he is now?"

Mrs. Waters brushed her hands across her eyes, then sat up straighter. "She didn't think it was right not to know how her son died," she said. "She asked me if I would find out what happened to him. That's when I discovered that Jamie was still alive and had been living with you all this time."

"This is outrageous," Wayne said. "If anyone had bothered to check in with us once in a while, this never would have happened."

"I'm so sorry," Karon said. "I...we didn't know you weren't having regular home visits. I've only been with the county for a month myself."

Mary pushed against the tremor in her stomach. The truth was, she'd been glad not to have any contact with the county or the Buckleys all these years. That was why she never called, never asked any questions about why there weren't any visits.

"It's been quite a shock for Jamie's parents," Mrs. Waters said, "as I'm sure you can imagine. I haven't talked with them yet about what they want to happen with Jamie now."

Mary's pulse quickened. "What does that mean?" She was on

the verge of panic. "I don't know what that means. Tell us what that means."

"We have to decide on a permanent plan for Jamie," Mrs. Waters said.

"Seven years isn't permanent?" Wayne was practically shouting. "How much more permanent can you get?"

Mary stared at him. She'd never seen Wayne that angry before.

"After having Jamie live with you all this time," Karon said with a sympathetic nod, "I understand why you would consider it a permanent placement."

"But I'm afraid it's not that simple," Mrs. Waters said. She sounded stern but she looked like she was about to cry. "Mr. and Mrs. Buckley are Jamie's legal parents."

"But they aren't capable of caring for him," Wayne said.

"Or any of their children," Mary added. "If they were, they wouldn't all be in foster care now, would they?"

"The other six Buckley children were returned home several years ago. They're doing well." The defensive tone was back in Mrs. Waters's voice.

"They better not..." Mary's fear choked off any other words.

"We love Jamie very much," Wayne said.

"I can see that you do," Karon said.

"We want to adopt him," Mary said. We've always wanted to, she screamed inside. Why didn't we say so years ago? Why didn't we do something about it before?

"Adoption might in fact be the best solution," Karon said.

Mrs. Waters frowned. "Let's not get ahead of ourselves," she said.

"I'm sure it will work out," Karon said.

Wayne reached for Mary's hand and gripped it like it was his lifeline and he would drown if he let go.

"The most important thing," Mrs. Waters said, "is to do what's best for Jamie."

"We all know what that is," Mary said.

"We just thought you should know," Karon said.

"I'll be talking with Jamie's parents soon. Then we'll take it from there." Mrs. Waters moved to the edge of the couch. "I know this must be difficult for you. Unfortunately, it's a difficult situation for everyone. Thank you for trying to understand." She stood up.

"I'll call you as soon as we know more," Karon Pate said. "Try not to worry."

Mary leaned against the doorframe. She watched the county car back out of the driveway and head down the street. She closed the door and turned to Wayne. His eyes were moist.

"What if...," he said.

She pressed her fingers to his lips. "No, Wayne. Don't even think it. Mr. and Mrs. Buckley don't want Jamie back. They don't even want to visit him. Don't you see? If they wanted him, they would have come here themselves instead of sending their social worker. We all know what has to happen. Didn't you hear what Karon said? She knows adoption is the best solution."

"I guess...yes...I'm sure you're right, Mary."

With those words and in that moment they made a pact. Wayne wouldn't give voice to his fears and Mary would refuse to consider the possibility that they could lose Jamie. It was unspoken but both of them understood it and would live by it. It was the only way they would be able to make it through.

———

Nonetheless, things went downhill between them each day that passed. It didn't help that Karon Pate called every few weeks to see how they were doing and to tell them that Mrs. Waters was still working with Mr. and Mrs. Buckley, but that no decision had yet been made about their son's future.

Mary's life revolved around Jamie more than ever. She anticipated his every need, and his needs multiplied. Whenever he whined, she jumped into action. Whenever he said he wanted something, she made sure he got it. Wayne tried to stay out of her way. But when he could no longer remain silent, he accused her of spoiling the boy. Soon they were arguing about everything from what she put in his lunchbox to what time he should go to bed.

When Jamie was with them, they acted like everything was normal. But when he wasn't around, the ghosts of fear took over and they turned their haunted faces against each other. The slightest thing would set them off. It didn't matter who started it. If Mary snapped, Wayne snapped back. If he criticized her, she retaliated. Not since that painful time before Jamie had come into their lives had there been this much tension between the two of them.

Nights were the hardest for Mary. She wandered the house, rearranged things, wiped down the already spotless kitchen counter. Some nights she would go into Jamie's room and sit next to his bed. She listened to his breathing, watched his eyelids flutter in the glow of his Mickey Mouse night-light. But lack of sleep inevitably took its toll, and the love Mary had for Jamie during her nocturnal watches turned into weariness in the light of day. His needs started to feel like obligations, his feelings a burden. What she wished most for her child she was less and less able to provide.

The days went by at a snail's pace. The weeks piled up as permanent plans for Jamie were being considered by others, yet no word arrived about what those plans might be. Mary wanted to hear, and then didn't want to hear. One minute she tried to believe everything was going to be all right; the next minute she was sure nothing would ever be all right again. She knew Wayne felt the same way. Never before had the two of them been so synchronized and yet so insufferable to each other. So Mary turned from Wayne and clung more tightly than ever to Jamie. But now, in an ironic and sad twist of fate, her son started to turn away from her. It seemed things could not get worse.

got ... need ... come ... these ... It's ... on ...
... for neither cup of ... coffee ... this second grade of
jaw-dropping details about the last Apollo manned mission to
the moon earlier this month.

Maybe he hoped no wonder she had the power I knew that
she thought he might at school He'd been on first He seemed I might
he'll ... enough I've seen inside of him. She didn't make
... he'll ... I've seen inside of him ...
they ... when ... some ... Why ... and ... class in
gloves and ... out yesterday, that the way he ran he knew
how to fight look of his harmless father-son horseplay.

"This is the best tree ever!" Jamie announced to Goldah, a little
pine sturdy with his small hand. Isobel's ... eyes adjusted, the scent
and positioned the tree, then he ran to the kitchen to get water.
Even though he was big enough to carry the pitcher, it had been his
job to keep the tree ... from slipping out.

It was Jamie's first ... was gone ... down ... is now.
It seemed silly to set ... bunch ... but ... the long dinner
... and his father followed their tried-and-true system
for putting on the lights. Then everyone dug into the boxes in
search of their favorite ornaments. Jamie pulled out the seven
ornaments that he'd his picture on them and laid them out on
the floor, organized by age.

"This is a baby," He held up the first ornament and walked
around the tree in search of the perfect place to hang it. "Who ...

FIFTEEN

The day after meeting with Officer Bradley Finch, we set out to find Paul Mellon's ex-wife. It was rush hour and the chaos and horn honking grated on my nerves but J. B. Harrell navigated the traffic on the interstate with the calmness of a pro. When a car surged in front of us as we emerged from the downtown Big Hill tunnel and J. B. slammed on the brakes, I gasped and pressed my hands against the dashboard.

"Watch out, idiot," I yelled out the open window. "You're not the only one on the road, you know."

J. B. glanced at me sideways with a look that said he was glad I wasn't the one driving.

"I'm sorry," I said, shielding my eyes from the morning sun with my hand. "I don't know what's happening to me." I looked out the passenger side window for a few minutes before continuing. "I keep going over everything we know. Two children die in the same foster home and another one breaks her arm. A baby dies and no one bothers to record it. Pages are missing from the case record. Officer Finch lies to us. Inez Koreskovsky is evasive, and looks guilty as hell to me. The agency administration won't let me read the case file. What the hell is going on?"

"There's obviously more to this story," J. B. said with a nod. "Let's hope Paul Mellon's ex-wife will shed some light on it for us."

"What if she isn't there? What if she won't talk to us?" I put my hands over my ears and held my breath as if I were drowning and my head was underwater.

"It might be a waste of time," he said. "But I don't think so."

"What makes you so optimistic?"

"The way loose ends usually get tied up. How each lead follows the one before and then takes you to the next lead."

"It can't always work that way," I said.

"No, it doesn't," he said. "Look, it's not too late to change your mind. I can get off at the next exit and take you home if you want. It's okay."

"No, don't," I said. "I just have the jitters. None of this is in my job description, you know."

We rode along in silence for several miles until I saw the sign for the exit near the east campus of the university. "I used to live in an apartment near here," I said. Memories of my time in graduate school rushed through me, the heavy drinking and casual sex interspersed with bouts of heavy studying. "It was an intense time," I said.

"Like now?" J. B. said. He looked amused.

"Different," I said after thinking about it for a second.

Several miles later we crossed the bridge that marked the state line. I looked out over the scenic river and after that the rolling hills and vibrant colors of the rural landscape. But none of it held any charm for me today.

"She might not remember much," I said. "A lot of time has

passed since she and Paul were married."

"Sometimes," J. B. said, "the best clues lie in buried and long-forgotten histories."

"Some people prefer to keep the past buried." I lapsed into silence, realizing the truth of what I'd just said. It wasn't that my own growing-up years had been terribly unpleasant. My parents weren't the ones who expected me to be perfect; I'd put that one on myself, with a bit of help from the church.

J. B. kept his eyes on the road. "What?" he said, without turning toward me.

"Would you want people digging around in your history?" I asked.

"Nope," he said.

He kept on driving, with the closed-up look on his face that I'd come to recognize for what it was. So far he had told me virtually nothing about himself.

"I sure hope this isn't a wild-goose chase," I said.

"You'd make a lousy investigative reporter," he said with a grin.

I crossed my arms over my chest and decided to keep any other doubts to myself. Several miles later, J. B. slowed the car to a near stop. He turned left onto a paved road by a wooden sign with two overgrown bushes flanking the words that announced the Rivers Mobile Home Park. Two-bedroom mobile homes angled all in the same position lined the road, a blend of pastel colors against a backdrop of mature maple and birch trees, a scattering of towering pines. There were no signs of children. J. B. parked by a white mailbox with the number twenty-two and a red cardinal painted on it. It stood in front of a white mobile home with a metal roof, metal siding, and a postcard-size deck. There was an air conditioner in one window. All the others had attached window boxes containing a profusion of pink, red, fuchsia, salmon, and a few light purple geraniums.

"Ready?" J. B. said.

"It's too late to quit now," I said resignedly as I got out of the car.

J. B. knocked on the front door. A stocky middle-aged woman swung the door open with a dramatic sweep of her hand, like a performer making her entrance onto a stage. Her T-shirt said "I'm a Virgin" in shocking pink letters, under which, in smaller black letters, it said, "but this is a very old T-shirt." I smiled for the first time since we'd started out this morning. Then the woman winked at J. B., and the look of bemusement that crossed his face made me laugh out loud.

"Are you...would you...happen to be Blanche Mellon?" he asked.

"Sure am," the woman said. "And now that you know who I am, maybe you can tell me who you are."

"My name is J. B. Harrell, and I'm an investigative reporter with the *Monrow City Tribune*...in Monrow? This is Sylvia Jensen. We'd like to ask you a few questions about your ex-hus-band, uh, if you don't mind."

Blanche Mellon stepped to the side of the door. "What kind of trouble is that son of a bitch in now?" She ushered us into the trailer with a wave of her hand. "It's been a good twenty years since I slammed that man's ass with the back of the door. Best thing I ever did in my life."

We glanced around the small wood-paneled living room for some place to sit down. A threadbare couch leaning against the wall looked like something the Salvation Army would reject, but after another quick scan of the room, J.B. settled on it as the best alternative. He loosened his tie, tugged at the long sleeves of his starched white shirt, and lowered his lanky body down onto the couch. The springs squeaked when he landed, and he jumped. Blanche Mellon giggled. I sank into an overstuffed beanbag chair and let it wrap itself around me like a blanket around a baby. The rich aroma of roasted coffee beans and other more mysterious smells—some ginger maybe, a little chocolate, a hint of almond—brought me back to sleepovers at my grandma's house when I was little. Blanche Mellon carried over a wooden chair from the kitchen area. Just when she sat down on it, a low *deeeet, deeeet, deeeet* sound brought her back to her feet.

"Blasted timer," she said. "It's on its last legs. Lucky for you, I bake farm cookies on my day off. You're gonna love 'em."

"Don't go to any bother for us," J. B. said, shifting his weight on the couch.

"They smell delicious," I said.

I liked everything about Blanche Mellon—the way she hummed as she pulled the tray of cookies from the oven; the swaying of her ample and unencumbered breasts, nipples poking through the threadbare white T-shirt; her candid and crusty sense of humor; her simple, second- and third-hand furniture designed for neither comfort nor style; the impracticality of baking cookies on a sweltering summer day.

"So, what's this about?" Blanche set a tray of coffee and cookies on a low table in front of us. "Is it drugs? Is he using again?"

"No, nothing like that," J. B. said. "At least not that we know of."

"Drugs were Paul's sugar. This, on the other hand, is mine." Blanche bit into a warm cookie. "Mmmmm. Told you they were good, didn't I?"

"To die for," I said, licking the crumbs from my lips.

"How long has it been since you saw your ex-husband?" J. B. asked.

"I haven't seen or heard anything from Paul since I kicked him out for the last time. Neither have the kids." She waved her hand at the array of pictures around the room of two children, a boy and a girl, at various ages. "They turned out all right, I must say. They both graduated high school. Got good jobs. Best thing ever happened to them was to grow up without a father, don't let anyone tell you otherwise. So, what's he up to? Why are you here?"

"He and his wife are foster parents," I said.

Blanche's eyes went huge. "You're joshing me," she said.

"Wish I were," I said.

Blanche's eyebrows were furrowed into a deep frown now. "Not possible. Not. Possible. A foster home? No way. That's just not right."

"Pretty surprising, huh?" J. B. said.

"Shocking is more like it," Blanche said. "The bastard couldn't take care of his own kids."

"We heard Paul wasn't allowed custody," I said, "when you got divorced."

"He was in jail then," Blanche said. "My kids didn't need to see their father like that. When he got out he didn't show any interest in them anyway. It was just as well. What I don't understand is why anyone would let him be a foster parent, or why he would want to be one."

"His wife's the one who wanted it. You see..."

J. B. cut me off with a sharp shake of his head. He must have sensed that I was on the verge of telling her about the five-year-old girl who broke her arm, and the baby and Anthony Little Eagle. I usually knew better than that. I really hadn't been myself these past few days. My usual compass was no longer working. It was like I'd lost my senses while thinking I'd found them.

"His wife?" Blanche said. "Rumor has it she was half Paul's age and already had a two-year-old girl when he married her."

"Why is it so hard for you to imagine Paul as a foster father?" I said. "Was he abusive to your children?"

"No, not that. He was mostly neglectful. Irresponsible." She paused and looked up at the ceiling, then added, "Sometimes he was a little weird with kids, but not with mine." She waved her hand in front of her face. "I'm sure about that. I would know if he was."

"How was he weird?" I asked.

"One night he took a bunch of pictures when we were drinking at a friend's house. I looked at them later and saw they were mostly pictures of my friend's daughter."

"Did he do that again? Did he do anything else that you thought was weird?" I asked.

"It was just that once. He was super drunk that night. We all were."

Alarm bells started going off in my head. I opened my mouth but once again J. B. cut me off.

"You said Paul was in jail when you divorced him," he said. "What did he do to end up in jail?"

"Nothing," Blanche said. "Ironic, huh? All the things he did that could have landed him in jail, and then he doesn't do anything and they haul his ass in there."

"What do you mean?" I asked.

"His best friend lied about a drug deal. That bastard let Paul take the rap for him. Paul was loyal, I'll give him that. He never told anyone the truth. Just served the time for something he didn't do."

Blanche paused. She looked sad, but after a few seconds her smile was back. "It ended up being the best thing that ever could have happened for us, though. I got a divorce, and jail kept Paul away from my kids. Life got better after that. Normal-like."

"Do you know if Paul remained friends with...what was his name?" J. B. asked.

"Adin Boyle," Blanche said. "If Paul stayed friends with that son of a bitch then he's more of a fool than I thought he was."

J. B. pulled a pad of paper and a pen from his shirt pocket and wrote the name down. "Do you have any idea what happened to Adin? How do you spell his last name?"

"B-O-Y-L-E. Funny you should ask about him now." Blanche scooted to the edge of her chair. There was a gleam in her eye. "A friend of mine showed me a picture of Adin in the paper not long ago. He was at some glitzy shindig, standing arm in arm with your governor. Really. There's Adin with a damn governor. Like he's some damn big shot. Under the picture it said he was a successful real estate developer from Spring Lake— can you believe that? Spring Lake? Well, let me tell you, he may be rich, but you can kiss my ass if his money comes from real estate."

"Maybe he grew up and became a respectable businessman," J. B. said.

Blanche rolled her eyes and made a snorting sound through her nose. "Paul and Adin both had so far to go before they were grown up that it would take them more than one lifetime to get there. I'm telling you. Anyone who sets up his best friend like Adin did to Paul is rotten to the core. You don't think Paul's into something with him now, do you?"

"We don't know," J. B. said, "but we're going to find out.

You've been a big help."

He scooted to the edge of the couch, unfolded his long legs, and pushed himself up. His eyes were sharp again, focused with renewed confidence.

"If Paul and Adin are still friends," Blanche said as she stood up, "then you can bet they are up to no good. You be sure to let me know what you find out, okay."

"Sure will," J. B. said.

I rolled myself out of the beanbag chair and stood up as J. B. strode toward the door. Blanche tucked a bunch of cookies wrapped in a napkin into my hand. Then she stood on the deck and watched us leave, waving and smiling as we drove off.

"Well, blow me away," I said.

"Oh ye of little faith," J. B. said.

"Next lead, Adin Boyle," I said triumphantly. "I bet we can find his address on the Internet."

"Now you're talking."

J. B. threw me his smartphone. I found the address and jotted it down on a piece of paper, gave him back his phone. A wave of anticipation rose inside me as we crossed the river. It swept me forward as we drove through downtown Monrow City. By the time we reached the west edge of the city it had swelled to the magnitude of a tsunami.

"You're really good at this stuff," I said.

"You're surprised?"

"No, not at all. Your reputation precedes you. But watching you work is something else. I mean, the way you know what to say, when to push, when to back off."

His lips turned up at the corners and his eyes moved off to the side.

"But why is this case so important to you?" I asked. "You

haven't covered any of the lawsuits or other cases involving foster children, so why this one? Why Anthony Little Eagle?"

"The boy was only seven years old," he said, as if the answer was obvious.

"Yes, but I was wondering if...never mind."

He glanced over at me, frowning. "And you," he said.

"You mean, why do I care so much?"

"No, I mean it was you that got me into this," he said.

I frowned. "Me?"

"Yeah. You pissed me off," he said. "The way you wore your guilt on your sleeve, decorated your office with it."

I pushed the air through my nose and then my mouth and a funny sound came out. "My first impressions of you," I said, "weren't all that flattering either, you know."

"And yet here we are," he said.

"Yes, here we are," I agreed. "The only two people who know that Mr. Mellon hurt one foster child and killed two others."

I thought about how J. B. had despised me at first, about my irrational need for his acceptance, but first impressions no longer mattered. I still preferred the beauty of his light brown face and the cut of his high cheekbones and square jaw to the business-executive look he so carefully cultivated. I suspected he still questioned my motivation and considered me a culture thief. But working together had changed our attitudes toward each other. He had been shocked and gratified, I thought, by the lengths I had been willing to go to to get my hands on the Mellon file. I was pleased at how astute he was at digging up information. We were an unlikely alliance, albeit an uneasy one—the only two people who knew the truth and were determined to expose it.

"Welcome to the land of the haves." J. B. slowed the car down. The speed limit was posted as twenty miles an hour on the winding road along the Spring Lake shoreline.

We drove by one palatial, multimillion-dollar home after another. The audacity of people who thought they had a right to live like this made me want to throw up. "Why do people need swimming pools when they live on a lake?" I said. "Look at those boats. Are we supposed to call them ships or something?"

J. B. slowed the car to a crawl when we reached a large estate surrounded by an ornamental wrought iron fence. The ornate arched gate stood open. "A Rolls-Royce like that will cost you at least two hundred and fifty thousand dollars," J. B. said. He pointed at a white car parked in front of the stone mansion. "Looks like Paul's friend Adin is doing all right."

With my mouth open I stared at the winding driveway flanked on both sides by a cornucopia of manicured bushes and golf-course-green grass. An array of grand old-growth trees near the lakeshore looked like it was keeping watch over the vast estate. Wide stone steps led up to an arched double front door of hand-carved mahogany with an ornate lion's-head knocker in the middle.

Just as I was thinking we should go in and see if anyone was home, J. B. pressed his foot down on the accelerator. I flew back on the seat as the car sped off, tires squealing. I grabbed onto my seat belt until we slowed down to a reasonable speed.

"We're not getting anywhere near Adin Boyle," J. B. explained. "Did you see those two guys standing outside, one on each side of the mansion? And the two black cars with tinted windows in the driveway? Security cameras on the gate, probably everywhere else, too. I wouldn't be surprised if they got a picture of my car and license plate when we slowed down."

"Scary," I said.

"There's a drive-in not far from here," he said. "Best burgers around."

———

My stomach was in knots and I thought the last thing it needed was food. But when the smell of our basket specials wafted through the car, I couldn't devour my cheeseburger and French fries fast enough. It was like I hadn't eaten for a week.

"What now?" I asked as I wiped some ketchup from the corner of my mouth with a napkin.

"We find out what Paul's friend is hiding," he said. He pushed a button on his smartphone, popped a fry in his mouth, and waited. "Hey, Mel," he finally said. "Glad you picked up. I need you to find out everything you can about a guy named Adin Boyle. B-O-Y-L-E. Lives on Spring Lake. Yeah, as soon as you can. Text me when you get something. Thanks. And, Mel? Dig deep, okay?"

J. B. put his phone away and started the car. I looked at my watch. "It's later than I thought," I said.

"Tomorrow's another day," he said. "And another day means another lead."

SIXTEEN

My alarm rang at six o'clock and I turned it off without waking up. I'd lain awake for too long last night ruminating about the next lead J. B. and I should follow. At seven thirty the sun shining on my face jolted me upright. I jumped out of bed—no time for coffee or reading the paper this morning—brushed my teeth, took a one-minute shower, got dressed, and got in the car.

When I reached my office, Brion Kacey was waiting outside the door.

"Glad you're here," he said, with a quick glance at his watch.

"I'm late," I said. "Sorry. Overslept."

"I want to talk about what happened," he said.

I put the key in the lock without looking at him. My first thought was that somehow Brion found out I'd broken into his office and made copies of the Mellon case record. Maybe Craig had been blamed for not locking up properly and they'd followed the trail to me, the only other person in the building at the time. Or he could have found out that I'd read the file online. He was the only one with access to the e-file; maybe an electronic alert of some kind had been set to go off if someone other than he opened it. I scrambled in my head for excuses for each of the possible scenarios, none of them remotely convincing.

Brion waved the morning edition of the *Monrow City Tribune* in the air and then placed it on my desk with a sweep of his hand. With a jubilant smile, he opened it to the metro section, tapped his fingers on the headline, and hovered over me as I read it: Local Authorities Rule Foster Boy's Death an Accident.

At first I thought I must have read it wrong. It couldn't be true. It must have said that they were *investigating* whether or not Anthony Little Eagle's death was an accident. I opened my eyes and read it again, and then again. I grasped the edge of my desk to steady myself. Then I covered the headline with my hands as if that would make the words go away, make it not true.

"I guess you didn't know." Brion's smile looked like a smirk to me.

"Why are you here?" I said. "What do you want me to say?"

"This is *good* news, Sylvia. You should be relieved. The truth won out."

A hissing sound escaped through my teeth.

He raised his hands in the air, palms facing me. "I just came to thank you for your cooperation, Sylvia. That's all. This whole thing's been an unfortunate situation." He reached for the newspaper, folded it, and tucked it under his arm like a trophy.

A burning sensation seized my chest and moved up to my throat. Long-ago memories came flooding back to me—of my former supervisor, Elaine, talking about a case of intolerable neglect by the foster care system as an "unfortunate situation" that I would have to "deal with." As furious now as I had been back then, I stood up and planted my hands on my hips.

"Anthony Little Eagle's death was *not* a situation and it was *more* than unfortunate," I said, with a quick intake of breath that made the words come out in a sizzle. "It was a disaster, a tragedy, a...a..." I stopped short of saying "murder." At least I had that much control left.

"Everyone is doing the best they can, Sylvia." Brion's smile was gone. "Now it's time to move on," he said.

"Stop it with the damage control language." My voice sounded like a hiss.

"I think you should take some time off, Sylvia. You need to pull yourself together. A couple mental health days will do you good."

"You're an attorney, not a therapist, Brion." I refused to listen to any more of his drivel. But I knew he was right about one thing. I *was* losing it. I was on the verge of behavior that was not only completely out of character for me but unforgivable—like throwing or breaking something or screaming at the top of my lungs.

He shrugged his shoulders and left my office, not a minute too soon. I had to get out of there. I rushed from the suite without speaking to or glancing at anyone. I took the elevator down to the parking garage and the safety and privacy of my car. Then I bent forward slowly and pressed my forehead against the top of the steering wheel.

There was no police investigation. There was no explanation about how the police could have made a ruling only nine days after Anthony Little Eagle's death. They didn't bother to pretend there'd been any kind of inquiry. J. B.'s voice joined with mine in my head. *He's just another dead Indian kid to them.* I grabbed my cell phone. My finger shook as it pushed the instant call button.

"Harrell. Leave a message."

"I just saw the paper. Call me."

I pounded my fists on the steering wheel. I let out a scream, screamed again, and again. I was mortified by what I was doing and tried to stop but I couldn't. After a while the only sound coming out of my mouth was a raspy croak that was barely audible. I wiped away the tears from my face with my sleeves. I reached for the phone and pressed the button again.

"Harrell. Leave a message."

"Damn it. Where are you, J. B.? We need to talk."

I dropped the phone and it bounced on the seat. I started the car. I was in trouble. I needed help. I had to talk to someone who would understand, someone who could calm me down and help me focus my anger. Peter Minter. The Indian Child Welfare Act compliance officer was the most level-headed person I knew. That's who I had to see. After working for fifteen years on individual cases and fighting together for changes in the system, Peter and I trusted each other implicitly. I'd already talked to him about what happened to Anthony Little Eagle. He knew ICWA procedures hadn't been followed, and how upset I was. I drove out of the parking garage, hoping against hope that Peter would be in his office and that he'd have time to talk.

With my jaw tightened and my lips pursed, I headed for the American Indian Community Center. I drove past a church I'd seen many times and slowed down. "All religions are oppressive," I muttered under my breath. Then I pressed my foot down on the accelerator and, with the tires squealing, made a sharp turn at the corner. That particular church was known in the community for its top-notch child care center and food bank. But I didn't take back what I said. I was in no mood to abandon my anger for fairness.

I wiped a tear from my cheek as I drove by the Indian-run public housing complex. The complex looked orderly, serene, not at all like the place where the combination of a gun and alcohol had set off a series of recent events that resulted in the death, the murder, of an innocent child. I kept driving, noting other neighborhood landmarks that I'd seen many times but had never entered out of a fear of intruding where I didn't belong, or maybe a more selfish fear of rejection.

I pulled into the parking lot behind the community center, the only building in Indian country where I felt comfortable. The lot was filled to capacity so I created a new space for my car in between two others. There was barely enough room for me to open the door so I had to squeeze my body out like a contortionist, in the process knocking my side mirror off. I tossed it into the back seat, untwisted my skirt, and walked as calmly as I could to the entrance. But once inside the building I was thrust into the middle of a tense crowd, and the muscles on the sides of my neck twisted into a coil.

"Sylvia?"

I turned around. "Thank goodness," I said. "I came to see you." Peter Minter's eyes radiated warmth. His oversized black glasses and matching shirt set off his silver-gray shoulder-length hair and made him look grandfatherly.

"Come on, I'll buy you coffee," he said.

He walked ahead of me through the crowd as we headed over to the Red Fox Den Café on the other side of the atrium. A group of elders, none of whom I recognized, stared at us as we passed their booth. Sam Chasa appeared as soon as we sat down at a table in the back. He was wearing his trademark grease-spotted vest that branded him as owner and chef of the café.

There were red and black beaded ribbons intertwined in his long braids, which meant that today he would be performing additional duties in his role as an American Indian Movement leader.

"News travels fast here in Indian country," Sam said.

"Big turnout all right." Peter tipped his head in the direction of the auditorium.

"What's going on?" I asked.

Sam looked down, shifted his weight from one foot to the other and wiped his hands on his vest. I'd never known him to come right out and say what he was thinking, but today he was more reticent than usual.

"You know we know you around here, don't you?" he finally said after a few minutes.

I nodded and waited for him to say more in his own time. That's what I'd always done with Sam, that's what everyone did with Sam.

"Okay, then," he said. He was silent for a few seconds before adding, "I'll get your coffee."

"So you came to see me," Peter said.

"It's my fault," I said. "I should have monitored Lynn Winters more carefully. I should have made sure she followed ICWA procedures."

Peter held his hand up to stop me. "We've been through all that," he said.

I nodded. "I know we already talked about it. But I can't help but think that Anthony Little Eagle would still be alive if... if I had just..." I looked off to the side, blinked away tears.

"How long have we known each other, Sylvia?"

"A long time," I said, "which is precisely why..."

"Exactly," he said, interrupting me again. "I know you. You know me. That counts for something around here."

I sat back in my chair, grateful to be on the receiving end of Peter's forgiveness.

Sam returned with two mugs of coffee and a pitcher of cream and placed them on the table. He tugged at one of his braids and ran his tongue over his top and bottom lips. After an interminable silence, he finally spoke, his words quiet and low so as not to be overheard.

"As much as life takes," he said, "it also gives. If you find the lesson in it, the road isn't as rough." Then he turned and walked away.

I didn't know why Sam cared enough to share his wisdom with me, only that I was grateful whenever he did. Maybe he was just used to seeing me here. I wanted to call him back and tell him I wasn't sure what he meant. I wanted to ask him to please help me understand. But that wasn't something you did with Sam.

"Tough stuff," Peter said, as if that explained everything. His warm smile today was tinged with sadness and worry.

"Why are there so many people out there?" I asked.

"There's a meeting in the auditorium. Should have started by now. They're planning a protest at MCPD headquarters. They're going to demand that the police reopen the investigation. People around here don't believe Anthony Little Eagle's death was an accident."

"It wasn't," I said.

Peter leaned forward. "How do you know that?" he asked under his breath.

"We don't have proof yet, but we're working on it."

"We?"

"Me and J. B. Harrell," I said.

Peter sat back in his chair and snorted. I'd never heard him do that before. "That investigative reporter for the *Monrow City Tribune?*" he said. "That white apple with the red skin peeled off and no core? He could care less."

"That's not true. You don't know him. He does care. He thinks Anthony Little Eagle was murdered. So do I."

Peter's eyes widened. "If people hear someone like you saying that," he said, "they'll get more riled up than they already are."

"Good," I said. "Then maybe the police will pay attention." I stood up. "Come on. Let's go."

Peter hesitated at first. Then he dropped a few dollar bills on the table, stood up, and followed me out of the café. We went to the auditorium and walked down the center aisle. There were two empty seats in the middle of the front row. Up on the stage three people were sitting at a table. One was a heavyset white woman with a permanently angry face I'd seen at Foster Care Alumni Association meetings. I couldn't recall her name. The other two, a man and woman, I didn't recognize. A young man with a ponytail was testing the sound equipment, making sure the microphone on the table was working. When he was finished, Sam Chasa walked onto the stage. He put his hands up to quiet the crowd.

"I want to express our deepest condolences to Anthony Little Eagle's parents, who are with us today," Sam said. "I've asked Mrs. Little Eagle to speak first." He moved the microphone on the table closer to her and then stood back.

Mrs. Little Eagle brought with her a thunderstorm of grief too massive to be contained in the auditorium. She looked out at the audience, her dark eyes blinded by sadness. She didn't seem to be aware of the missing button on her plain, dull-gray blouse. No one spoke. The silence in the auditorium was interrupted only by sporadic sniffling, blowing of noses, shuffling of feet.

Anthony's mother pulled the microphone to within inches of her mouth. Her hand was shaking. "We made a mistake, a big mistake," she said in a barely audible voice. "But our son didn't." She pushed the microphone away. It made a scraping sound on the table. She fell back in her chair and dropped her head down.

"Thank you," Sam said, and he moved the microphone over to Mr. Little Eagle.

Anthony's father cleared his throat. He tugged at the turquoise and white bolo tie at his neck. He moved closer to the microphone. "We have people that are supposed to take care of our children, but they don't." He sucked in his breath. "What does 'Protective Services' mean? What does it do?" He stopped and wiped a tear from his eye. "I'm crying out to all of you who are parents and grandparents. If you have kids in Child Protective Services, straighten yourselves out and get them out of there before it's too late."

Mr. Little Eagle slumped back in his chair. He placed his hand on his wife's arm. The heavyset white woman grabbed the microphone.

"Our children are being ripped out of supposedly abusive or neglectful environments only to be placed in more dangerous situations," she yelled. "The police don't care about protecting our kids." The microphone, too close to her mouth, screeched.

"We have to make them care!" someone shouted from the back of the auditorium.

"We have to make them do what they're supposed to do!"

"That's right!"

Several people yelled. Others joined in, and soon everyone was talking at once. Some men stood, their fists in the air. One man jumped up on his chair.

I stood up and started walking toward the stage, ruled by

my passion like never before. There had been other situations that had enraged me, to be sure, but this one was remarkable in its power to make me risk everything to do whatever had to be done. Maybe it was an accumulation of all the injustices I'd borne witness to, and sometimes colluded with, before, all the times I felt powerless. Or maybe at the age of sixty I had nothing to lose. Maybe I was just fed up. It didn't matter why. I went up the steps, not thinking about what I was doing or why I was doing it. I stood next to Sam on the stage and reached for the microphone in his hand. He held it up in the air, out of my reach.

"I have something to say," I whispered to him.

"I'm not sure that's a good idea right now, Sylvia."

"I know something that can help."

Sam shifted his weight from one foot to the other. He looked down at the floor. I glanced over at Peter in the front row. He was mouthing "no" to me, shaking his head vigorously.

"I have to tell them, Sam."

He shrugged, held the microphone behind his back.

"Please. I'm begging you. It's urgent. I have to do this."

He coughed, cleared his throat. He lifted the microphone and brought it to his mouth. "Can I have your attention?" he said. "Your attention, please." He waited for the din to quiet down. "There's someone here who wants to speak." He raised his shoulders in surrender and handed the microphone to me. The auditorium went silent.

"My name is Sylvia Jensen," I said. "I'm a foster care supervisor at the Human Services and Public Health Department. The police aren't doing what they're supposed to be doing."

"*You're* not doing what you're supposed to be doing!" a lone voice shouted.

"We have to get the police to reopen the investigation," I continued. "They want to forget about Anthony Little Eagle, but we can't let them."

"Your foster care system wants to forget about him," the white lady shouted into the microphone on the table. "Your system doesn't care about protecting our kids any more than the police do. All our children who are dead or abused had two things in common, a child welfare system that didn't care what happened to them and police that didn't care what happened to them."

"That's right," someone shouted from the back of the auditorium. "Our children are falling through the cracks!"

"You're right," I said in a louder voice, "and we have to change that for Anthony Little Eagle."

"*We* will speak for Anthony Little Eagle!" someone yelled. "Not someone like you."

"That's right," another person said. "We speak for our own children."

"You're the one sent that boy to his death!"

"The system is broken!"

Pandemonium broke out. People talked over each other. They shouted out their ideas about what should be done. Protest at the MCPD. Protest outside the Health Services Building. Sit in at the mayor's office. Storm City Hall.

"You better leave," Sam whispered. He took the microphone from my now-trembling hand. "Go out the back door."

"But I can help."

"Go."

He pushed me toward the side of the stage. I heard the crowd booing as I ducked behind the curtain. I didn't leave because I was afraid or because I wanted to, but because I trusted

Sam. If he thought I should go then I should go. Maybe I didn't belong here, but I didn't belong at the agency either. I ran out to the parking lot and squeezed my body into my car again, talking to myself the whole time. *They only see me as part of the system. They don't know me. But Peter does. He knows how hard I work to change things, from the inside. Sam does, too. All those people in the auditorium, they don't know it. To them I work in the system, so I am the system. I'm the enemy. But I'm not the enemy. I'm on their side.*

I pulled out of the parking lot and kept driving until I had left the neighborhood. *You don't belong there,* I told myself. *You're not wanted there.* But where did I belong? I spotted a bar that I used to frequent in the adjacent, middle class neighborhood. *That's where I belong,* I thought. I slowed down and looked for a parking space. It would be so easy to go inside, erase everything from my mind, obliterate my loneliness by sharing intimacies with people I didn't know, have drunken sex with whoever I wanted or whoever was available. But then I remembered what it was like to wake up in the arms of a stranger, my loneliness worse and smothered with shame.

Get off your pity pot, Sylvia. I heard Hehewuti's voice in my head. I knew what to do. I knew where I belonged. I kept driving past the bar and headed for home. My recovery partner, my lifeline, would be waiting in the online chat room, like always, ready to help. I wasn't alone after all. How could I have forgotten?

I parked my car in the lot behind my apartment, rushed into the building, got on the elevator. That's when it hit me. Hehewuti couldn't understand what had just happened at the community center unless I told her where I was and what was going on. And now she'd know who I really was. I'd planned to tell her the truth someday but I couldn't tell her now. Not today. Not in the shape I was in.

A wave of nausea came over me and my knees buckled, my spine contracting as I pressed my fists into my crushed guts. Then the elevator stopped with a thud and I straightened up. The door opened and Alex, an irritatingly perky girl with a sing-song voice and a miniature poodle always in her arms, got on.

"Say hello to our nice neighbor, Little Mutt."

Alex's habit of talking through her dog instead of speaking to me was always annoying but today it was more than that: it was further confirmation of my invisibility and aloneness. I unenthusiastically patted Little Mutt's fluffy white head. Alex made odd cooing sounds while rubbing her nose in the dog's neck until the elevator finally stopped at her floor. Then she waved good-bye to me with Little Mutt's paw. I watched her hop down the hall, her two orange-red puffs of hair, one on each side of her head, bouncing in rhythm with her equally bouncy dog.

The door closed and the elevator continued its gloomy journey up one more floor. Dark images of empty caves and stark, lonely rooms filled my head. Sounds of people laughing in the distance and silent echoes pummeled my ears. The acidic taste of self-pity filled my mouth and made its way down into my stomach's hollow, empty cavern. The elevator finally stopped and the door opened. I forced my feet to move and trudged toward my empty apartment. Never before, not during the most desperate moments of my life, had I been so completely and utterly alone.

And then I saw J. B. Harrell standing outside my door, waiting for me.

SEVENTEEN

April 1973

Finally the foster home worker called with some news. It was a
rainy afternoon and Mary Williams was curled into herself on
the couch with the afghan wrapped around her shoulders. A
flash of lightning outside followed by a loud crack of thunder
dealt a blow to her empty stomach. She felt a dull ache in her
chest left over from an argument she'd had with Wayne the night
before. She couldn't remember how it started, but she couldn't
stop thinking about how it ended. After the shouting stopped
they'd found Jamie slumped over on the floor with his head
between his legs, arms clasping his knees to his chest, rocking
back and forth. Wayne picked him up and Mary put her arms
around both of them. Tick jumped up on the backs of their legs.

"I don't like it when you yell." Tears spilled from Jamie's eyes
onto Wayne's shoulder.

Mary vowed she would never let anything like that happen
again. From now on she would focus only on what was best for
Jamie, nothing else.

Just then the phone rang. She threw the afghan off to the

side and rushed to the kitchen.

"Hi, honey," she said, thinking it was Wayne calling to say he was sorry, too. "I'm so glad you called."

There was a quiet laugh on the other end of the line. "Hello, Mrs. Williams." Karon Pate paused. "I finally have something to tell you."

Mary closed her eyes and pushed the air out of her lungs. "We've been waiting to hear," she said. Was this the good news she'd been hoping for or the bad news she'd been dreading? She stood still, afraid to move.

"The Buckleys have decided to terminate their rights to Jamie," the foster home worker said. "They go to court in two weeks."

"What?" Mary gasped.

"They think it's best for Jamie," Karon Pate said. "They think he should stay with you permanently."

Mary slid down onto the closest chair. "Now we can adopt him."

"I don't see any reason not to start the process right away. At least get the adoption home study scheduled. Nothing's final, of course, until the Buckleys parental rights are legally terminated, but I've never heard of a single case where a judge didn't grant a parent's voluntary petition. It's pretty much pro forma."

"But what if...I mean, you're really sure?"

Karon Pate laughed. "I wouldn't be telling you this, Mary, if I weren't one hundred percent certain that everything is going to work out."

Mary placed her palm on her chest and looked out the window. A double rainbow had arched over the back yard. The clouds were breaking apart and the sky was brightening like a host of blooming flowers. Never again would she doubt that Jamie was meant to be her son.

"Mary? Mrs. Williams?"

"I knew you were on our side," Mary said. "I have to call Wayne. Thank you, Karon. Thank you so much for everything."

—

As soon as Wayne picked up the phone, before he had a chance to say hello, Mary was already talking.

"Everything's going to be okay. I love you, Wayne. I'm sorry about last night. Karon Pate just called. It's all working out. Jamie'll be free to be adopted in two weeks. Of course, we won't tell him until it's for sure but..."

Tick crashed into the kitchen, a ball of white fur barking and jumping up on the back door. "He's here," she said. "Can you come home now? So we can celebrate?"

She hung up the phone and ran to Jamie, laughing. Tick was already in his arms so she pulled both of them to her. She kissed Jamie's face and neck, ran her fingers through his hair.

"Mom, cut it out. You're squishing Tick."

"I'm just happy to see you, sweetie," she said. "I love you so much."

He looked up at her, his brow wrinkled. "Do you love Dad, too?"

"Of course I do. I'm sorry you heard us arguing last night. No more fights, I promise. From now on, only good stuff."

"I'm hungry," he said.

"Dad's on his way home," she said. "Then we'll go to the Dairy Queen."

She saw the relief in his eyes. He dropped his backpack on the floor.

"Guess what, Mom? Matthew's dog borned five puppies

last night and he said it was the grossest thing he'd ever seen. Are we going fishing after school is out? Remember that huge fish I caught last year? I can't wait to go back to that cabin on the lake. That was so cool. When is it time to start planning my birthday party? Can I watch Bugs Bunny until Dad gets home?"

———

For the next two weeks, Jamie was back to himself, chattering nonstop. The only other time Mary had experienced so much joy was the day Jamie was first placed in her arms. She relished the signs of spring that suddenly were everywhere—shy snatches of green peeking through the drab yellow vestiges of last year's dead grass, ripples of crocuses fluttering in the breeze, light green leaves sprouting tiny and translucent on the fingers of tree branches. Now that she had been freed from anxiety, she was able to release Jamie from her clutches. She allowed him to grow with unfettered abandon like the plants she released from their soil-bound pots to the earth at this time of year. Her spirit sang as he ran through the fields behind the house, inhaled the fragrance of each new blossom, and planted his own garden for the sheer joy of doing it just the way he wanted.

———

When the day of the court hearing arrived, Mary woke early, excitedly counting the final hours that were left before the Buckleys would appear before a judge and terminate their rights to Jamie. She noticed but didn't let the furrows in Wayne's forehead squelch her enthusiasm. She was sorry he was spoiling things for himself by worrying about what might go wrong, especially when nothing was going to go wrong. He'd made it clear that he didn't want to go to court today, and in turn she'd

made it clear that she was going with or without him. Because
he didn't want her to go alone, he'd reluctantly agreed. If it had
been up to him, they'd be staying away out of respect for Mr.
and Mrs. Buckley and waiting for Karon Pate to call when the
hearing was over.

"You look handsome," she said when they were in the car.
She was glad she'd insisted that he wear his best suit.

"Just so we're not counting our chickens before they're
hatched," he said gloomily.

"That's your father talking," she said. "Remember, one hundred percent is one hundred percent. That's how sure Karon Pate
is."

During the hour's drive from Basko to the county seat,
Mary found it hard to sit still and not comment on every little
thing she saw along the way. With his eyes on the road, Wayne
stoically kept whatever negative thoughts he had to himself. At
the courthouse, Mary slipped her hand through his arm. She
nudged him into the building and up the wide marble steps. A
woman with blond-beige hair pulled back in a French twist was
half a landing ahead of them. Mary assumed from her tailored
three-piece suit and matching two-inch pumps that she was
an attorney. But when the woman turned around, she poked
Wayne's arm and pointed.

"That's Mrs. Waters," she said in a low voice. "I hardly recognized her."

Wayne tugged at Mary to hold her back. They stopped and
watched Mrs. Waters shake hands with a man and woman at
top of the stairs. The man looked like he was about to disappear
inside a threadbare light blue suit that was several sizes too big
for him. An unexpected pang of pity hit Mary when she saw the
woman's face, carved with sadness and looking as worn out as

the faded dress hanging loosely on her slight shoulders.

"That's them," Mary whispered.

Wayne put his hand on her arm. "Wait," he said. "They don't need to know we're here."

They watched as Mr. and Mrs. Buckley, like shadows fading into the dark mahogany walls and shrinking under the ornate chandeliered ceiling, trailed behind Mrs. Waters and went into the courtroom. They waited a few more minutes before going in themselves and then slipped in quietly and sat on the last bench in the back.

The courtroom was dark and quiet with a slightly moldy smell to it, the stale aroma of stagnant air combined with aged wood. Mary sneezed. She reached for a clean white handkerchief from her purse and blew her nose.

"Shh," Wayne said with a sharp shake of his head.

Mr. and Mrs. Buckley were in the front of the courtroom. They sat next to Mrs. Waters in straight-backed wooden chairs, their hands folded as if in prayer on top of a heavy mahogany table. Karon Pate sat on the bench right behind them. Mrs. Waters turned around to say something to her, and when she spotted Mary and Wayne in the back row she looked irritated.

Wayne flinched. "We shouldn't have come," he mumbled under his breath.

Mary shrugged her shoulders. She didn't care what Mrs. Waters or anyone else thought. She hadn't told Karon Pate they were coming. She hadn't told Wayne's parents either. She wanted this to be a special moment just for her and Wayne.

The door to the courtroom creaked open. Three men stood in the darkness in the back of the room and glanced around. With slow, deliberate steps they walked to the other side of the aisle. Instead of sitting on the bench, they stood erect in front of it with their hands behind their backs, jaws set. There was a distant clank, clank, clank sound from construction going on outside the building.

Mary leaned forward to get a better look at the three men. The one in the middle looked familiar to her. His hair was in two long braids adorned with beads and ribbons, and he wore a white shirt and red vest. When she saw the multilayered choker of white, turquoise, and black beads around his neck, she realized who he was.

She moved closer to Wayne and took his hand. "One of them was on TV," she whispered. "On the news. He was talking about AIM and Wounded Knee and stuff."

A side door opening at the front of the courtroom caught their attention. A mousy-looking woman with a crook in her neck walked with measured steps to a little table in front of the dais.

"The court transcriber?" Mary said.

"Shh."

Right after the woman, a tall, imposing man wearing a light-weight seersucker suit and light blue tie came through the same side door. He walked over to the dais and sat down. The woman smiled at him.

"Is that the judge?" Mary muttered. "Aren't we supposed to stand up? Why isn't he wearing a black robe?"

Wayne warned her to be quiet with a shake of his head.

The man ran his fingers through his thick curly hair and scanned the courtroom. His eyes settled for a few seconds on the back of the room, first one side and then the other, before focusing his attention on Mr. and Mrs. Buckley sitting behind the table in front of him.

"Good morning, Mr. and Mrs. Buckley. I'm Judge Johnson."

Mary pulled Wayne toward her and brought her lips close to his ear. "Karon Pate says Judge Johnson is known for doing what's best for children," she whispered. "Do you think he noticed us?"

"He will if you keep talking," Wayne said.

Judge Johnson riffled through the papers in front of him, and then looked at Mr. and Mrs. Buckley. "You have petitioned the court to terminate your parental rights to your son, Jamie, who is...let's see, how old is he?"

He'll be eight in a few months, Mary shouted out in her head.

"Ah, yes," the judge continued. "Your son is almost eight years old. Is that right, Mr. and Mrs. Buckley?"

The Buckleys didn't move. There was the sound of a hammer pounding on metal in the background.

"They don't know how old Jamie is," Mary muttered under breath.

"So that is the reason for this hearing today," Judge Johnson said. "I have your petition here."

Mr. and Mrs. Buckley sat as still as statues. Mary leaned to the left and then to the right, trying without success to see the expressions on their faces.

"I would like to begin by asking you a few questions," the judge said. "Is that all right with you, Mr. Buckley?"

Mrs. Waters looked at Mr. Buckley and gave him an encouraging nod. He turned away from both her and the judge.

"Why doesn't he say anything," Mary whispered.

Wayne leaned forward. She didn't have to touch him to feel the tenseness in his body.

"According to Mrs. Waters's report, you and your family had some troubles in the past, but you're doing okay now. Is that right?" The judge waited for a response, and when there was none, he continued. "All your children, with the exception of Jamie, are living with you now, are they not?" Slight nods. "And I think I understand what happened with your youngest son. Have you folks seen the social worker's report?" He held it up.

"What's wrong with them?" Mary said under her breath.

Wayne shuffled his feet and tightened his jaw. She recognized the signs. He was expecting trouble, big trouble.

"Mrs. Waters." Judge Johnson paused to let out his breath. "Did you go over this report with Mr. and Mrs. Buckley?"

"Yes, your honor," Mrs. Waters said. "I read it to them and I gave them a copy of it."

"Do you have any questions about it, Mr. and Mrs. Buckley?" the judge said. "Do you dispute anything in it?"

Mrs. Buckley tipped her head ever so slightly but said nothing. Mary let out a sigh of relief.

"Do you understand what it means," the judge persisted, "to give up your rights as Jamie's parents?"

No response. Mary grabbed Wayne's shirt and pulled him back onto the bench. He placed his hand on top of hers but his gesture of reassurance was cancelled out by the fear in his eyes. She turned away from him.

The judge looked at the Buckleys like he was probing their faces for some sense, any sense, of what they understood or didn't understand about what was going on. He glanced ever so briefly, just a twitch of his eyes, at the three men standing in the back before looking back at Jamie's parents.

"I understand you wish for Jamie to be adopted by his foster parents." Judge Johnson frowned and rubbed his forehead with his fingers.

Mrs. Buckley nodded. "Yes sir," she said in a barely audible voice.

Mary let her shoulders go down. It's okay. Everything is going to be okay. They're just nervous, that's all.

"And you understand," Judge Johnson said, "that if Jamie is adopted, as you say you wish him to be, that his surname will be changed...and he will then be named..." He looked down at the papers in front of him.

Mary squeezed Wayne's arm.

"Williams," the judge said. "Your son's legal name will become Jamie Williams. His name will no longer be Buckley. Do you understand?"

A sharp intake of breath from Mrs. Buckley could be heard all the way in the back. Judge Johnson looked alarmed. Tiny beads of sweat glistened on his forehead.

"I am appointing a lawyer for you," he said. "We will reconvene in two weeks. I believe you folks need legal counsel before we can proceed."

Mary gasped and covered her mouth. Wayne bent over with his hands on the back of his neck.

"May 14, 10:00 a.m.," the court transcriber said after scrutinizing the calendar on the table in front of her.

"Okay, Mr. and Mrs. Buckley, I'll see you again on May 14," Judge Johnson said. "*After* you meet with your attorney." Then he strode over to the door off to the side and left the courtroom.

EIGHTEEN

J. B. Harrell was leaning against the wall with his arms crossed over his chest and a look of impatience on his face. I tripped over the questions that raced through my head from the elevator to my apartment. *Why are you here? Where have you been?*

"Took you long enough to show up," he said.

His scolding words were music to my ears, lyrics singing that I wasn't alone—it didn't matter that the police had ruled Anthony Little Eagle's death an accident, it wasn't too late to prove them wrong, we weren't giving up. I skidded to a halt in front of him with a grateful smile on my face. J. B. reached down to pick his briefcase up from the floor and my outstretched arms fell to my sides.

"We have to talk," he said, and I unlocked the door.

We went inside and walked down the hall. As we passed my bedroom, I closed the door. "Sorry about the mess," I said. "I overslept this morning."

Other than a crooked poster on the wall and a stack of magazines and papers on the scratched desk in the corner, my living room was in fairly good order. Compared to his loft condo, though, it must have seemed incredibly tiny and dark to J. B. He spurned my faux-leather couch and sat down on the burgundy velvet of my pulpit chair.

"Where have you been?" he asked.

"You didn't call me back," I said.

"You didn't answer."

"Oh, I forgot," I said. "I turned my cell phone off. I was at a meeting at the community center. They're planning a protest at MCPD headquarters."

"A waste of time," he said with a snort. "Beating on drums and acting like a bunch of savages."

I frowned and thought about Peter Minter's accusation that J. B. was red on the outside and white on the inside. "That's not fair," I said. "A protest could put pressure on the police to reopen the investigation."

He waved his hand dismissively.

"I tried to speak at the meeting," I said. "They booed me off the stage."

"What were you going to tell them?" He looked worried.

I shrugged. "I don't know." I looked down at my hands. *Just what was I planning to say when I jumped up on that stage,* I asked myself. "They wouldn't have listened to me anyway," I said.

"Nope," J. B. said. "They wouldn't have."

I lowered my head. "Peter Minter would have listened. So would Sam Chasa."

"They know you," he said with a smile.

"And you? What about you?"

He responded with a wry look that told me to let it go. I took it as a reminder that this wasn't about me.

"What's next?" I asked. "We have to figure out what to do

now."

"Follow our leads," he said with a nod. He took out his designer fountain pen and a pad of legal-sized paper and printed the words *What We Know* on top of the first page. Then he looked up at me with his eyebrows raised.

"Well, we know that Paul Mellon has a history of drug use and criminal activity," I said. "And he lied about it."

"Or maybe someone else made sure it was kept secret," he said.

"Or," I said with an involuntary twitch, "a worker screwed up the foster parent application process."

"Everything's possible." J. B. looked thoughtful. "What we do know is that the secrets and lies are piling up. Paul's history isn't the only secret." He wrote as he spoke. "There's no information about the baby's death. Pages are missing from the case file. Bradley Finch lied about the incident report."

"Inez Koreskovsky lied, too," I added. "She knows more than she told me." Inez had been more evasive and defensive than usual when I asked her about the baby's death and the missing pages.

"And then there's the fact that the agency attorney wouldn't let you, the supervisor in charge, see the case file," he said.

"I don't want to be around Brion Kacey when he finds out I got my hands on that file not only once, but twice."

"You haven't told me how you did that," he said.

I laughed. Then it came to me. "Wait a minute," I said. "Now that the investigation is over, they have to let me see the file, and..."

"And?" J. B. put his pen down and looked at me.

"And no one has talked to Mrs. Mellon yet. I think I can use the case file as an excuse to contact her and do just that." I glanced at my watch. "I'll do it tomorrow. It's too late today and I have a meeting to go to now." I paused before adding, "An AA meeting."

J. B. dropped everything in his briefcase and snapped it shut. He opened his mouth to say something, then I guessed he thought better of it and closed it. We both stood up and headed for the door.

"What about Paul's old friend who he went to jail for?" I asked as we got on the elevator.

"Mel's still digging," he said, "but I'm betting we're going to find out that Adin Boyle isn't the person the governor of our state thinks he is."

The elevator stopped at the first floor and we got off. As we walked to the parking lot I went over the steps I would take once I got to my office tomorrow. I assumed J. B. was busy planning his next moves, too. We reached my Suzuki and stopped to say good-bye.

"Thank you," I said. "I was ready to give up."

I unlocked the car door and then noticed that J. B. hadn't moved. "What?" I asked.

"I know you, too," he said.

I jiggled the car keys in my hand.

"I know you're part of the system..."

I yanked my car door open. "Maybe you don't know me," I said with a sharp shake of my head.

He held the door with his hand, and his arm blocked me from getting into the car. "Come on, Sylvia, where does your paycheck come from?"

He moved his hand. I got into my car and pulled the door closed. He leaned down and put his hands on the frame of the open window.

"I do know you, Sylvia," he said. "You're a bureaucrat, but a lousy one. I know you're not the enemy." Then he smiled and turned to leave.

I bit my bottom lip and swallowed the lump in my throat. I rested my head against the back of the seat for a few minutes. Then I started the car and backed out of the parking space. I pulled up next to J. B.'s car just as he was about to drive away.

"Talk to you in a couple of days," I called out to him.

"Or as soon as there's something to report," he said with a wave of his hand.

—

The next morning I parked in the underground garage of the Health Services Building, took the elevator up to the third floor, and headed straight for Betsy Chambers's office. Her door was open and she was sitting at her desk. I went in and sat down. Yesterday's edition of the city newspaper was still on her desk, the Mellon case file lying next to it.

"I suppose everyone's relieved," I said.

"How about you?" Betsy asked.

"I guess I was wrong." Betsy visibly relaxed. "Maybe Brion's right, that it's time to put it behind us," I added.

"The police investigation is over," Betsy said, "but not the internal child mortality review. I hope the local panel will make some recommendations that will help us better protect the children under our care. The panel will want to hear from you about what happened and what we could have done differently—what improvements we need to make."

"Believe me, I'm already doing a lot of thinking about that," I said. I paused for a moment and then continued. "I don't think we should place any more children in the Mellon home. I wouldn't be surprised if they've already decided that they don't want to take children anyway, on their own."

"Well, at least not until the internal review is completed," Betsy said, with that cautious look that I was beginning to think was permanently etched on her face.

"We can always reopen the case later," I quickly assured her. *Over my dead body,* I said to myself.

"Closing their home isn't punitive, though," she said. "The police didn't find them to be culpable of any wrongdoing. They may need to be reassured about that. I want you to handle this, Sylvia. Don't delegate it to anyone else."

"Of course," I said. "And don't worry. I'll be sensitive to their feelings."

"I'm sure you will," she said, and she pushed the Mellon case file across the desk to me.

I hadn't expected it to be this easy. Not only did I now have an excuse to talk to Mrs. Mellon, I didn't have to ask for the record. Apparently Betsy had faith in my competence after all. Maybe she hadn't been hiding anything; maybe she really had just been following protocol when she agreed with Brion that no one should see the case file until the police had concluded their investigation. A sense of unease came over me about the secrets I was keeping from her. But when I thought about what she might do if I told her what J. B. and I were learning...it was too big a risk. I stood up to leave.

"I know how hard this has been on you, Sylvia."

Betsy looked smaller than usual to me. Her upper torso was shrunken inside her bright crimson jacket, as if she had somehow been diminished by my deception. Maybe I could tell her part of the truth, without letting her know why I still had doubts about the police ruling. Would it hurt to tell her that the whole thing had shaken me up, that it might take me a while to move on after all? What was I doing to our relationship, the trust there'd always been between us?

"Is there something else?" she asked.

I hesitated for a few seconds. "I just wanted to tell you," I said, "that I'll be sure to take care of this right away."

———

As soon as I got back to my office, I looked up Mr. and Mrs. Mellon's phone number in the case file and made the call. When Linda Mellon answered the phone and I identified myself as the foster care supervisor, I heard a little gasp.

"I know how hard this must be for you," I said.

"It shouldn't..." Mrs. Mellon's voice cracked. "It shouldn't... have happened."

"What shouldn't have happened?" I didn't know whether she was referring to Anthony Little Eagle's death or the police ruling.

Mrs. Mellon lowered her voice. "I don't know what to do," she said.

"About what?"

"I just don't think..." She was whispering. "I've tried, but...I always watched him."

There was a voice in the background then, harsh and demanding. A man's voice. I couldn't make out the words.

"Thank you so much for calling, Miss Jensen." Mrs. Mellon's voice turned bright and chipper. "We'll be sure to let you know if we need anything." Then she hung up.

I held the phone in my hand and listened to the dial tone. All the pieces were falling into place, and they all pointed to Paul Mellon's guilt. He was a control freak. He was in charge of his wife now, just as he had been in charge whenever something happened to a foster child. He had been denied custody of his own children. He'd lied about his prison record and his involvement with drugs. His wife hung up when he overheard her talking to me because she was afraid of him, an indication that he was abusing her.

I knew what I had to do. I had to protect Mrs. Mellon. Her conscience was pushing her to tell me something and I had to make it safe for her to do so. I had to find a way to meet with her alone, before she had time to change her mind. But how was I to do that? It took me a while, but by the end of the next day, I had worked out a plan.

NINETEEN

It was sunny and a pleasant seventy degrees at nine o'clock Sunday morning when I began my vigil in front of the Mellons' house. My plan was to watch for Mrs. Mellon to leave for church, follow her there, and accidentally bump into her after the service was over. I'd read that she attended services regularly, and since the case file was silent about Mr. Mellon's church attendance, I assumed that if she went today it was likely that she would be alone.

Thinking my faded orange car would raise suspicions in this upscale urban community, I rented a black Chrysler PT Cruiser for the weekend.. I sat in it now, in a spot partially hidden under a mature maple tree. The two- and three-story houses in the neighborhood built in the early 1900s were well-maintained. Most of them had large porches and all had manicured lawns, some enclosed by ornate latticework fences. The relative disrepair of the Mellon house made it stand out on the block. Its dull paint was chipping away in places and the front porch was sagging at one end. Their pale green station wagon in the driveway was a junker compared with the BMWs and Mercedes-Benzes parked by some of the other houses.

At ten to eleven, just when I was about to give up, Mrs. Mellon walked out of the front door. As soon as I saw her I felt sorry for her. She was the size of a child, under five feet tall and less than a hundred pounds, but with the watery eyes and thinning hair of someone much older than her thirty-eight years. Her shoulders drooped as she walked from the porch to the car. I waited until she'd driven halfway down the block and then followed a safe distance behind. Less than ten minutes later, she turned into a parking lot next to a red-brick church. I parked across the street and watched her drag her feet up the front steps as if they weighed as much as bowling balls. When the door closed behind her I settled in to wait with the Sunday paper and my thermos of coffee.

At noon I went into the church and stood in the vestibule to wait for her to come out. The congregation stood for a closing hymn, then a white-robed minister gave the benediction and walked down the aisle toward the exit where I was standing. I moved off to the side. Mrs. Mellon left the sanctuary behind the minister and shook hands with him at the door.

"It's good to see you, Mrs. Mellon," he said. "You've been in my prayers."

I followed several feet behind as she held onto the railing and made her way down the stairs. When she reached the parking lot, I headed her off.

"Mrs. Mellon!" I acted surprised to see her and held out my hand.

She turned around, puzzled.

"I'm Sylvia Jensen, from the Health Services Department. I'm the foster care supervisor. I called you a couple of days ago?"

"How did you recognize me?"

"I was behind you in the church. I heard the minister say your name."

Her mouth formed a suspicious O but made no sound.

"I'm so glad to run into you," I said. "We didn't get to finish our phone conversation. Do you have time to talk now?"

She squinted at me. She glanced down at her wrist but I didn't see a watch on it.

"I'm sorry," I said. "Maybe this isn't a good time." I paused to justify the guilt I felt about manipulating her. "Or I could come to your house if you'd rather talk there?"

She looked down at the ground. Looked up at me. Her face was contorted with the effort of trying to decide what to do.

"Maybe you'd prefer that I talk to both you and your husband together."

Her head went up in a seemingly involuntary movement. "Now is fine," she said.

"There's a little coffee shop around the corner." I tipped my head and took a step in that direction.

She hesitated at first, then started walking beside me. The coffee shop was only half a block away but it took forever to get there. Every once in a while she looked at me like she expected me to say something, but I didn't want to start until we were sitting down and it didn't seem right to make small talk.

"Go ahead and sit down." I held the door to the coffee shop open for her. "I'll bring you something. Would you like coffee or tea?"

"Tea, please," she said. "Herbal, mint if they have it."

She dragged herself to a table in the back corner. I brought tea for her, coffee for me, plus two almond croissants and some napkins. I sat down and took a sip of coffee. I watched her stir sugar in her tea. Her hands were trembling. She unfolded one of the napkins and placed it on her lap. I looked for signs of bruising on her arms, neck, and face. When she noticed I was studying her I glanced down at my cup and took another sip of coffee.

"This has been a difficult time," I said.

She nodded, her eyes watery.

"When we talked on the phone," I went on, "you said that you did everything you could. I've been thinking about that and wondering what you meant."

She stared down at her cup of tea.

"Were you referring to Anthony Little Eagle?"

She picked a piece of lint off her skirt and flicked it onto the floor. She folded her hands on the table. "Tony was such a sweet boy." I heard tears in her voice.

"You said you always watched him. That sounded to me like you tried to keep him safe."

Mrs. Mellon blinked. She opened her mouth like she was going to say something, but then clamped it shut. Her eyes dimmed.

"Did you think Tony might be in danger?" I spoke in a soft, gentle voice. I didn't want to push too hard and frighten her, but she was already starting to shut down. She sat so still I began to wonder if she'd become catatonic. I offered her a croissant and she whispered no. I took a bite of one. I sipped my coffee.

"You said on the phone that it shouldn't have happened," I said.

"The case is closed," she said, still looking down.

"Is that what you meant, that the case shouldn't have been closed? Or did you mean Tony shouldn't have died?"

"It's over now. There's nothing to be done." There was a look of resignation on her lined face.

"I can only imagine how hard it's been for you." I paused, then added, "To have two children die in your home."

Mrs. Mellon's hand flew up to her mouth. Tea splashed over the rim of her cup and onto the table. "Haven't we been through enough?" she said.

I wiped up the tea with a napkin. "I'm sorry," I said. "I thought, maybe, since we're alone, this would be a chance for you to talk about it."

She frowned in a way that made me think she was giving serious consideration to what I said. "My husband tries," she finally said. "He does. He tries."

"What do you mean? What does he try to do?"

"I'm not like him," she said.

I moved a little closer to her. "What do you mean, Mrs. Mellon? What *is* Paul like? How are you different from him?"

"I'm too nervous to enjoy the kids like he does. He plays with them, teaches them things. His work keeps him busy, but he makes time to spend with them upstairs in his office. I'm always too afraid something's going to go wrong, that there'll be an accident or something, to relax like that."

"You mean like Ellie Moon's accident?"

"Paul fixed that step after Ellie broke her arm. Everything was okay after that. Until Tony..." She grabbed her napkin and wiped the corners of her eyes.

I put my hand on her arm. "What does Paul do when you get nervous, Mrs. Mellon? Does he yell at you? Does he hit you?"

She jerked her arm away and glared at me. "Why are you asking me that?"

"You and I were talking on the phone, and when I heard him in the background your voice changed and then you hung up. I thought you might have been afraid."

She nodded. "I was. I was afraid Paul was going to worry. You see, he always thinks I'm going to have a nervous break- down. He doesn't like me to get upset. That's why I tried to act like everything was fine. To keep him from worrying about me."

"But he's not here now," I said. "Do you want to finish what you started telling me on the phone?"

She drew her lips together and wrinkled her brow. "There's nothing more to tell," she said. "I'm afraid I have to go now. Thank you for the tea."

She stood up faster than I'd thought she was capable of and headed for the door. There was no point in trying to stop her. She wasn't going to give her husband up.

TWENTY

The next day was the fourth of July and I didn't have any plans. I was in my apartment feeling discouraged about my talk with Mrs. Mellon when J. B. called.

"How soon can you get to my office," he said. "I've got something."

"You're working on a holiday? You want me to come to the newspaper?"

"The fifth floor," he said.

At the *Monrow City Tribune* building I stepped off the elevator and into a fast-paced, high-pressure world that I'd only imagined from watching movies and television shows. The buzzing of voices and ringing and binging sounds from phones, TV screens, computers, and radios surrounded me. Young, tech-savvy people stared at screens and typed at top speed on keyboards; others zipped from desk to desk in the room with reams of papers in their hands and arms. I was so mesmerized by the intense, data-driven atmosphere in which I stood that I wasn't aware of J. B.'s presence until his hand was on my shoulder.

"I reserved a room," he said. "We'll swing by my desk on the way."

His cluttered workstation was in the center of the massive open room and enclosed by a glass wall no more than four feet high. J. B.'s excitement was palpable as he shuffled through a stack of papers on his desk to retrieve a large brown envelope near the bottom.

"Wait until you see this," he said.

It took two of my steps for each one of his to keep up with him as we made our way through the hectic beehive of the newsroom. When we got to a small conference room and went in, J. B. closed the door behind us. The silence was sudden and jarring. So was the whiteness. Other than a flatscreen TV hanging from the ceiling and a view of downtown Monrow City through the picture window, everything in the room was white: the walls, a round table and four chairs, the carpeting.

We sat next to each other at the table. J. B.'s eyes were shining as he opened the brown envelope. He pulled out some papers and slid them over to me.

"Bradley Finch's bank statements," he said. "Look at the list of his account balances from 1999 to 2001."

"How did you get these?"

He answered my question with a shrug. "Look at them. What do you notice?"

I pored over the list of checking and savings account balances for a while. "His checking account looks like mine," I eventually said. "There's a couple-thousand-dollar boost the first of each month, must be payday, and then it keeps going down pretty regularly, probably paying bills, then another infusion on payday just before the balance gets to zero. I don't see anything unusual. Oh? Wait a minute. It says his balance is thirty dollars

here, but then the next balance is, what? One hundred thousand
and thirty?"

J. B. sat back in his chair with a one-up, one-down nod of
his head.

"So how do you get that kind of money on a cop's salary?"

"That's exactly what I asked him. I went to his house yesterday and caught him by surprise, showed him the statements."

"What did he say?"

"He threatened to have me arrested for violating his privacy."

"That's what I'd do if you ever got a hold of my bank
account."

He shrugged and went on. "I told him I'd love for him to
take me to court. It would give me a chance to submit his bank
statements as evidence of foul play, see what the judge would
think about a cop getting a hundred thousand dollars in his
checking account right at the same time that a baby dies."

My palms started sweating. I thought about some of the
things J. B. and I had been doing, things that I never would have
imagined myself doing in a million years. For starters, I broke
into an office and stole a case file. I lied to my supervisor, and
our relationship was most likely destroyed. And now J. B. somehow stole Finch's bank statements without seeming the least bit
concerned about suffering any consequences.

"So then Finch tried to tell me that his uncle died and he'd
inherited the money from him. I laughed in his face. Then,
when I asked him who gave him a hundred thousand dollars
to not complete the incident report when that baby died in the
Mellon home, he started to talk."

"He admitted taking a bribe?"

"He said it never set right with him but he had no choice.
He said they threatened him."

"Who?"

"He said it was a man but he claimed he didn't know who he was. So I told him if he didn't give me the man's name I was going to report him to the IRS, tell his supervisor about the bribe, and write an exposé in the newspaper. That's when he told me the man was just a lackey who was hired by someone else."

"Paul Mellon," I said. "That's who was behind it?"

"Good guess, but you're wrong." He put the papers back in the envelope and went on with his story. "I told him if he'd tell me who it was, I'd tear up the bank statements, destroy all the evidence, and forget about his involvement, and he still insisted he didn't know. But you should have seen him. The sweat was pouring down his face in buckets. I tell you, that man was scared shitless."

"So how did you find out who it was?"

"I called his bluff. I told him I already knew who it was, and it was too bad he hadn't cooperated when he had the chance because now he was going lose his job, his pension, and his reputation. He acted tough then, and gave a little snort like he didn't believe me, so I said, 'Look, I already know Adin Boyle was behind it.'"

I stared at him, wide-eyed.

"Finch literally collapsed in his chair. He might as well have confessed on the spot, it was so obvious I was right."

"Why would Adin Boyle go to such lengths to cover up the baby's death?" I said.

J. B. raised his shoulders and brought them down with a little shake. "That, we don't know yet."

"This is getting scary," I said. "I think we should turn these bank statements over to the police."

He nodded in agreement. "We will. But we're not ready to

do that yet," he said. "All we know is the who, not the why. We still have to find out what Adin Boyle is up to and what it has to do with Paul Mellon. We still don't have any evidence to prove that Paul killed Anthony Little Eagle."

I frowned and pursed my lips. "But I know he did," I said. "That's why Adin Boyle and Mrs. Mellon are both protecting him."

J. B. raised his eyebrows. "His wife is protecting him?"

"I was busy yesterday, too," I said. "I was able to get her alone."

"How did you manage that?"

"Don't ask," I said. "Let's just say it wasn't exactly professional. From the way she talked, though, you'd think her husband was a saint."

"Do you think she's afraid of him?"

"I didn't see any physical signs of abuse on her, but she's scared about something. Bottom line is, she's not going to talk. If she won't tell the truth about her husband, who will?"

"Maybe Ellie Moon?" J. B. said.

"That's it!" I jumped up. "Ellie knows whether she really fell down the steps or if Paul Mellon broke her arm. I'll talk to her. See what I can find out."

TWENTY-ONE

May 14, 1973

Even when the court hearing was rescheduled, Mary didn't allow her confidence to be shaken. Judge Johnson had to assign an attorney to Mr. and Mrs. Buckley, she reasoned, to ensure that all legal protocols were followed. All it meant was a three-week delay. She could remain absolutely certain the judge would terminate the Buckleys' parental rights as long as she took an action every day to ensure that he would.

Most of her actions were small, like bringing good luck by doing a good deed for someone and warding off bad luck by knocking on wood. The most drastic action she took was mailing out the invitations to Jamie's eighth birthday party way ahead of time. Doing so would guarantee that they would be celebrating both his birthday and his adoption next month. She didn't consult with Wayne before doing it. He would have insisted that she wait until after the court hearing. *Just to make sure,* she could hear him say. If she told him that making sure was exactly what she *was* doing, he would accuse her of being superstitious. So she didn't tell him what she believed or about

any of the actions she took. Nor did she acknowledge his wor-
ries. That would definitely bring bad luck.

On the morning of the rescheduled court hearing, Mary got
up early. When she saw the rising sun brush the distant pine and
birch trees outside the kitchen window she knew everything was
going to be okay. But, just as further insurance, she insisted on
getting to the courthouse well before the scheduled ten o'clock
hearing and sitting on the back bench to the left rather than the
right side of the aisle this time. As an added precaution, she was
adamant that she and Wayne wear different clothes this time.
She picked out a cotton dress for her and a polo shirt and tan
slacks for him. Casual attire, she reasoned, was a way to capture
her sense of confidence.

They arrived at the empty courtroom a good half hour
early. It was eerily quiet, no construction noise outside like last
time—another positive sign for Mary. She closed her eyes and
visualized the next time they would be coming to court, when
they finalized Jamie's adoption. Wayne's parents were there with
flowers and balloons, expensive champagne, airplane tickets to
Disneyland.

Her fantasy was interrupted by the sound of the heavy door
opening. She opened her eyes and saw a man walk into the
courtroom with Mr. and Mrs. Buckley behind him. She broke
out in a smile. If the man was their attorney, his appearance was
definitely a sign that everything was going to be all right. His
suit was rumpled, he wasn't wearing a tie, and a tuft of curly
red chest hair sprouted out from just below the stained collar of
his wrinkled, off-white shirt. His red freckles and crooked teeth
reminded her of a boy in elementary school named Charlie, who
couldn't seem to do anything right.

A few minutes later, two of the AIM men who had been at

the first court hearing arrived, this time with an older woman instead of the man with his hair in braids. The woman wore a loose summer dress and her gray hair was pulled back in a tight bun. Mary took her matronly appearance to be a positive sign. Her optimism soared when the three of them sat down instead of standing like they did last time. And when Judge Johnson came in wearing a bright multicolored tie dotted with the faces of happy children, she broke out into a smile. She believed from the top of her head to the tip of her toes that everything was going to be all right, and thus it was inevitable that it would be. It was as simple as that.

"Good morning and welcome back," the judge said. "Mr. Greenwater, I assume you have met with Mr. and Mrs. Buckley?"

"I have, your honor."

"And have they told you what their wishes are in regard to their son Jamie?" Judge Johnson asked the attorney.

"Yes, your honor. They wish to terminate their parental rights to him."

"They told you that?"

"Yes...your honor."

Mary stifled an urge to jump up and down. She was barely able to contain her excitement.

"And do Mr. and Mrs. Buckley fully understand what that means?" the judge asked.

"I have explained it to them in detail."

"Answer the question, Mr. Greenwater. Do they understand?"

"Your honor...I find them to be...ambivalent."

"What does that mean?" Wayne mumbled under his breath. He moved toward the edge of the bench and craned his neck toward the front of the courtroom.

Mary tugged at the bottom of his shirt and pulled him back.

"Stop worrying," she whispered.

"Your honor," Mr. Greenwater continued, "Mr. and Mrs. Buckley do wish to terminate their rights, but with two conditions—a guarantee that Jamie's foster parents adopt him and that he keep the Buckley surname. In other words..."

The judge cut him off with an impatient wave of his hand. He rubbed at his temples with the tips of his fingers as if trying to massage away a knotty problem.

"Your honor, if I may." Mr. Greenwater waited until Judge Johnson nodded before continuing. "Mrs. Buckley, in particular, feels strongly about these conditions."

"What the hell?" Wayne blurted out.

"Shh." Mary poked him in his ribs with her elbow. The legal system was fundamentally fair. The judge was on Jamie's side. There was nothing to worry about.

"And what did you tell Mrs. Buckley about the viability of her conditions, Mr. Greenwater?" Judge Johnson asked.

Mr. Greenwater said something to Mrs. Buckley and she nodded. "I explained to her that such guarantees were not customary," he said, "but she wants me to convey her wishes to the court in any case."

"And it is these conditions that lead you to believe that Mrs. Buckley is ambivalent about terminating her parental rights. Is that correct?"

"Yes, your honor."

"Why doesn't he ask *her*?" Wayne hissed. Mary slapped his arm.

"Mr. and Mrs. Buckley, has Mr. Greenwater accurately stated your wishes?"

They both nodded.

"Now, I am going to ask you one more question. It is critical that you answer honestly." The judge drew his words out. "Do you have any doubts about terminating your rights as Jamie's parents? Any doubts at all?"

Mrs. Buckley looked down at her hands. Mr. Buckley looked straight ahead. Someone in the courtroom coughed. There was a sound of shuffling feet. Silence...then one sharp strike of the judge's gavel on the dais. A collective gasp echoed off the courtroom walls.

"Mr. and Mrs. Buckley," Judge Johnson said. "I am denying your petition. You are Jamie's rightful parents. I am ordering that he be returned to you."

A short cry, quickly muffled, hit the high ceiling and fell down onto the floor. Wayne, the blood drained from his face, gnawed at his thumb. He put his arm around Mary's shoulder and pulled her close.

Judge Johnson's upper body was stretched across the dais. "Jamie has the right to live with his parents and siblings," he said. "Mr. and Mrs. Buckley, you have a right to your child, and he has a right to his parents and his culture. Your community has a right to its children. The county was remiss when it left Jamie to languish in foster care after your other children were returned to you. You are owed an apology for the grave injustice done to you."

Mary drifted away on the ocean of a growing storm. The judge's voice was a distant foghorn in her cloudy head. She grasped for a towline but it was beyond her reach. She saw the judge's lips move, heard his faint murmurings: "Birth parents... returned...injustice." Why was he looking at Mrs. Buckley with such intensity? Why did he look so sad? Why did he sound so angry?

"Mrs. Waters," the judge said, "I am ordering you, as Mr.

and Mrs. Buckley's social worker, to transport Jamie home within three days' time. The foster parents should be commended for their service. I trust they will prepare Jamie for his return to his rightful parents and visit him during the transition period...although I want to make clear that that is the sole decision of his legal parents, who are John and Josephine Buckley."

A deep animal-like groan rumbled through the cavernous courtroom. Then the moaning started, a long low sound that pushed its pain into Mary's womb. She pressed down on her stomach and prayed for the wailing to stop.

TWENTY-TWO

I had to find Ellie Moon. Maybe by seeing and talking to her a little I'd get a sense of how she was doing and in the process be able to discern the truth about what happened five years ago when she broke her arm. I went to the foster care database for basic information. Ellie was born in 1995, so she was ten years old. She first entered the system at age five after her mother died, and was placed in the Mellon home where she'd lived until two months ago. Her new foster parents were Tisha and Lamont Parks and the social worker assigned to their home was none other than Lynn Winters.

I called Lynn to my office at once. She stood in the doorway with her hands clasped in front of her. It looked as if she'd aged ten years in the days since Anthony Little Eagle's death, although her appearance was somewhat improved from the last time I saw her. Her hair was pulled back in a neat ponytail and there was some natural blush to her cheeks. She waited for me to invite her in, then sat down in the chair on the other side of my desk. She looked at me warily.

"How are you?" I asked, genuinely concerned.

"I'm sorry, Sylvia," she said. "I know how bad I messed up. I don't blame you for firing me."

"I'm not going to fire you, Lynn. But the child death review panel will no doubt hold you accountable for the placement procedures you didn't follow. I'll be held accountable for not providing you, as a new, young social worker, with closer supervision and monitoring. The agency is accountable as well for assigning too many cases and not putting enough resources into training."

Her mouth opened a little and her eyes filled with moisture. I pushed the box of tissues toward her.

"I didn't expect it to be this hard," she said. "They don't tell you in grad school...I can't help but think that Anthony Little Eagle would still be alive if I...but you see, I don't know what..." She blew her nose. "It's just obvious that I'm not a good social worker."

"It isn't about whether you're a good social worker or not," I said. "It's about how you can develop into a good social worker. You and I will work on that together. There's something else related to the case that we can work on. Tell me, what do you know about Tisha and Lamont Parks?"

Lynn Winters brightened a little. She leaned forward. "Their home was just licensed about three months ago. They're an older African American couple. Tisha is sixty-five, a retired teacher, and Lamont is a few years older and just retired this year from the post office. They have three adult children and five grandchildren. When they applied to be foster parents they said they missed raising children and they still had a lot to give."

"Ellie Moon was recently placed with them," I said, "after living in the Mellon foster home for five years."

Her shoulders drooped. "I would have known that earlier," she said with a groan, "if I'd read the Mellon case file like I was supposed to."

"But now you have," I said. "So you know about Ellie Moon's broken arm."

Lynn nodded.

"I don't think it was an accident," I said. "I don't believe Anthony Little Eagle's death was an accident either."

Lynn's eyes widened. Her mouth dropped open.

"I want the police to reopen the investigation," I said. "That's where Ellie Moon comes in. If it was Mr. Mellon who broke Ellie's arm, I think we could convince the police to take a closer look at what might have happened to Anthony."

"I have a home visit scheduled with Mr. and Mrs. Parks for eleven o'clock tomorrow," she said.

"Perfect," I said. "I'll go with you. Tell the foster parents I'm coming along to observe you, that it's part of your in-service training, which it is. I'll find a way to talk to Ellie Moon alone while you talk to the foster parents. Maybe between the two of us, we'll learn more about what happened to her."

Lynn Winters hesitated, then placed her hands flat on my desk. "Thank you," she said, "for giving me a second chance."

—

The next morning Mr. and Mrs. Parks greeted us at the door with the confidence and generosity of people who knew and liked themselves. Their modest and comfortable home teemed with life, decades of laughter, tears, and love infused into the worn furniture. An oversized Bible dominated the scratched coffee table. Family photographs were on the walls, piano, fireplace mantel, and every other available and highly polished surface.

"Ellie, sweet pea," Mrs. Parks called out. "Where is that child now?"

Mr. Parks laughed. "Want to bet, Tish, that she's up in that tree again? I'll go out back and find her."

Mrs. Parks led us into the dining room. The smells of freshly brewed coffee and cinnamon sugar made my mouth water. Mr. Parks and Ellie Moon came in from the kitchen. They were holding hands.

"This is Miss Lynn," he said. "And this is Miss Sylvia."

"Have they come to lunch, Poppa?"

Mr. Parks chuckled. "Indeed they have," he said. "Can you say hello to the nice ladies."

Ellie tipped her head and pressed it against her foster father's arm. "Hi," she whispered, looking up at us with a timid smile.

"Let me see those hands, honey," Mrs. Parks said. Ellie showed her palms, and then turned her hands to show the other sides. "I swear, sweet child, there is more dirt on you than there is on the ground. Now you go on in and wash up before you touch anything." She kissed Ellie on the forehead, then placed her hands on her shoulders and turned her to face the door, gave her an affectionate nudge in the back.

"She seems to have adjusted well," Lynn said. "She's calling you Poppa already. That's a good sign."

"Heck, we've been Momma and Poppa ever since our first one was born," Mr. Parks said. "That's what our grandkids call us, too. I doubt they know what our real names are, so it didn't take little Ellie long to get with the program. You two can call us Tish and Lamont, though." He chuckled again.

Tish brought in a plate piled high with open-faced egg salad sandwiches. She set it on the table next to a bowl of potato chips, a plate of cucumbers and carrots from the garden, and a stack of homemade snickerdoodle cookies. Then she stopped Ellie, who was on her way to her seat, and pulled her close. Ellie held up her hands. "Just look at this girl of ours, Poppa. She sure does know how to wash up good, doesn't she? And look at her face, all scrubbed shiny."

I unfolded the red and green plaid cloth napkin by my plate and laid it on my lap. It was obvious all through lunch that Ellie Moon was in a good home now. Lamont asked her if she wanted to play soccer or go for a bike ride later and Tish praised her for tucking her napkin into the neck of her T-shirt, for eating two whole sandwiches, crust and all, and for saying please and thank you without being reminded. Ellie didn't say much, but when Lynn Winters asked if she had a favorite toy, she lit up and said she liked to play with her dolls. When lunch was over, she asked if she could please be excused. I wiped the crumbs from my mouth and laid the napkin on the table.

"Do you have a favorite doll, Ellie," I asked.

She nodded and smiled shyly.

"Will you show me?" I stood up.

Ellie nodded and took my hand. "This was Uncle Mathew and Uncle Mark's room," she said pointing into the first room we passed. "Momma uses it for sewing now except when little Christian or Joseph or Gabriel or Joshua comes to stay overnight. This is Poppa and Momma's room. And this one's my room. Aunt Esther grew up here."

"Wow, you have two beds," I said.

Ellie smiled. "This one's mine and the other one is for Kayla when she stays overnight."

"Such a nice room," I said. "Pink is one of my favorite colors."

"Mine, too."

"That's a beautiful bracelet you're wearing," I said.

She looked down at her wrist and ran her fingers over the bracelet. "It was my momma's," she said. "I wear it all the time."

"It's beautiful," I said.

"Yes," she said. "It is."

"Are all those dolls yours?" I pointed to the shelf at the foot of her bed.

She nodded.

"Which one's your favorite?"

She lifted her shoulders, tipped her head, and smiled.

"Is it this one?" I picked out a pink pajama-clad baby doll from among the more than half a dozen African American dolls arranged by age.

Ellie smiled shyly. "No."

"This one?" I pointed to a toddler dressed in a red and blue gingham dress.

She smiled wider and shook her head.

"I'll bet it's this one. She looks like she's your age."

Ellie giggled. She covered her mouth with her hands.

I laughed. "Well, I give up," I said.

She reached for the Black Barbie on the top shelf and held it up.

"I can see why she's your favorite. She's very pretty. What's her name?"

Ellie shrugged.

"Is her name Ellie?"

"Not Ellie." She giggled again. "That's *my* name."

"I give up," I said.

"Eleanor," she said.

"I see. Kind of like your name, only longer."

"She has lots of clothes." Ellie pulled a box down from the shelf. "She wears something different every day."

"I like the turquoise gown she's wearing now," I said, "especially the sequins. And look at those matching earrings!"

Ellie set the Barbie doll on the bed and pulled the gown over her head. "See? Her underwear matches, too."

She moved the doll's arms and legs into different positions. She laid her on her back on the bed with one of her legs up in the air. She placed her on her side with one arm under her head. She put her on her stomach with her buttocks raised in the air and her head turned upward.

"Is Eleanor a model?" I asked.

All of a sudden Ellie's eyes filled with terror. She yanked the Barbie doll up by its arm and slammed it down. Then she scooted away from the doll and crossed her arms over her chest. I put my arm around her. She was trembling. After a few minutes she picked the Barbie doll up and hugged her. We sat in silence for a while, my arm around her, her arms enfolding the Barbie doll. Several more minutes passed and Ellie's little body started to relax a bit. Then she hugged the Barbie, kissed her cheeks.

"You're not bad, sweet pea," she whispered to the doll. "There's just some things you don't want to do, that's all. It's okay, Eleanor. You don't have to do anything you don't want to do now. I promise."

I gave Ellie's shoulder a little squeeze. She looked up at me. "Eleanor does have to wash her hands before eating," she said, "but she wants to do that. She wants to go with me and Poppa on our bike ride but I don't let her do that."

She moved to the edge of the bed and placed the Barbie doll back on the shelf, then took my hand and led me from the room. Having never worked as a therapist, I knew my limits, knew not to push her, not to try to get more information from her. But after many years of experience as a social worker, I understood the significance of what had just happened.

TWENTY-THREE

J. B. Harrell and I sat on the bench looking out over Island Lake. It was a scene worthy of a Monet palette, a lone canoe caught in the pink and orange glow of the sunset over the still water. It had been warm all day, and the temperature still hovered around eighty degrees, yet my fingers were cold as ice cubes.

"Peaceful here." J. B. breathed in the dusk-filled air.

I rubbed my hands together. Island Lake was one of the few places in the city where I had found introspection without angst to be possible, but it didn't have its calming effect on me today. My insides were as jumpy as if we were sitting in the middle of the shirtless, deeply tanned frat party of neighboring Lake Crosby, a place I'd frequented in my youthful drinking days but now assiduously avoided.

"Beautiful houses along the parkway," J. B. said.

I snorted and crossed my arms. "Ridiculously huge and fancy."

A couple walked by on the inside jogging path and a gray-haired bicyclist rode by on the separate biking path going in the opposite direction, all three with contented looks on their faces that I envied. My shoulders tensed, the muscles in my neck ached.

"I saw the terror in Ellie Moon's eyes," I said. "I've seen that look before." I shook my head and looked down at the ground. "Something happened to her. Something bad." My mouth went dry as my head filled with images of Ellie—her violent outburst with the Barbie doll, her sudden mood swing.

I slipped into silence. A family of ducks swam by on the lake. A shiny bald-headed man walking by on the inner path tipped his head to us with a friendly midwestern smile. J. B. nodded back.

"The foster parents told Lynn Winters that Ellie startles easily," I said. "They think her behavior seems overly compliant." I paused, thinking about how polite Ellie had been. "We'll get her the help she needs. At least she's safe now and with loving people. Mr. and Mrs. Parks told Lynn they want to adopt her."

My mind was a jumble of confusion. Something had happened to Ellie Moon in the Mellon home, something possibly related to her broken arm, or something worse. Whatever it was, it had traumatized her. I knew I was obligated by law to report any new information about possible abuse, but I worried that if I reported my suspicions now, it could interfere with our attempts to prove that Mr. Mellon killed Anthony Little Eagle. Maybe it wouldn't hurt to wait a while and report my suspicions later. After all, Ellie was safe now and there were no longer any foster children at risk in that home. A more propitious time to make the report might be after we had other evidence pointing to Mr. Mellon.

I also knew that failing to report my suspicions now could result in my losing my license and my job. But then, weren't those the consequences I was expecting for the other things I'd already done?

A great blue heron watched me from a distance as my head filled with thoughts and memories. I went back to the meeting at the community center right after the police ruled Anthony Little Eagle's death an accident. His father's warning screamed in my ears: *If you have kids in Child Protective Services you need to get them out before it's too late.*

"How right you are," I muttered under my breath. "How right you are."

J. B. cleared his throat and looked at me, his eyes curious.

"We say we rescue children from life-threatening situations and place them in loving homes," I said, "but we don't say we save them from our own foster homes, do we? Nor do we say how often we take kids like Anthony away from their homes not because of cruelty or abuse, but because of poverty. We don't talk about children like Ellie Moon being traumatized, sometimes permanently, from being in foster care, or about how many kids end up dead, like Anthony. And what about the children who are abandoned and forgotten by the same system that is supposed to protect them? How often do we talk about them?"

J. B. spotted something on the ground. He leaned down to pick it up. It was a penny. He held it in his open palm and stared at it. He offered it to me but I kept my hands folded on my lap and the penny fell down into the grass.

"I'm sorry," I said. "I'm just not in a mood for a lucky penny." I leaned down to retrieve it, handed it back to him.

J. B. turned the penny over in his hand, then turned it over again, and again. He leaned back on the bench with his long legs straightened out in front of him. The sun was low against the water now.

"I worry that I've made things worse," I said through gritted teeth. "At least for Mrs. Mellon but hopefully not for Ellie. And we still can't prove Paul Mellon killed Anthony Little Eagle and maybe a baby. We can't prove that he broke Ellie Moon's arm either."

J. B. flipped the penny in the air and it landed in his palm. "Heads," he said with a shrug. "It's not over. Mel's still digging. He's pretty sure it was more than real estate that made Adin Boyle this rich. He's got a forensic computer expert by the name of Clyde Bloesdell checking out his suspicions."

I perked up a little. Maybe we weren't out of leads after all. "Where does Mel think Boyle's money is coming from? Does he think he's dealing drugs? Does he think Paul Mellon's involved with it?"

"Too soon to tell," he said.

Just then J. B.'s phone rang and he pulled it from his pocket. He raised it to his ear and smiled as he listened. When he was finished, he stood up and motioned for me to do the same.

"That was Mel," he said. "He's at Clyde's house. They've got something. Come on, I'll drive."

TWENTY-FOUR

May 14, 1973

Mary Williams tried to suffocate Judge Johnson's words. She held her breath. *No, no, no, please don't do this. I'm begging you. Please.* A moaning sound echoed through the courtroom and she covered her ears, only to realize it was coming from deep inside her. Her rage-laced keening rose to a pitch, silenced only by the exhaustion that finally overtook her. Her face was crushed against Wayne's chest. Her eyes stung from tears and the sharp scent of his Irish Spring soap.

"I'm sorry." It was Karon Pate's voice. "I didn't see this coming, Mr. and Mrs. Williams. Really I didn't."

Mary was off the bench and on her feet in a flash, her fists clenched. "You promised...you said...damn it," she hissed. "You know what you said."

"I believed what I said to be true." The foster home worker's voice went formal, the tone of an expert.

"You didn't say you *believed*. You said it *was* true. You said the adoption was a sure thing. You never talked about anything that could go wrong. Never."

Karon Pate stepped back, her hands up in the air. She turned toward Wayne. "Mr. Williams," she said, "maybe you could?"

"Don't you turn away from me," Mary said, her eyes blazing. "I want to talk to the Buckleys. Now."

"I don't think that will be possible," Karon Pate said.

Wayne's arms hung at his sides. His face was that of a man whose world had just been annihilated. "Isn't there some way we could work this out together?" he said.

"The judge's decision is final," Karon Pate said with a shake of her head.

Mary flew to within inches of the foster home worker's startled face. "The *Buckleys* have the final say about Jamie." She paused and stood on her toes, her body an exclamation mark. "The Buckleys, I said, *not* the judge."

Karon Pate flinched and stepped back. She glanced around the courtroom, seemed distressed to see that everyone else had left.

"What could it hurt to talk to them," Wayne said, his voice a little stronger than before.

"We have to find them. Now! Before they leave." Mary's voice was a shriek more than a demand, loud enough to be heard beyond the courthouse.

Karon Pate opened her mouth, then closed it and looked down at her hands.

"Try," Wayne said. "Please."

The foster home worker hesitated. "I'll see what I can do," she finally said. "Come with me."

She led them down narrow back steps to the basement of the courthouse. She ushered them into a conference room and told them to wait. The room had no windows, no pictures or green plants to soften its stark, institutional gray walls. The door was closed but they could still hear the sounds of chaos coming from the County Department of Income Maintenance and Social Services reception area. Exhausted mothers shushed their rowdy toddlers. Every now and then a baby howled. The receptionist called out numbers.

Mary sat ramrod straight in a flimsy metal chair, focusing every ounce of energy she had on how to save Jamie. This was no time for self-doubt. She had to act and act fast. *Do whatever you have to do,* she told herself. *Jamie's life is at stake. All our lives are at stake.* She looked at Wayne sitting next to her, looking like a broken man.

"We have to fight," she said.

She placed her hand over his.

"With all we've got."

He nodded.

"I think the Buckleys know that what's best for Jamie is to stay with us. But if they don't, we'll have to convince them. We start by making sure they know how happy and loved Jamie is."

"*If* they'll talk to us," Wayne said.

"Stop it." Mary squeezed his hand. "I'm serious. Don't go there. Not today. Not now."

Wayne started to say something but was stopped by a soft knock on the door. Karon Pate came in. "They've agreed to meet," she said with a nervous smile on her face. "Everyone's here."

Mary nodded at each person as they walked in, made a point of looking each one straight in the eye. There were eight of them crowded into the small conference room. Mr. and Mrs. Buckley sat on one side of the table next to Mr. Greenwater, their court-appointed attorney. Mary and Wayne, along with Karon Pate, sat across from them. Mrs. Waters claimed the head of the table.

As if she's in charge, Mary said to herself. *Wasn't I the one who called this meeting?* The matronly-looking woman Mary had seen with the two men in the courtroom was there, too. She tugged at the hem of her dress like someone who wasn't used to wearing dresses and tucked a loose strand of her gray hair behind her ear. Then she claimed a chair at the other end of the table.

"This is May Goodheart," Mrs. Waters said as the woman sat down. "She's a good friend of Mr. and Mrs. Buckley."

Mary's ears burned from the scraping sounds of metal chairs on the concrete floor. She waited for everyone to get settled, rehearsing in her head the words she'd use to start the meeting— *Thank you for agreeing to meet with us. Let me tell you why we wanted to talk to you and what we hope to accomplish.* But before she was able to get the words out, Mrs. Waters beat her to it.

"We have a lot of planning to do," she said, "but before we get started, is there something you'd like to say, Mr. and Mrs. Buckley?"

There was no response. Mary looked at Mrs. Waters with her lips pursed as if she were sucking on a lemon. It was clear whose side Mrs. Waters was on by the way she hovered over Mr. and Mrs. Buckley and invited them to speak first. She might be wearing a suit instead of a miniskirt to make it seem like she was a professional in court, but it only made her look like someone in her twenties trying to act grown up. The pained expression on her face showed that she wasn't at all the objective professional she wanted everyone to think she was.

"Mr. and Mrs. Williams, is there something you'd like to say?" Mrs. Waters asked.

Mary cleared her throat, sat up straight. "We want to talk about the judge's decision. You see..." She looked around the table, ready to take over, but Mrs. Waters interrupted her.

"Judge Johnson's decision was a surprise," she said, "for *all* of us."

May Goodheart jumped in then. "And it was the *right* decision." Her voice was filled with such depth and certainty that everyone looked at her as if *she* were the one in charge. Mary tried to object but the words got stuck in her throat.

"We have a lot to do but little time," May Goodheart continued. "A boy Jamie's age can only handle one thing at a time, so each thing needs to be done in order. First, he has to be told what's going on. So, who's going to tell him? Second, he needs to meet with his parents. So, when and where will that meeting take place? Third, he needs to be moved. The judge already settled that. Mrs. Waters here will drive him to the reservation in three days." She counted the steps on her fingers as she spoke.

"What about the others," Mrs. Buckley asked. Everyone stared at her as if she'd just shouted, although her voice was barely audible and not directed at anyone in particular.

"Josie's right." May Goodheart raised a fourth finger and directed her words to Wayne and Mary by way of explanation. "John and Josie haven't told their other children about Jamie yet."

"Jamie doesn't know us," Mr. Buckley said. With his head down, his whisper got swallowed up by his much-too-large suit jacket.

Mary moved her chair closer to the table. "That's *exactly* why we wanted to meet with you, Mr. Buckley," she said. "We're the only parents Jamie has ever known. That's why we need to talk about the judge's decision."

Mr. Greenwater coughed, loudly. "In the interest of time," he said, glancing at his watch, "I'm sure we can all agree that our job is not to question the judge's order but to carry it out."

Karon Pate and Mrs. Waters nodded.

"That's a given," May Goodheart said. "But John is right that Jamie doesn't know them. That's why we need to plan how he should meet with his real parents."

"*Real* parents?" Mary shot up in her chair.

Mrs. Buckley shifted in her chair, like she wanted to say something. Mary noted that her faded and worn dress was starched and freshly ironed, which meant she had dressed up for today. She craned her neck toward Mrs. Buckley, looked at her hopefully. Their eyes locked. A baby out in the reception area started crying. When Mrs. Buckley finally spoke, it was with a voice that was surprisingly firm.

"Jamie is at the center," she said.

"*Exactly,*" Mary said. "We have to do what's best for *him*."

"He has to be at the center."

"Absolutely," Mary said with tears in her eyes. "Absolutely."

"What that means," May Goodheart said, "is that we will all do everything we can to help Jamie get through this."

"Everyone wants what's best for Jamie," Karon Pate added.

"Very good," Mrs. Waters said. "We're all on the same page about that so we should start with how Jamie should be told." She paused. "I think it would be best for him if Mr. and Mrs. Williams talked to him first."

Mary raised her palms in the air. "Wait," she said. "We can't decide *how* Jamie should be told until we decide *what* he should be told."

"That is something we already know." May Goodheart's voice was sharp yet surprisingly devoid of malice.

Mary swiped at her eyes, fought off tears. It felt like a steamroller was coming down on her and she didn't know if she had enough strength to hold it off.

Wayne put his hand on her arm. "Mr. and Mrs. Buckley,"

he said, "Mary and I want to talk to you about what alternatives there might be. We think you still want us to adopt Jamie. We want you to know that we don't have any problem with your conditions. None at all."

Mr. Greenwater cleared his throat. His nose, down to the smallest freckle, was aimed at Wayne. "I think I know where you're going with this, Mr. Williams," he said. "So let me save all of us some time by setting the record straight right up front. It's true that Mr. and Mrs. Buckley expressed an interest in having you folks adopt their son on the condition that he keeps their family name. But they've come to understand, and so must you, that it's not that simple."

"It *is* that simple," Mary said. "Let us adopt Jamie, Mr. and Mrs. Buckley, and we promise we will not change his last name. He will keep the Buckley name."

"I believe you folks are sincere," Mr. Greenwater said, "but here's what you don't understand. Before you could adopt Jamie, Mr. and Mrs. Buckley would have to give up all their rights to him, which means they would then have no say about what happens to him. No say at all. If you changed your mind about adopting him there's nothing they could do about it."

"We will never change our minds about Jamie," Mary said.

"Okay, let's say, hypothetically, that you adopt Jamie and he doesn't want to keep the Buckley name. What if he insists on taking your last name?"

"We'd explain it to him," Wayne said. "We'd work it out."

"Or maybe his last name could be Williams Buckley," Mary said. "Only if that would be all right with you, of course." She nodded at Mrs. Buckley.

"I believe you folks are missing the point here," Mr. Greenwater said. "Once Mr. and Mrs. Buckley's parental rights are terminated, they can't do anything if you change your mind."

"We said we wouldn't," Mary said. "Why don't you let these people speak for themselves?" A flush of heat jabbed her in her neck. Mr. Greenwater might look like a loser, but the way he was gripping his pen and pointing it at her right now was downright menacing.

"We could draw up a contract," Wayne said, looking at the Buckleys. "Make it legally binding."

"You could visit Jamie anytime," Mary said. "And we would bring him to see you whenever you wanted."

"We'll put visitation rights in writing, too," Wayne said. "Make it legal."

"Mr. and Mrs. Williams," Mr. Greenwater said with an exasperated sigh. "Stay with me, okay? Let me walk you through this. You can't adopt Jamie unless Mr. and Mrs. Buckley terminate all rights to him. So let's say they do that. At that point Jamie automatically becomes a ward of the state until the adoption is final."

Mrs. Buckley's head jolted up. "No! No child of mine will be a ward of the state!" She dropped her face into her hands as if the outburst had plunged her into an abyss of fatigue.

Mr. Greenwater smiled. "As you can see," he said, "Jamie's mother clearly knows what's at risk. If the state had total say about her son, she understands that anything could happen. That's what you folks need to understand, too. Think about it. One of you could get sick or, heaven forbid, one or both of you could be killed in a car accident before the adoption was final. Then what happens? The state decides."

"We're not going to die," Wayne said.

"What we're talking about here is a little boy," Mr. Greenwater said, "and a mother who refuses to put her son's fate in the hands of the state."

"Never," Mrs. Buckley said with a lift of her head.

Mary was reeling. Jamie's parents hadn't said they wanted him back. Nor had they said they didn't want him to be adopted. What they did say was that they didn't want to take the risk of him being a ward of the state. That was an entirely different matter. This could be worked out. They just had to find an alternative. She tried to reach across the table for Mrs. Buckley's hand but Jamie's mother inched back in her chair and placed her hands on her lap.

"We don't want Jamie to be a ward of the state either," Mary said.

Wayne quickly jumped in. "I'm sure there's a solution. Let's find it. Think about this. The judge gave you all legal rights to Jamie, so whatever happens to him now is *your* decision, your *sole* decision. As his legal parents, it's your right *and* your responsibility to do what's best for him, which we know is what you want to do. And if you think that it's best for him to continue to live with us, and I think you do, *you* get to decide that. We wouldn't have to legally adopt him. He could live part-time with you and part-time with us, whatever works best for Jamie."

Mary gripped Wayne's hand, dug her fingernails into his palm. *Please, please, please,* she begged Mrs. Buckley with her eyes.

"Jamie belongs with his *real* family," May Goodheart said. "He belongs with his own community. He needs to learn Indian ways. He needs to know who he is. I know this must be tough for you to hear, Mr. and Mrs. Williams, but what's best for Jamie is to be with his parents, his people."

Mary let go of Wayne's hand, gripped the edge of the table, and stood up. The chair tipped with a metal clang onto the floor. "Jamie is with his parents now," she said. "Jamie already knows who he is."

She stood there on the verge of tears. Everyone was looking at her, waiting for what she would do or say next. The silence in the room screamed in Mary's ears. The glare of the fluorescent light on the ceiling burned her eyes. May Goodheart stood up then and walked over to her. She picked up the chair, put her hands on Mary's shoulders, and helped her sit down. Then she handed her a tissue and went back to her place at the table.

Mary blew her nose and wiped her eyes. "I'm Jamie's mother," she said. "I may not have given birth to him but for eight years I've fed and clothed him, loved him, nursed him when he was sick, sat with him when he was upset, laughed and played with him, done everything with and for him. I know him better than anyone and I know the loving home he has now is just what he needs. And I know the rest of you know that, too."

She sank back in her chair then and didn't speak again for the rest of the meeting. In the background she heard the others talking and planning. Mrs. Waters wrote down the steps they would take and in what order. Someone read the list out loud. Mary and Wayne would tell Jamie about what was going to happen. Mr. and Mrs. Buckley would tell their other children about Jamie. They would visit Jamie in the foster home the next day. Mrs. Waters would pick Jamie up at noon the day after that. There would be a tribal ceremony to celebrate his return, et cetera, et cetera, et cetera. Their voices sounded farther and farther away to Mary. The plan had no meaning for her. Nothing they said mattered anymore. She had turned a corner and she'd seen what was on the other side.

TWENTY-FIVE

"Well, folks, I've got a few answers for you."

The muscles in my calves tensed with anticipation at the serious and authoritative sound of Clyde Bloesdell's voice. He stood before us in a threadbare sweater vest that protected his slightly stooped shoulders and a soiled, off-white T-shirt that matched his thinning hair. Neither his X-ray eyes nor his understated persona hinted at the significance of what he was about to tell us.

Mel Commer, J. B., and I were crammed together on flimsy metal chairs in Clyde's corner basement office, the four of us an unlikely alliance of computer specialist, freelance detective, investigative reporter and foster care supervisor. Five computer monitors faced us, two of them rising above the others on tripods, plus two laptops, multiple keyboards, two printers, and a mass of cables and wires. A blackboard illuminated by a clip-on light filled the wall to our left, and behind us there was a height-adjustable computer workstation attached to a treadmill.

Mel's chest expanded like a balloon and he pointed to the

framed documents hanging on the wall behind the mound of equipment. Clyde Bloesdell, Certified Computer Forensic Examiner. Regional President of the Investigative Technology Association. Advanced Trainer in Data Recovery and analysis. Retired with special commendations after thirty years as special agent with the Department of Justice, Bureau of Alcohol, Tobacco, and Firearms.

"Like I told you," he said proudly, "if anyone can hack through to the truth, it's Clyde." Mel brandished his chubby hands in front of the computers as if they were about to unveil all the secrets in the universe.

The three of us sat on the edges of our seats, holding our collective breath, our shoulders touching. I was wedged between wiry J.B on one side, with his long legs stretched out so his feet were under the table holding the computers, and portly Mel on the other, with his short legs tucked under his chair.

"Well, I was more or less lucky," Clyde said with a self-effacing blush. "Adin Boyle, like most people, doesn't seem to understand that the delete key on the keyboard is not the equivalent of a paper shredder." He unfolded a metal chair and sat down facing us knee to knee as if what he was about to say was too heavy for him to stand.

"Boyle and his cronies aren't stupid, though," he said. "They use multiple computer systems that contain hundreds of gigabytes of data and several different types of computers, too, each one either with a different operating system or serving a unique function. All that made the retrieval process a bit complicated. Fortunately, I was able to recover enough data from desktop hard drives and networked servers and backups anyway."

He paused and pointed to the blackboard. We turned to the left as if our bodies were one, craning our necks and squinting our eyes. The board was covered with tiny scribbles that were connected by squiggly lines and arrows.

"It was a challenge to determine which chain of events or activities were relevant and how they fit together," Clyde said after an interminably long wait. "But I was able to piece together the Internet cache files on Boyle's hard drive, including files he'd deleted, and figure out what was going on."

"And?" the three of us said in unison.

"Well, first of all," Clyde said, staring at the blackboard, "it appears that the money Boyle makes from his real estate business is legitimate. At least there's no reason to suspect it isn't."

I battled an impulse to feel disappointed and told myself to be patient and hear him out. But in my head I was screaming at him to get to the point.

"That doesn't mean, however, that Boyle isn't up to no good," he went on. "It seems that he's been investing his money in a shell company called Global Distributions Unlimited or GDU for short."

"Didn't I tell you," Mel said.

"So is GDU connected to the drug cartel that's been dealing heroin in the Midwest?" J. B. asked.

"That was my first thought, too," Mel said.

I turned my head from side to side, staring at each of them in turn. Never, in my wildest imagination, would I have predicted any of this. I'd read J. B.'s series in the *Monrow City Tribune* about the epidemic of middle school kids in small midwestern towns getting hooked and dying from heroin overdoses. I didn't know J. B. then, and yet here we were, working as a team that was on the verge of proving that Paul Mellon was responsible for Anthony Little Eagle's death. But bringing down a drug cartel, too, how remarkable was that? Then I noticed that

Clyde was shaking his head.

"I didn't turn up any evidence that GDU is distributing drugs." He paused. "But of course that doesn't necessarily mean it isn't."

"Then what does it do?" J. B. asked.

Clyde took in a deep breath and ran his fingers through his hair like he was stalling, like he really didn't want to tell us whatever it was he was about to tell us. J. B.'s body tensed up on one side of me, Mel's thick thighs pressed into mine on the other side. My legs started jumping up and down. Fortunately, Clyde continued without keeping us waiting too long.

"It seems that Adin Boyle," he said through gritted teeth, "is raking in tons of money from the distribution of child pornography."

A scream rushed up my throat. Its sharpness cut my lips as it burst through my mouth and pierced the musty air. Dealing drugs would have been bad enough, but this? There were no words for this.

"Here." Clyde stood up and handed J. B. two large manila envelopes that had *CONFIDENTIAL* written on them with a black Magic Marker. "I made copies of some of the evidence for you. There are two identical sets here. Now, you know, folks, that what I've done isn't exactly legal, so if any of this is going to be used as evidence, we'll have to figure out a way to make it stick." He let out one last long breath and sat back down. His job was done.

J. B. held one of the envelopes out to me. I stared at it, unable to lift my hand to take it from him, unable to move. He placed the envelope on my lap and I stared down at it. The dank smell of the basement stung my nostrils and brought tears to my eyes. I grabbed at the goose bumps springing up on my arms.

"Can someone turn the lights up?" I said.

Clyde reached for the switch on a gooseneck desk lamp and turned it on, but it didn't seem to make any difference. We sank into silence, each of us submerged in our own pits of horror, trying to grasp the sides and pull ourselves out.

"Paul Mellon?" J. B.'s voice cut through the silence. "Where's Mellon in all this?"

"His name didn't appear anywhere," Clyde said, "but that doesn't necessarily mean he's not involved."

"It doesn't mean he is, either," I said. "Drugs, maybe, but not something like this." I was sweating and shivering at the same time.

"But remember, Boyle protected Mellon by threatening Bradley Finch," J. B. said. "So we know the two of them are connected. If they're both involved with GDU, I'm guessing they wouldn't want to risk exposure due to any sort of negative attention or publicity, like the death of a baby. That could explain why Boyle didn't want that incident report to be completed."

"There are other explanations for that," I said. "Maybe Paul was afraid his wife was going to have a nervous breakdown and he asked Boyle for help protecting her. Boyle could have thought he owed Paul a favor for going to prison for him."

"Anything's possible," J. B. said with a shrug.

"I stopped being surprised a long time ago about what people are capable of," Clyde said.

"But there isn't any evidence that connects Paul Mellon to Boyle or to the shell company, right?" I said.

"Not at this point," Clyde said.

"Don't you see?" I gripped J. B.'s arm with both of my hands and squeezed it like a vise. "I can't bear to think that one of our foster homes could be involved in something this...this sordid..."

"Don't forget," J. B. said. "A seven-year-old boy and a new-born infant died in this foster home. Something happened to a little girl that terrorized her. Paul Mellon's wife is afraid of him."

"I know," I said. "But I refuse to believe that Mrs. Mellon would be so supportive of him if she knew he was involved in something like this. Never. *Never.*"

"Maybe she doesn't know," he said.

I released my grip on J. B.'s arm and threw my hands up in the air, accidentally grazing his cheek in the process. He flinched and I touched his face apologetically. "All I'm saying," I said, "is just because Paul Mellon and Adin Boyle were friends in the past doesn't mean they are now."

"That's what we have to find out," J. B. said.

"We have to tell the police about Boyle," I said. "He needs to be arrested."

"There's enough evidence here for the police to nail Boyle for distributing child pornography," Clyde said. "But only if it's admissible in court, of course."

"But it's not Boyle we're after," J. B. said.

My eye twitched. "Are you suggesting we let him get away with this?"

"What I'm suggesting," J. B. said, "is that we still haven't been able to link Paul Mellon to Boyle or to Global Distributions Unlimited."

"Maybe because there isn't any connection."

"But what if Mellon is involved? We don't want him to get away with it either, do we?"

"No, of course not." I crossed my arms over my chest.

"Okay. Okay." J. B. said. "So let's say we do it your way. We tell the police about Boyle and GDU but we tell them we don't have any evidence tying them to Paul Mellon. So what happens?

The police investigate Boyle and maybe see if Mellon might be involved, too. But they still have no reason to reopen the investigation into Anthony Little Eagle's death, and isn't that what we're after?"

I didn't have an answer for that. My brain was scrambled and nothing made sense anymore. I replayed the events of the past few days in my head. The talk I had with Mrs. Mellon. How she praised her husband for being so good with children. How I was still sure she was afraid of him. Then there was little Ellie, the look of terror in her eyes.

"I'll keep digging," Mel said. "See what I can find out about the current relationship, if any, between Mellon and Boyle."

"What we know so far is that they communicated around the time the baby died," J. B. said. "But that was five years ago. We don't know if they've been in contact since then."

"I'll see if I can find some deleted email messages between them," Clyde said. "I can also hack into more of Mellon's data, like bank accounts and such."

"What do you think, Sylvia?" J. B. said.

I didn't respond. I didn't know what I was thinking. I was incapable of thinking at all.

"Why don't you folks take some time to study those copies I gave you," Clyde said.

"Tomorrow," I said as I looked down at the envelope on my lap. "I'll look at them tomorrow. I can't bear any more right now."

TWENTY-SIX

The next morning I saw the manila envelope on the kitchen table where I'd left it after I got home last night, the word *CONFIDENTIAL* written on top in bold block letters. The residual chemical smell of Magic Marker attacked my sinuses and left me nauseous and light-headed, my nose stuffed up. I turned the envelope upside down and pushed it away. What if I recognized some of our foster children in the pictures?

I downed two cups of coffee and a toasted bagel. Then I unsealed the envelope. I had to drink another cup of coffee before I had the courage to pull the papers out. I reminded myself that Clyde Bloesdell had made it clear that Paul Mellon's name hadn't come up in any of his searching. There was no proof of any connection between Anthony Little Eagle's death and Adin Boyle's involvement in child pornography. Wasn't that what Clyde said?

I worked up my courage to stare at copy after copy of the website pages. Children of all races, both boys and girls, from as young as two or three years old up to twelve or thirteen, were posed in sexually provocative ways, some fully clothed, others scantily clad, a few nude. A sticky note on the top copy said, "This is just a sample. Others much worse. CB."

I pushed my chair back from the table and stood up. I went to the sink and drank some water only to have it fill my mouth with more bitterness. I went back to the table and sat down. I picked up the pictures again and studied each image, carefully focusing on every detail. It made my flesh crawl but I owed it to these children not to turn away.

Then I saw it. I might have missed it if I hadn't been paying such close attention. The bracelet on the wrist of one of the girls looked like the one Ellie Moon was wearing when I saw her. *It can't be.* I pulled my magnifying glass from the drawer and looked at the picture again. The girl, four or five years old, was posed in a red polka-dot bikini. She had a shy smile—or was it a grimace—on her lips but her hands covered her eyes and the rest of her face. Her brown skin was the same color as Ellie's. I steadied the magnifying glass with both hands. The bracelet had delicate round crystals interspersed with silver-plated roundels, the same heart lobster clasp, and two sterling silver blocks engraved with the letters EM. It was Ellie.

I dropped the magnifying glass on the table and ran into the living room. My cell phone was on the coffee table. I grabbed it, my fingers shaking as I pressed J. B.'s number.

"Harrell. Leave a message."

"Ellie," I cried out. "She's in one of the pictures."

I threw the phone onto the table and ran into my bedroom. I grabbed my purse and left my apartment, still wearing the raggedy T-shirt and frayed shorts that I'd slept in. I heard the door slam shut behind me. I don't know why I didn't take the elevator, why I took the stairway instead. I found myself plunging two and three steps at a time down to the lobby. Once outside, I started running. I ran and ran until I was out of breath and on the verge of collapsing. I stopped in front of a liquor store, *my* liquor store, until five years ago my daily stop on the way home from work. I stared in the window at row upon row of bottles that promised relief, salvation, revenge, escape, oblivion, and more. I went in.

Back home I found myself slouched on the couch. A bottle of white zinfandel wine glared at me from the coffee table. *You were so sure, weren't you,* the bottle said. *Only goes to show how much you don't know. What the hell made you think you could make any difference when you can't see what's right in front of your face? You can't manage to do even a tiny drop of anything right in an ocean of wrong. Just like before. You can't make things right. You can't make things better. You're incapable of saving yourself, much less anyone else.*

I picked up the bottle and ran my fingers around the top. When I was in treatment, they made me get rid of my corkscrew, but there were other ways to open a bottle. I could push a screw into the cork and pull it out with pliers. I could twist the cork out with a knife. Once, on a camping trip, I used a corncob holder, but it wasn't easy and it took a long time. I went over to my desk and rummaged through the drawer, grabbed a Magic Marker. I could use it to push the cork into the bottle. I turned to go back to the couch to do it and saw that my computer was on and reached to turn it off but sat down instead.

I got online and opened the screen to the NAICS chat room. I typed in my screen name and then the name of my recovery partner.

"Hehewuti?"

"How you doing, Numees?"

"I bought a bottle of wine," I typed.

I waited but no reply came back.

"Are you there?" I typed.

"I'm here."

"There's a bottle of white zinfandel sitting on the coffee table."

"Your favorite."

"Well?"

"Well, what?"

"Aren't you going to tell me what to do?"

"You know what to do, Numees."

"I can't face what's happening anymore, Hehewuti."

"So things are bad and now you've got yourself some wine to make them worse."

"I'm white."

"What?"

"I'm not an Ojibwe from Canada. I'm a white woman from the United States. I live in Monrow City."

"I see."

My cheeks burned. I bit my bottom lip, started to cry. "I lied. I thought it was okay as long as I was honest with you about everything else but I was wrong. I'm sorry."

"Well, Numees..."

"Sylvia," I typed. "Not Numees."

"Well, Sylvia, I can't blame you for wanting to be Ojibwe, but I know you were created beautiful just the way you are."

I sucked in my breath. That was it? Hehewuti was accepting my amends and forgiving me, just like that? I rocked back and forth in my chair as a tsunami of grace flooded over me, washing me clean and making me whole.

"Numees? I mean, Sylvia? Are you still there?"

"I love you," I typed. My chin quivered as I uttered the words out loud.

"I love you, too," Hehewuti wrote. "Now get rid of that damn bottle of wine, okay?"

"Okay."

"And go to a meeting. Go to ninety meetings in ninety days. Without fail."

"Okay."

"And Sylvia? Remember that your sobriety requires rigorous honesty."

I swallowed the lump in my throat. I had been telling so many lies that it was like my life was becoming one big lie, and I was pretty sure I hadn't seen the last of them.

"Sylvia? Are you still there?"

"Yes."

"Check in with me every night and be honest with me. We'll start with that. I don't know what you're up to but I suspect there are some amends you're going to need to make to others besides me."

"Okay."

After logging out of the chat room I grabbed the bottle by its neck and carried it into the kitchen. It was quicker to hit it against the side of the sink than to try to figure out how to open it. It shattered to pieces and I watched the wine disappear down the drain.

I had started to pick up the shards of glass when I heard a knock. I wiped my hands on my T-shirt, walked down the hall, and opened the door. J. B. stepped inside and started talking without saying hello first.

"Okay, now we know what Paul Mellon has been doing in his upstairs office." He followed me down the hall. "All that's left for us to do is get Boyle to admit not only that he knows Mellon but that he's been in contact with him. Once we've connected those dots, we'll have all the evidence we need to go to the police."

We stopped at the kitchen doorway and stared down at the pornographic images on the table. J. B. took in a deep breath, turned up his nose, and sniffed the air. He scanned the room, his eyes growing wide when he spotted the broken bottle in the sink. He looked at me curiously.

I pointed to the wet wine on my T-shirt, unable to speak. J. B. glanced down at the floor, then back up at me. He shuffled his feet ever so slightly. He looked like he was going to say something but then thought better of it and instead opened his arms to me.

"It's okay," I said. "I poured it all down the drain. I'm ready to go get those bastards. Just give me a minute to get dressed and call the office to tell them I won't be coming in today."

TWENTY-SEVEN

We stood side by side outside the iron gate fronting the historic Tudor mansion that served as Adin Boyle's real estate headquarters. The brick exterior of the first floor was topped by a second floor of stucco and timber that rose to opulent gables. I could admire the beauty of the stone and brick mansions on Swan Boulevard as long as I ignored their history: they were built by the wealthy in the latter half of the nineteenth century so they could escape the industrial stink and clamor of downtown and live in the elegance to which they considered themselves entitled.

"Ready?" J. B. had a glimmer in his eyes, the look of an investigative reporter on a quest. He was his debonair and smartly dressed self while I was completely out of character in my classic but decades-old suit that I assumed, perhaps erroneously, made me look like a journalist.

"Let's hope this works," I said. I smoothed down the knee-length linen skirt and tugged at the hem of the jacket.

The gate opened with a squeak and I pulled my shoulders back. I checked the tape recorder inside my purse one more time. It was set up, ready to record. All I had to do was remember to turn it on.

The central hall inside the front door was a two-storied gallery paneled with hardwood. I was looking at the fireplace and winding staircase when a balding man with the unlined face of a forty-year-old suddenly materialized and I about jumped out of my skin.

"How can I help you folks?" The man's smile was friendly and he looked professional in a navy blue suit, white shirt, and peach-colored tie. But I wasn't fooled. The way his polished black shoes dug into the oriental carpet and his arms tightened over his chest told another story.

"Good afternoon, sir," J. B. said. "We're with the *Monrow City Tribune.* We'd like to see Mr. Boyle."

The man uncrossed his arms and reached out with his right hand, palm up. J. B. took out his press card and showed it to him. Then the man looked at me questioningly. I hadn't expected to be asked for my identification. I hoped there wasn't anything else I hadn't thought of. I fumbled around in my purse.

"I'm sorry," I said. "I always carry my card, but I must have left it at the office today." I loosened the scarf around my neck.

"Please, wait over there." The man pointed to two over-stuffed chairs in front of the fireplace. Then he disappeared into a room off the side of the hall and closed the door.

"Look," I whispered. I pointed to two stone grotesques snarling at us from each side of the fireplace, vicious-looking dog gargoyles with wings.

"Just a little creepy," J. B. said under his breath.

A sucking sound echoed through the open space when I sat down on the chair. The hall felt cold. I picked up a real estate magazine from the table and leafed through the pages, trying not to speculate about where the man had gone or what he was doing, why he couldn't have just called up to Adin Boyle's office or, better yet, directed us there.

"Come with me." I jumped again. What was it with this man, creeping up behind us like that? Was he trying to intimidate us?

We followed him up the winding staircase, past posts adorned with mother-of-pearl. Halfway up, a stained glass window with mauve crystals cast a rainbow effect onto the landing. When we reached the second floor, a young receptionist with short blond hair greeted us.

"Welcome to Boyle Real Estate Headquarters," she said in a singsong voice. "How can I help you?"

"What a pretty scarf," I said.

"We're here to see Adin Boyle," J. B. said.

"I'm afraid Mr. Boyle isn't in right now. Would you like to talk to Mr. Priester?"

Just then a man with glasses perched on his forehead walked over to the receptionist's desk. His crisp white shirt was unbuttoned at the top and its sleeves were rolled up. "Priester," he said with his hand outstretched, "Guy Priester. How can I help you?"

"We'd like to get Mr. Boyle's take on a story we're doing about the current housing market," J. B. said.

Guy Priester tipped his head like he didn't believe us. "We're investigating the financial sector's involvement in the real estate market," I said. "It's mostly exploratory right now, but we're looking for insights from large real estate companies like yours about foreclosure rates, who's buying and selling houses, things like that."

"And of what interest could any of this possibly be," Mr. Priester said, "to a foster care supervisor from the human services department?"

I froze. There was moisture under my arms. "I'm interested in..."

J. B. jumped in with an obsequious smile on his face. "I'm sure it seems a bit unusual," he said. "Ms. Jensen and I are working different angles of the issue. Might Mr. Boyle be in later this afternoon?"

"I'm afraid not. He's at the University Club for the rest of the day," the receptionist said.

The man from downstairs glared at the receptionist. He gave me a stern look, placed his hand on my arm, turned me to face the stairs.

"Thanks for your help," I said over my shoulder to the receptionist.

The man kept a grip on my elbow while ushering us down the stairs. At the front door J. B. shook hands with him and said good-bye in a pleasant voice, thanked him for his time.

"How did he know who I was?" I asked as we hurried away from the mansion.

"They had cameras on us," J. B. said. "They must have run it through a facial recognition program or something."

"I shouldn't have blabbered on like that," I said. "But at least now we know where we can find Boyle.

"It's not far from here," he said. "We can walk."

TWENTY-EIGHT

The University Club sat on a high bluff on Swan Boulevard over-looking downtown and the river. Adin Boyle's Tudor building, impressive as it was, was dwarfed next to this one. We stopped outside the grand entrance next to the perfectly arranged flowers and plants in the middle of the circular drive while J. B. checked the day's scheduled events on the club's website.

"There's a fundraiser in the Terrace." He put his smartphone back in his pocket.

"What if it's an invitation-only event?"

J. B. raised one finger in the air and reached for his smart-phone again. I sat down on a bench. I'd only been to the University Club once before, as a wedding guest in one of the private rooms. My palms started sweating, like they always did when I found myself in places reserved for the elite. I smarted from not belonging and at the same time had no desire to belong. I tugged at the skirt of my beige linen suit. The color was wrong, out of style. I was going to stand out like a country bumpkin inside the clubhouse.

"All set." J. B. was smiling like he'd won the lottery. "My editor's a member of the club. We can use his name to get in if we have to."

I stood up and followed him inside. With every step we took across the marbled floor, and with each column and each valuable antique furnishing we passed, I expected someone to stop us and ask for proof of our right to be here. The muscles in my neck were a coiled spring waiting to be released. In the Franklin Room, as I looked up at the ornate plaster ceiling, I nearly tripped, but no one was there to notice. We sauntered, as if we belonged, into the adjacent Terrace, where scores of the überwealthy were gathered in chattering clusters. The only person who noticed our arrival was a waiter, who offered us hors d'oeuvres from a tray filled with nothing I could identify and all of which I graciously declined.

J. B. reached for a cocktail napkin and placed an array of appetizers on it. "Blue cheese and pear tartlets," he said, licking his lips. "My favorite."

A second waiter stopped with a tray filled with glasses of wine. J. B. took one and requested a glass of Perrier for me.

I stood on my tiptoes and scanned the crowd of elegantly dressed men and women, searching for someone who looked like the photographs I had seen of Adin Boyle. I spotted him standing by the window looking out at the pool. He was a vision of respectability and success with his hands in the pockets of his shiny blue silk suit, not a strand of hair out of place on his head. I wanted to strangle him, wipe the self-satisfied half smile from his face, announce to everyone in the room who he really was. *Be smart and stay cool,* I warned myself. *The sleazebag will get what he deserves in due time. All in due time.*

We made our way quickly yet politely through the crowd. As

we approached the window where Boyle stood, J. B. called out to him.

"Adin Boyle. How are you?"

An automatic smile crossed Boyle's face, the Cheshire cat smile of a man who was used to pretending he knew people he'd never met.

"J. B. Harrell from the *Tribune.* I don't expect you to remember me. How'd you like that picture we ran of you with the governor a while back?"

Boyle's eyes widened and he nodded as if he'd just put two and two together. "Good to see you again," he said with a vigorous shake of J. B.'s hand. "Glad you're covering this worthy event."

"I'd like you to meet a friend of mine," J. B. said. "Sylvia Jensen, this is the infamous Adin Boyle."

"Nice to meet you." Boyle eyes roved from my face all the way down to my feet. I slipped my hand into my purse and pushed the on button on the tape recorder.

"And you," I said, forcing a smile. "I think I know a good friend of yours."

"Oh? Who's that?"

"Paul Mellon."

"Oh yes. We grew up together." Boyle paused. He rubbed his chin and looked down at the floor. "It's been years since I've seen Paul," he said. "How's he doing?"

"I haven't seen him in a long time either," I said. "You've probably kept up with him better than I have."

"I doubt that," Boyle said.

I kept smiling and nodding at him, but inside I was cursing. The man was too shrewd for words. J. B. put his hand on my shoulder. He had a "let's get out of here" look on his face.

"Good to see you again, Adin," he said. "I'm afraid we were on our way out. It was good to run into you."

"Nice to meet you," I said with a slight wave. "If I see Paul, I'll be sure to tell him I ran into you."

"Do that," Boyle said.

I had to run to keep up with J. B.'s long strides as he led the way through the crowd and out the door.

"Hold on. Geez, let me catch my breath," I said, once we were outside the building.

"He's suspicious," J. B. said. "He's probably on the phone with his headquarters right now asking them to investigate us. If Boyle doesn't already know what we're up to, he soon will. Who knows what he'll do then."

TWENTY-NINE

May 14, 1973

After Mary declared to everyone at the meeting that she was Jamie's mother, she refused to say anything else. The others probably assumed she fell silent in shock or despair. But they were wrong. While they were all discussing how to prepare Jamie for his return to his birth parents, she was doing her own planning. The meeting ended, and she remained silent, leaving Wayne to shake hands and say good-bye to everyone. She didn't speak when they were in the car on their way home, just sat in the passenger seat with her arms folded across her chest.

"What's happened to you?" Wayne asked. "Did you give up? Why won't you say anything? Talk to me. Please."

She waved her hand in the air and looked out the window.

"I tried, but they wouldn't listen," he said. "I really tried, Mary."

She shrugged away the tears in his eyes and watched the birch trees go by on the side of the road.

"It was a conspiracy," he said. "They'd all decided what they were going to do before they came into the room. Mr. and Mrs.

Buckley are coming to see Jamie tomorrow and we're supposed to tell him tonight. How are we going to do that? Tell me, Mary. What are we going to say to him? How are we going to do this?"

She looked directly at him for the first time since they'd left the courthouse. "How much money do we have?" she asked.

"What?"

"I've got it all worked out," she said, tapping the side of her head with her finger.

He stared at her.

"Don't tell me you haven't considered it yourself," she said.

"It's the kind of thing desperate people may think about doing," he said, "but they don't actually do it."

"Giving up our son is *not* an option, Wayne."

He shifted his eyes from side to side as if he were afraid someone might hear them.

"Is it, Wayne?"

"No," he said, in a whisper. "Losing Jamie is not an option."

"I won't break his heart," she said.

They rode in silence for a few miles. Mary looked in her purse for some paper and a pencil, started to write down her plans.

"Where?" Wayne asked.

"We'll head south," she said, "until we get to Mexico. I'll pack as soon as we get home while you go to the bank. With what we've saved from your paychecks plus all the monthly foster care checks from the county that we put into Jamie's college account, we should have enough money to live on until we can get settled somewhere. I'll empty the food from the refrigerator into the big cooler. That'll be enough for the first couple of days, so we'll only have to stop for gas and to go to the bathroom. We'll leave after dark tonight and take the truck. You need to make sure the tank is full and check the oil. We'll leave the car in the driveway so it looks like we're home."

"What do we tell Jamie?"

"When he gets home from school, we'll tell him we're going on a camping trip. You know how he loves to fish."

"He'll want to know where."

"We'll tell him it's a surprise. It'll be an adventure for him."

"What happens when he realizes we're not coming back?"

"We'll cross that bridge when we come to it," she said.

Mary started making a list of all the things they had to pack. Wayne kept blowing out his breath like he was hyperventilating. When they got home, he pulled into the driveway and sat in the car looking straight ahead, thinking. All of a sudden his hand flew up to his mouth.

"My folks," he said. "What about my folks? They've been expecting me to call after the hearing. What do I tell them?"

"Tell them everything went well in court," she said. "Say you can't talk right now, that we're going on an overnight fishing trip to celebrate and we're in a hurry to get going before dark. Say we'll call them in a couple of days and tell them all about it then."

"And after that?" he said. "Do we wait until we get to Mexico before calling them again? They'll be worried sick by then."

"We'll have to figure that out later," she said. "Go. Call them now and then go to the bank."

Mary watched Wayne go into the house to lie to his folks and saw in his demeanor a glimpse of their future. From now on, it would be one lie after another, a life of dishonesty that she hoped God would not make them regret. There was no other way to save Jamie. Turning their own son over to strangers was not an option. And when there were no other alternatives, it was best not to think about things too much. She went into the garage to get the suitcases.

THIRTY

J. B. and I sat on the bench facing the University Club, both of us on the alert so we wouldn't miss Adin Boyle when he came out. My mind was a spider spinning a trap, my eyes on the front entrance watching for the prey.

"He knows who we are," J. B. said.

"That's why we need to be honest with him about everything," I said. "He won't trust us otherwise."

"What are you suggesting? That we tell him we know he's involved in the distribution of child pornography?"

"Not exactly. I'm suggesting we tell him we know a firm that he's invested in is involved in pornography. I don't want to get us killed, you know."

J. B. studied me with his brows knit and his eyes narrowed, as if he were trying to read whatever brilliant ideas might be percolating inside my brain. All of a sudden he lifted his head and straightened his back, leaned in closer to me.

"So if we made him think the police *were* on to him," he said, "what do you think he would do?"

"Book a flight and get out of the country fast," I said.

J. B. looked skeptical. "Not sure he'd walk away from everything he's got going for him," he said. "It'd be more like him to try to beat the rap. He'd mobilize that cadre of high-powered attorneys and influential people around him, and probably succeed."

"Unless...unless we gave him another way out."

He practically jumped off the bench. "That's it," he said. "We offer a trade. He's a wheeler-dealer. That's just his style."

But before we had time to do any more planning, Adin Boyle walked out the door of the University Club looking down at his smartphone.

"Wait here." J. B. said.

He strode over to the entrance. A startled look on Boyle's face quickly turned into a frown. I couldn't hear what they were saying, but when J. B. leaned closer, like he was whispering in Boyle's ear, Boyle flinched and stepped back. I untied the scarf from around my neck and used it to wipe the sweat from my brow. J. B. pointed toward me and Boyle lifted his head up once, then down. My blouse was wet under my arms. I unbuttoned my suit jacket. When the two of them walked over to me, the hot sun was nothing compared to Adin Boyle's eyes drilling through me.

"Well, what is it?" he said.

I swallowed hard and placed my hands on my lap, tipped my chin up. *Time to be smart, Sylvia. Be shrewd. Trap the bastard. Whatever it takes.* Damn it, I wished I knew what J. B. had already said to him.

"I apologize, Mr. Boyle," I said with a stammer. "We weren't straight with you in there. I should have told you. I'm a foster home supervisor, and J. B. and I are investigating the death of a boy under my agency's care."

"And what does any of that have to do with me?" he scoffed.

I hesitated. If only J. B. and I had had time to talk about how to pull this off. I decided to go with the truth. "The boy was placed in the Mellon foster home," I said. "That's where he died. That's why we wanted to talk to you. I'm sorry I misled you. I'm not a personal friend of Paul's." I glanced at J. B. and he nodded. "But you *are* a friend of his."

"I don't know what you're talking about." Boyle sounded annoyed. "Like I told you, Paul and I grew up together, that's all. I haven't seen him in ages. Why did you want to talk to me about this?"

"Well..." I paused, tried to think of what to say next. *Don't panic. Don't show him you're nervous.*

"Actually," J. B. said. "When Sylvia and I were investigating what happened to the boy, we happened onto some evidence that concerns you. We thought you should know about it before we turn it over to the police."

"That's right," I jumped in. "It's about your investment in a company that's in the child pornography business."

"What?" Boyle's eyes doubled in size, his mouth fell open.

"Global Distributions Unlimited," I said.

"We know that you have financial holdings in GDU," J. B. said.

"Of course I do." Boyle's voice was indignant. "GDU is a trading company that specializes in tourism and has some import/export holdings."

This guy's good, I said to myself. Really good.

J. B.'s mouth opened as if he'd been taken totally by surprise. "So you're telling us," he said, "that you actually don't know GDU is a shell company for a pornography ring?"

"Are you deaf?" Boyle shouted. "That is exactly what I am telling you. This is shocking! It's outrageous!"

J. B. and I glanced at each other and shrugged. I placed my hands under my thighs, decided to follow my instincts. What else did I have to go on?

"We have evidence," I said. "Website pictures of children, financial records of your investment in GDU. The whole business."

Boyle's face reddened. "This is absurd," he sputtered. "I know nothing about any of this."

"Frankly," J. B. said. "We'd be surprised if a successful and highly respected businessman like you would knowingly invest in something like this."

"Well," Boyle said with a snort. "I'm certainly glad to hear that."

"The problem is this," J. B. said. "I've been in the newspaper business long enough to know that once we turn the evidence over to the police, it really won't make any difference what you know or don't know. I've seen other men's reputations destroyed by a whole lot less. It didn't matter if they were innocent, in the end they lost everything. All it'll take is a newspaper headline linking you to pornography, and it'll be all over for you. But look, Mr. Boyle, we didn't go looking for this information. The trouble is, now that we've got it, we're obligated to turn it over to the police."

J. B. glanced at me, his eyes telling me it was my turn. "We don't have any choice," I added, not quite sure what to say next. "We can't withhold evidence."

"How many times do I have to tell you?" Boyle said. "I would never, ever be involved with anything so sordid, so horrible. How could anyone think that?"

"I understand." J. B. raised his palms. "It seems, Mr. Boyle, that you were duped as an investor, clear and simple."

"We were all duped," I said. "We were duped by Paul Mellon. We have evidence that he's been harming children in his house. We know he's involved in child pornography. We know he killed Anthony Little Eagle."

Boyle didn't say anything but I could tell he was listening.

"It's Paul Mellon we want," J. B. said. "We're not out to get you."

"So maybe we can help each other," I said.

J. B. raised his finger in the air as if he'd suddenly thought of something. "Here's a possibility. Instead of us giving the evidence to the police, and having your reputation destroyed because of your investments with GDU, we could give the evidence to you and *you* could hand it over to the police. That way you can tell them you were set up and knew nothing about it. Since you'd be turning the evidence over to them, they'd have to believe you. You could come out of this a hero."

Adin Boyle's eyebrows went up. "Why would you do that?" he asked.

I jumped in. "Like we said, we know that Paul Mellon murdered a child, but we need someone to testify against him."

"Where's the GDU evidence now?" Boyle asked after a few seconds of consideration.

"In a safe place," J. B. said.

"And you'd actually give it to me," he said with disdain.

"Paul Mellon's a murderer," I said. "We want him. We have no beef with you."

Another moment of silence passed.

"It's up to you, Mr. Boyle," J. B. said. "Meet us at MCPD headquarters at four o'clock this afternoon. We'll give you the evidence then, and you can turn it over to the police. If you're not there by four we'll turn it over to them ourselves. Fair enough?"

Adin Boyle turned and walked away. People were starting to leave the fundraiser, hopping into their fancy cars in the circular drive in front of the University Club. I thought they looked a lot more comfortable than Boyle did as he walked down Swan Boulevard in the direction of his real estate headquarters.

"What do you think he'll do?" I asked once he was out of earshot.

"Who knows? He's a shrewd one."

THIRTY-ONE

J. B. thought we should brief the MCPD in advance, so we provided copies of the evidence to the deputy chief right after we left the University Club. We went back to the city courthouse a few hours later and, after passing through security, stood off to the side to wait for Adin Boyle. The late-afternoon sun was pouring through the oval window at the top of the wide marble stairs. It was a few minutes after four o'clock.

"I thought he'd be here," I said. I glanced around.

"Let's wait five more minutes," J. B. said.

My pulse beat in time with the ticking of the big clock on the wall. Every time someone entered the courthouse and it wasn't Boyle, my anxiety level shot up another notch. At ten minutes after four, I began to think that Boyle was on to us. He wasn't coming. I had agreed with J. B. that we should give the police a heads up before Boyle came in...*if* he came in...but now I worried that somehow Boyle had found out. Maybe he had an informant in the department.

The front door opened and outside I caught a glimpse of the

entrance to the Human Services and Public Health Department building. I imagined Betsy Chambers sitting in her office right across the street and thought about what she would say or do if she saw me here with J. B. Harrell. Eventually, of course, she would have to be told everything we'd been up to. And then I would be fired. It was just a matter of time.

"I guess he's not coming," J. B. said. "We might as well go back to the deputy chief's office and tell her."

But just then Boyle, still in the blue silk suit he'd worn to the fundraiser, walked through the front door. He was deep in conversation with a man dressed in a gray suit, maroon shirt, and maroon and gold striped tie, obviously one of his many high-powered attorneys. We walked over to them and stopped. J. B. reached into his briefcase and pulled out the large manila envelope containing the evidence.

"Deputy Chief Anderson is expecting you." He handed the envelope over to Boyle. "The Violent Crimes Investigations Unit is down that hall behind you."

Boyle and his attorney turned and left without having said a word.

———

J. B. and I waited behind the staircase. From where we stood we would be able to see Boyle leave the building, without him seeing us. We speculated about how long he would meet with the deputy chief and made a bet with each other about what time he would leave the building. But we kept our own counsel on any fears and speculations about what might be happening right now and what might happen next. A half hour went by. Thirty-five minutes. Then forty minutes.

"What if they didn't go in there?" I said. "What if they just took the evidence and ducked out through another door?"

Just then we saw Boyle and his attorney walking across the marble floor, with their heads huddled together.

"Is he smirking?" I said. "That bastard looks like he actually thinks he pulled it off. Look at that. He's strutting like he's some kind of big hero."

"That's what we want him to think," J. B. said. "He's sure going to be surprised when he learns we know he had a cop threatened to cover up a baby's death in the Mellon home."

"Didn't you promise Bradley Finch that you'd destroy all that evidence?"

"That was the deal I offered Finch if he gave Boyle up," he said with a shrug. "What can I say? Everything's locked up in my office, tape recording and all."

I laughed, and as if by silent agreement, we started walking down the hall toward the MCPD administrative offices. We stopped at the plaque on the door that said Violent Crimes Investigations Unit, and went inside.

"And now we're about to find out if Deputy Chief Anderson believed Boyle's story or not," J. B. said.

The receptionist saw us and waved us into her boss's office. I caught myself nervously clenching and unclenching my fists and stuffed them into the pockets of my suit jacket. Deputy Chief Anderson looked up over her reading glasses and stood up behind her desk to greet us. Once again I was struck by her exceptional height. She didn't have any makeup or jewelry on and her light blue shirt and navy slacks were as nondescript as her oversized, no-frills office. She motioned for us to sit down on the two chairs in front of her desk and sat down herself. Then she pulled out the stack of children's pictures from the evidence envelope and started shuffling through them.

"Mr. Boyle denies ever seeing any of these pictures before," she said. "He was very persuasive."

"Really?" This did not sound promising.

"We had a good interview." Her lips formed a little smirk. "Boyle was kind enough to provide us with a complete set of descriptive documents about GDU, including all his financial statements. I was impressed with how cooperative he was, and surprised that his attorneys didn't stop him from giving us everything he had."

J. B. and I remained silent. I bit my bottom lip.

"Boyle insisted that he was being set up by his old friend Paul Mellon," she went on. "He was quick to let us know that he believes Mellon to be untrustworthy. He said it was Mellon who got him to invest in GDU, but that Paul had never invested in it himself. He said he always thought that was because Paul didn't have the money, but now he thinks that Mellon got him to invest in order to get revenge. Apparently Mellon went to jail when they were young for something he thought Boyle did, and his life was ruined as a result."

"And?" I asked.

"Let's just say I've met more convincing witnesses. He thinks he was convincing, and I'm sure he expects that to be the end of it, but I can assure you it's not."

I released an audible sigh of relief.

"What happens now?" J. B. asked.

"We'll call in the FBI, for one thing. I'll send a couple of detectives over to Paul Mellon's house with a search warrant. If we find anything, we'll bring him in for questioning. But right now I'm afraid we have nothing concrete to connect him to GDU or the porn ring."

"There *is* some evidence," I said. "May I see those pictures a minute?" The deputy chief slid the stack over to me. I pulled out the picture of Ellie Moon and held it up to her. "This girl was a foster child in the Mellon home when this picture was taken."

Deputy Chief Anderson looked surprised. "How do you know that?"

"I've seen the file. Her picture is in it."

"So now it seems we may have evidence against both Mr. Boyle *and* Mr. Mellon."

The deputy chief paused, looked thoughtful. "Boyle seems to believe that Mr. Mellon is about to be arrested for murder," she added.

J. B. and I glanced at each other.

"We've been investigating the death of Anthony Little Eagle in the Mellon home," J. B. said.

"The police ruled it an accident, but we think Paul Mellon killed him," I added. "We've been gathering evidence."

The deputy chief raised her eyebrows. "I see," she said. "Then it seems we'll want to be talking to you some more." She suddenly stood up, with her hand outstretched. "But right now, you folks need to let my detectives do their jobs. And, Mr. Harrell, if you please, no press coverage about any of this without clearing it with me first."

J. B. and I both nodded.

We'll do whatever we have to do, I said to myself as we left her office. It was as simple as that. When you know what to do, you have to do it.

THIRTY-TWO

May 14, 1973

Wayne was standing with the telephone receiver in his hand, staring out the kitchen window at the clouds gathering in the sky, when Mary came in from the garage with the suitcases.

"The lawn needs mowing," he said.

She set the suitcases down on the floor.

"I'll get to it tomorrow," he said.

"Wayne? What did your folks say? Did you call them already?"

He looked like he was about to cry. "I can't lie to them."

"Do you want me to call them?"

"We may never see or talk to them again."

"We can't think about that now," she said.

"We'll be on the run for the rest of our lives. What kind of life will that be for Jamie?"

"What kind of life will it be for him if we don't go?"

"We don't speak Spanish. How will we get along in Mexico?"

Mary pressed her back against the counter. "We'll work it out," she said. "Maybe we'll find some small town in Texas where we can live instead of Mexico. Someplace nobody knows or cares about."

"Sooner or later we'll get caught."

"We have no other choice, Wayne."

"What about our house? Our car? If we leave we lose everything. My folks, our friends, our town."

"If we stay, we lose Jamie, and he loses everything, *including* us."

"There has to be something else we can do."

"That's just it, Wayne. There isn't."

Her eyes glazed over. She put her hands over her ears, but he took them from her and placed them on his chest instead. Her fingers moved up and down from the pounding of his heart.

"We could go to jail for kidnapping," he said.

"You can't kidnap your own child."

He put his hands on her waist and led her over to the kitchen table. "Please, Mary. Sit down. We have to talk about this."

She pushed his hands away. "Talking is the last thing we should be doing right now. You have to go to the bank. I have to pack."

"What happens when we run out of money? Or, God forbid, someone steals it? What happens if we're in an accident and the police trace us through our drivers' licenses and insurance cards?"

"Stop, Wayne!"

"Okay, let's say we make it to Mexico," he said. "Do you have any idea how to go about changing our names and getting new forms of identification there?"

Mary's legs grew weak. She sat down at the kitchen table. She hadn't considered that they might have to change their names. "We'll figure it out." She held her head in her hands.

"And how will we explain any of that to Jamie? How do we tell him why he has to have a new identity?"

Mary closed her eyes. "There's no other way."

Wayne rubbed his chin between his thumb and fingers. "We could drive out to the reservation right now and talk to Mr. and Mrs. Buckley again, this time without their attorney or that friend of theirs around to muddy things up. Maybe we can convince them to leave Jamie here at least for another week or a month, maybe longer, until we can sort things out. Didn't you see how uncomfortable they were about how fast things were moving?"

"Sure, we could talk to them. And as soon as we left," Mary said, "May Goodheart would talk them out of anything they agreed to with us. Even if that didn't happen and they agreed to leave Jamie here with us, they'd have the right to swoop in and take him anytime they wanted."

"What about our rights," Wayne said.

"Foster parents don't have any rights," she said. "Apparently Jamie doesn't have any rights either."

"Wait a minute," he said. "Maybe that's it. The judge was careful to protect Mr. and Mrs. Buckley's rights by getting them an attorney, but who was protecting Jamie's rights?"

"It was the judge's job to protect Jamie," Mary said with a shake of her head.

"Right. But Jamie's rights and the Buckleys' rights are in conflict," he said, "and the judge placed their rights over his."

"We don't have time to hash this over now, Wayne."

"Just let me think. Maybe there's something else we can do. The judge protected the Buckleys' rights by appointing an attorney for them, right? But what did he do to protect Jamie's rights?

Where was Jamie's attorney? The judge should have appointed one for him, too. That's the point. This is how we can fight this. Jamie should have had a lawyer. We'll appeal the judge's decision, take it back to court. We can do this, Mary. We'll win the appeal. I know we will."

Mary had never seen Wayne this certain of anything before. It made her want to believe. All that talk today about parents' rights and the community's rights and what was best for Jamie, but she couldn't recall anyone saying a word, not a single word, about Jamie's rights. What kind of parent would she be if she let others determine her son's future without making sure that he was represented by an attorney? It was her responsibility to protect him.

"But an appeal would take time," she said doubtfully. "The Buckleys are planning to come tomorrow to see Jamie."

Wayne reached for Mary's hands and took a deep breath, looked into her eyes. He hesitated before speaking, and then in a soft and gentle voice, he said, "Maybe we'll have to let Jamie go with them for while."

"No, no, no!"

"Only for as long as it takes to fight in court to get him back," he said.

"I couldn't bear it. Jamie couldn't bear it."

Wayne gripped her hands tighter. "Yes, you could. And so could Jamie. Especially if we told him that his parents want him to stay with them, just for a while. Especially if we tell him that we'll come to get him as soon as things are worked out. We need to tell him the truth. I'm not saying it'll be easy. We can win this, Mary. I know we will. We don't have to take Jamie and run away."

Mary covered her face with her hands. There was a panic

rising in her throat, confusion swirling through her brain. *Think, think, think.* If they ran away with Jamie, they'd be in hiding for the rest of their lives, or they could get caught and end up in jail. But if they didn't leave, the Buckleys would be here tomorrow and the plan would have to go forward. Jamie would have to leave for a while. Could she stand that? And what if their legal efforts failed? Then what? *Think, think.*

If they lost the appeal, couldn't they still find a way to run away with Jamie? No matter what happened in court, it wouldn't be over until Jamie was back where he belonged, with them. They had two chances. Two ways to get him back. If they won in court, they'd get him back legally. If they didn't win in court, they'd find a way to run away with him and get him back that way. Two options. Either way, they would be together again. Jamie would always be their son, no matter what.

She looked at Wayne with a combination of tears and fear in her eyes.

He nodded. "I'll put the suitcases back in the garage," he said.

THIRTY-THREE

There was no need for J. B. and me to talk about it. We both knew what we had to do next. As soon as we left the MCPD we headed straight for the Mellons' house. We pulled up to the curb in front and saw a police van in their driveway instead of their car. Stepping over the tufts of weeds poking through the cracks in the sidewalk, we made our way to the sagging front porch and rang the doorbell. Several minutes passed. J. B. pushed the button again. He had to ring the bell once more before the door opened, and then only a crack. Mrs. Mellon peeked out, and when she saw me, she opened the door a bit more. Her shoulders were crunched into a cringe like someone afraid she was going to be hit.

"Why are *you* here?" Rivulets of tears flowed down the lines in her cheeks and pooled in the crook of her neck.

"I thought we might be able to help," I said.

"My husband's not here."

"May we come in?" I asked.

"The police already looked."

"This is J. B., a friend of mine. We're here because we knew the police were coming."

"I don't know where Paul is." Mrs. Mellon hesitated. Her eyes flitted from side to side. "They're searching the house. They have a warrant. I don't know what to do."

"I know this is hard," I said. "Why don't we go in and sit down."

She didn't say anything, so J. B. and I stepped inside. Entering the living room was like walking into a catalogue filled with all the signs of questionable motivations I'd learned to look for over the years. Signs that a family might want foster kids in order to make ends meet, to look good for their neighbors or their church, to fill a hole or give meaning to their otherwise-empty lives.

It was obvious on first glance that a lot wasn't right about the Mellon home—cheap furniture protected like a shrine, a gold and red brocade sofa and boudoir chair enveloped in plastic protective covers, the relative shabbiness of their house compared with others in the upscale neighborhood.

We followed Mrs. Mellon in silence, she several feet ahead. In the kitchen we saw a teenage girl bent over a peanut butter and jelly sandwich on the table. When we walked in she jumped up from her chair. "I was just getting a snack, Mom," she said.

"My daughter, Cindy." Mrs. Mellon's chest caved in and she looked down at the floor.

The girl rolled her eyes and snatched up her sandwich. "The cops are upstairs," she said. She walked out of the kitchen with a look on her face that made my stomach twist into a knot.

Mrs. Mellon picked up her daughter's plate and it flew into the air. It fell to the floor where it shattered into pieces. She cried out and covered her mouth. I took her arm, guided her to a chair at the table and sat down next to her. J. B. grabbed a broom that was leaning against the back door and swept the shards of glass into a pile.

"What am I going to do," Mrs. Mellon sobbed.

"Just tell the truth." My voice was soft and gentle, yet firm.

She wiped her eyes and blew her nose. I pulled my chair closer to hers.

"I did," she said. "I don't know where Paul went. He just left, that's all."

Just then a detective in a dark suit appeared in the doorway. His light blue shirt was open at the neck and he had a computer in his arms. "So your husband is gone, and so is everything on his computer," he said. "Looks like he wiped this thing clean before he left."

A shadow of panic flew across Mrs. Mellon's eyes.

"We'll be taking this, ma'am. It's only a matter of time before we retrieve everything that was on it. It will go best for you if tell us what you know before we find out for ourselves."

"Paul didn't do anything."

"Just what is it, ma'am, that you think your husband didn't do?" the detective asked.

Mrs. Mellon clasped her hands tight on the table. A tear dropped onto her fingers.

"It's okay to talk now," I said. "Paul isn't here. This is your chance to tell the truth."

The detective scowled at me. "Who are you folks? What are you doing here?"

"No need to sound so impatient," I said. "I'm a foster home supervisor with the human services department. We're here to help Mrs. Mellon and her daughter. We've already spoken with Deputy Chief Anderson."

Another detective walked in. This one was older, his hair graying at the temples. He had kinder eyes than the younger one and a much calmer demeanor.

"Put the computer in the van, Joe," he said as he sat down at the table across from Mrs. Mellon and me.

We sat in silence. I was struck by the detective's patience, the look of sympathy in his eyes. I took my cues from him and waited. Finally Mrs. Mellon spoke.

"I don't know why that man's doing this," she said.

"What man?" I asked.

"Adin Boyle. Paul hasn't seen him in years. Why is he doing this to him now?" She stopped and looked at me sideways, as if fearful of having said too much.

"So Mr. Boyle must have tipped off your husband," the detective said.

He opened his mouth to say more but stopped when he saw the pained look on Mrs. Mellon's face. He tipped his head to the side and sat back in his chair. I handed Mrs. Mellon a napkin from the table and she dabbed at her eyes.

"Paul is not going to jail for that man. Not again."

I nodded. Out of the corner of my eye I saw J. B. leaning against the back door, his arms crossed over his chest.

Mrs. Mellon squared her shoulders. "He's despicable," she said.

"Yes," I said. "He is that."

She glared at the detective. "I know why you're here," she said. "But you're wrong. My husband would never do what you think he did."

I tucked my hands into my jacket pockets. I had been convinced that Mrs. Mellon knew what was going on, was sure she had been on the verge of telling me about it at one point. So why, when I was giving her a second chance to talk now, wasn't she taking it? I was starting to wonder if she really didn't know what her husband was up to, but it was hard to believe anyone could be that naive.

"The thing is," I said. "There was a picture of Ellie Moon on the child pornography website. It was taken when she was here, living with you." I knew telling her that was stark, but it had to be done.

Mrs. Mellon's head jerked up. "It couldn't have been her."

"Remember the bracelet Ellie's mother gave her before she died? The one she wore all the time? She was wearing that bracelet in the picture."

She pursed her lips. "I want you to leave. All of you. Now."

The detective placed the palms of his hands flat on the table. "It'll go better for you if you tell us the truth, Mrs. Mellon." He spoke slowly, his voice calm, nonthreatening.

"I *am*. Why don't you believe me?" She fell back in her chair and held her head in her hands. "I don't know what to do. I don't know what to do."

All of a sudden there was a loud crash and Cindy Mellon stood in the doorway. "You are so stupid!" She swayed back and forth, waving her hands in the air and screaming at her mother. "The only reason you don't know is because you don't want to know! What the hell do you think Daddy was doing all the time up in his office with those kids?"

Mrs. Mellon looked horrified. "Your father is a good man," she moaned. "He likes children. You know what he does, Cindy. He teaches them things."

"He teaches them things all right. I'm sick of this! I'm sick of you!" She grabbed for a vase in the middle of the table and smashed it onto the floor.

"Cindy, honey." Mrs. Mellon made a move toward her daughter.

The girl's glare was cold enough to freeze the air.

"How can you be so clueless, Mom?" Her rage was barely restrained, and the contempt in her voice made my stomach twist.

Mrs. Mellon got up from the table. She took a shaky step in one direction, then turned and took a step in the other direction. She walked back and forth like a caged animal, wringing her hands. She wobbled and grabbed the edge of the table. "I'm sorry, I'm so sorry," she said, looking at me. "My daughter has problems. She can't help it. She lies."

"Shut up, Mom!" Cindy screamed. "I am not lying. I can prove it."

"Why do you say that? You can't do any such thing."

The girl's mouth twisted into a hideous fury. "I know where the pictures are," she said.

"Show them to us, Cindy," I said. "Show us the pictures."

The girl tucked in her chin, clasped her elbows in her hands, and stomped down the hall. The two detectives, J. B., and I all followed her. Mrs. Mellon stayed in the kitchen.

"My daughter is sick," I heard her cry out. "I don't know what to do with her. I'm sorry."

Cindy Mellon led us up the stairs to her bedroom on the second floor. She stopped at the door on which, in permanent red Magic Marker, she'd drawn a skull and crossbones. Under the picture were the furious words, "You do not want to go in here. You'll be sorry if you do."

As soon as I stepped inside my body went cold. The bedroom was dead, lifeless, completely devoid of the excess energy typical of teenage girls. A lone lamp stood in the middle of the floor with its bulb painted black and no shade. Cindy Mellon leaped up on her unmade bed and reached for a DVD from a row of Disney movies lined up on a bookshelf attached to the wall. She stomped down onto the floor and threw it at me with a look of defiance.

"*Toy Story?*" I said, when I looked down at the label.

"Right," she said with a sneer. "You gonna be like my mom and believe that?"

My fingers trembled as I opened the DVD case. There was no label on the disc inside, just *Backup #5* written in black pen. I realized what it was and had to sit down on the bed. A sharp pain shot up my neck. I felt dizzy.

"I told you I wasn't lying." The girl crossed her arms and glared at all of us.

"How did you get these?" the older detective asked. "Why are they in your room?"

"Fool! I didn't see you thinking to look in here for them, did I?" She laughed, a menacing laugh that made my neck tighten.

"Cindy..." I was cold, then hot, then cold again. *Poor girl. Poor child. Poor girl.* I sat up straighter, tried to pull myself together. *She needs help.*

"Here, Cindy." I patted the bed. "Come sit with me."

To my surprise, she sat down next to me. I put my arm around her shoulder. She stared off in the distance but made no attempt to move away. "He...he never..."

I pulled her closer. "He never did what, Cindy?"

"He never did it to me," she said.

THIRTY-FOUR

May 17, 1973

Mary looked at her watch and a sob caught in her throat. Mrs. Waters would be here soon to take Jamie to the reservation. The final countdown had begun. She looked at the little brown suitcase by the front door, filled with enough clothes for a week, two stuffed animals, a puzzle and board game, and Jamie's favorite poster of a baby elephant with its mother. Tick's dog food, two ceramic bowls, and some squeaky toys were in the brown paper bag next to it.

A wave of nausea overcame her and she staggered to the bathroom, just in time. After flushing the toilet, she closed the lid and sat down. She wiped her mouth with a tissue and blew her nose. She had to pull herself together. For Jamie—everything for Jamie. She only had to hang on for a little while longer. She pressed the palms of her hands against her temples.

Wayne heard her whimpering and came into the bathroom without knocking. He sat down on the edge of the bathtub and put his hands on her knees.

"Focus on his return," he said, "not his leaving."

"He's sitting on his bed staring," she said. "He's a statue."

"He'll be back before we know it."

"He's already gone, Wayne."

She curled into herself and rocked back and forth.

The first time Jamie disappeared into himself had been three days ago. It was the day of the court hearing, after she and Wayne decided to appeal the judge's decision instead of running away. If it had been an ordinary day, Jamie would have come home from school to the smells of dinner and the sound of voices gossiping on the radio about people getting married, giving birth, dying of natural causes. She would have given him a snack while he chattered about his day. Then he would have run off to play with Tommy until dinner.

But it hadn't been an ordinary day. As soon as Jamie got home, she and Wayne had gathered him into a protective circle and told him about his birth parents. They told him that when he was born, his parents were unable to care for him, but they were better now, and he would be going to stay with them for a while. They emphasized that it wouldn't be for long, and that they would come to get him and bring him back home as soon as they could.

And the whole time they were telling Jamie all of that, he said nothing. They told him they loved him and that everything was going to be okay. Still he said nothing. The more they talked, the more he retreated. Soon he had disappeared into a space where it was impossible for anyone to reach him.

The vacant look on Jamie's face had horrified Mary that day. But then, when they went to the A&W for hamburgers and root beer floats, he sprang back to life. He acted completely normal again, as if nothing had changed. The next day he'd retreated again, yet seemed to recover when she tucked him in at bedtime.

But now the vacant look was back on his face, and this time Mary feared she'd lost him forever.

"Did he eat this morning?" she heard Wayne ask.

She uncurled her body and looked at him. "He's never passed on blueberry pancakes before," she said. "It's too much for him. Telling him about his parents was shocking enough. And then when they came to see him...he hasn't been the same since. I don't think he realizes what's going on."

She moved her hands up and down her arms, rubbing them. When Mr. and Mrs. Buckley came to see Jamie, they brought him a red woolen blanket with black and white horses on it—a gift from the tribal council—and a beaded bracelet his oldest brother, Jay, made for him. But Jamie hid in his bedroom and wouldn't come out. He finally agreed to let Mrs. Buckley come in, but only if Mary was there, too. Then he sat in the middle of his bed with his face buried in the fur of Tick's neck. When Mrs. Buckley tried to show him pictures of his brothers and little sister, he refused to look at them. When she told him stories about his siblings, he turned his body so he was facing the wall. The harder she tried to reach him, the more he retreated. As Mary watched, the silent screams in her head grew louder and louder. *Go away, leave us alone, disappear again like you did before, only this time, please don't come back.*

—

The touch of Wayne's hand on her arm brought her back to the present. "We have to keep telling him how much we love him," he said.

"He can't hear us, Wayne."

"We have to keep trying," he said. "We have to tell him that his birth parents love him, too. Tell him his brothers and sister are excited about meeting him today and that he'll make new friends. Tell him it'll be an adventure."

"He doesn't want to go," she moaned.

"We keep telling him he'll be back home before he knows it. We have to reassure him that we'll come and get him as soon as we can work things out."

"That doesn't mean anything to him. He doesn't know what kinds of things we have to work out. He never asked. I think he's afraid that..."

"We're going to win in court, Mary. We *will* get him back." He made one of his hands into a fist and pounded it into the palm of his other hand.

Mary wondered where her normally cautious and worried husband had gone. The past few days, Wayne had stepped up and taken charge in a way she'd never seen before. At first she had been suspicious, assumed he was just pretending to be optimistic for her benefit. But he picked her up over and over again with a confidence in the future that never wavered and she became convinced that he really did believe what he was saying. It was his faith, not hers, that made it possible for her to hold on and be there for Jamie. She never could have done it without him.

He reached for her hand now and pulled her to her feet. "Mrs. Waters will be here soon," he said. He put his arm around her waist and led her to the door. "Our son needs us."

Jamie stood stone still in his room, staring at himself in the mirror, mesmerized. Mary watched him touch his cheeks and run his fingers through his straight black hair.

He spoke, but his voice was flat, distant. "She looks like me," he said.

Mary held onto the doorknob to stay upright. "Yes," she murmured uncertainly.

"My hair is the same as hers."

"Yes. She's your...you have her genes." Wayne's voice trailed off.

Jamie studied the back of his hands. He looked at Mary's hands. "You aren't the same color as me."

"No."

"You either, Dad."

Wayne stood next to him and looked in the mirror. "I know who does look like you," he said. "Your brothers and sister. Aren't you excited to meet them?"

Jamie kept staring at his image in the mirror. When the doorbell rang he showed no sign, not the faintest flicker of his eyes or twitch of his mouth, that he heard it or Tick's sharp bark. Mary clasped her hands to her chest and hovered in the doorway.

"Mrs. Waters is here." Wayne's voice was hoarse and his eyes filled with tears. "It's time to go, buddy."

Jamie didn't move.

"We'll come to see you in a couple days," Wayne said.

Wayne put his arm around Jamie's shoulders and nudged him from the room and down the hall. Mary followed them to the front door with concrete blocks for feet and heavy sandbags for shoulders. Tick held back, uncharacteristically wary. Mrs. Waters stood on the porch. The smile on her face had a sadness in it that bordered on pity. *If you feel bad about what you're doing,* Mary wanted to scream at her, *then why are you doing it?*

Mrs. Waters crouched down in front of Jamie and put her hands on his waist. "You're going to be fine," she said. "Everything's going to be okay."

He turned his head to the side and stared down at the floor.

With one arm around Jamie and the other around Mary,

Wayne led them outside. Mrs. Waters picked up the suitcase and paper bag and followed behind. When they reached the county car in the driveway, Wayne scooped Jamie up in his arms and breathed into his neck.

"You'll have fun, buddy. You'll see." His eyes were red and his voice quavered as he lowered Jamie into the front seat.

Mary reached through the open door and gave her son a fierce hug, at once protective and possessive. Tick jumped up on his lap and licked his face. Jamie was wooden, nonresponsive. Wayne closed the door and kissed the dog's nose through the open window. Then he hurried to the back of the car where Mrs. Waters was putting the suitcase and paper bag into the trunk.

"We're going to fight this," he said, under his breath so Jamie couldn't hear. "We're going to get him back."

"Jamie knows how much you love him," Mrs. Waters said. "That will not only help him get through this, it will help him through other normal heartbreaks of life, too."

"You think this is a normal heartbreak of life?" Wayne hissed in a voice bordering on contempt. "A normal heartbreak is not getting what you want for Christmas—or being bullied at school—or not being invited to someone's party. Losing your parents, your home, and everything you've ever known without any warning? That's not a normal heartbreak of life. You know this is wrong. You know this isn't fair to Jamie."

Mrs. Waters bit her upper lip. "No child should have to go through something like this," she said with a shake of her head. "No, it's not right, Mr. Williams. Nothing about it is fair. It's a tragedy for everyone."

"Tell that to the judge," Wayne said. "We'll see you in court."

Mrs. Waters looked shaken as she sat behind the steering

wheel. She turned the key in the ignition switch and backed the county car out of the driveway. Jamie stuck his arms out of the open window and waved.

"Don't worry," he called out. "I'll be home in time for my birthday."

The sudden bravery in his little voice was a sledgehammer that almost brought Mary to her knees. She waved and blew frantic kisses to him until the car was out of sight. Then she fell to the pavement, tearing at her hair. Wayne wrapped himself around her body as if that could keep her from breaking apart. She clawed at his face.

"He'll be back, Mary. He'll be back. Focus on that."

Several minutes passed before her body stilled. Then he placed his hands under her arms and pulled her up to her feet. She moved toward the house as if walking through water.

"Are you okay? Can I get you anything?" he asked when they were inside.

"I'm going to take a bath," she said.

She stood in front of the bathroom mirror. A dispossessed stranger with tangled hair and a body bloated with grief stared back, pleading with her to take away the pain. She turned away from the unkempt creature's dull and lifeless gaze. She took off her clothes and lowered her spent body into the bathtub. The steamy water burned her skin until it was blood red like the hole in her tortured heart.

It was over. Jamie was gone. No matter what Wayne said and no matter what they did, her son was never coming back. She lay back and rested her head on the rim of the tub. She closed her eyes and cried out with a pain that was too deep for sound. The truth showed her no mercy. It slapped away at the countless layers of denial she'd so delicately constructed over the years until they lay shattered in a million pieces. She was not Jamie's mother. She never had been. She was his foster mother. The two were not the same. They never had been. She loved Jamie as if she'd given birth to him, but in the end, could love that was based on a lie really be love, or was it something else?

She heard a knocking. "Mary? Open the door. Are you okay?"

There was nothing Wayne could say that would change anything. She knew, in that moment, what she had done, what she had become. She lowered her body into the tub until her head was submerged. She let the water take her, cleanse her, praying that it would release her from the clutches of grief and guilt.

THIRTY-FIVE

For the next six hours, the Mellon house was filled with cops. The detectives trashed every room in the place looking for evidence and carried out boxes of it, in addition to the DVDs that had been hidden in Cindy Mellon's bedroom—cameras, pictures and more DVDs they found in a locked cabinet on the third floor, two computers, other items that didn't seem on the face of it to have any significance.

"We'll be putting out an APB for your husband," one of the detectives told Mrs. Mellon before he walked out with the last box. "But right now all you folks need to come down to the station."

I thought his brusqueness was unnecessary and told him so. A cluster of neighbors stood out in the street gawking as we left the house. I tried to comfort Mrs. Mellon by placing my hand on her arm as she and her daughter walked to the police van, but she shook me off. J. B. and I drove in his car down to the station.

After the police had finished interviewing all of us and had taken our statements, Mrs. Mellon accepted J. B.'s offer of a ride home. She and Cindy sat in the back seat as far apart from each other as was physically possible. Neither of them said a word. J. B. pulled into the driveway and I turned around to face them with a sympathetic smile.

"J. B. and I will stay with you for a while," I said.

"No. Leave."

"What about your daughter?" I said.

"I'll see to her."

"But...I'm..."

"Go. It's enough that the police called Child Protective Services." Mrs. Mellon got out of the car and gripped the edge of the car door, poised to slam it behind her. Her back was stiff and straight, the tears gone from her eyes, and her skin was drawn tight over her jaw.

I didn't know whether to be concerned or relieved about the change in her. I worried about leaving her daughter with her in the state she was in. I looked at J. B. for help but he just shrugged. I tried to ask Mrs. Mellon one more time if she needed help. She shook her head more vigorously than before and started to close the door.

"I'm worried about you," I said. "Cindy is going to need help. Both of you are."

Mrs. Mellon slammed the car door closed, then she and Cindy went into the house.

—

Neither J. B. nor I said anything for several minutes. We were several blocks away from the Mellons' house when he finally broke the silence. "Mellon can't have gone far," he said. "The police will have him in custody soon. Why don't we wait at my place for them to call?"

I nodded, not because I shared his optimism but because I didn't know what else to do, and I didn't want to go home. It wouldn't be good for me to be left alone, not with all the thoughts spinning through my head right now. Each time car lights approached us I blinked and another new thought popped up. By the time we got to J. B.'s condo, I was afraid I would burst if I didn't let some of them out.

I settled in on his genuine leather couch with a glass of ice water. He faced me in the matching chair and we reviewed the day, starting with our visit to Boyle's real estate headquarters and then on to the fundraiser at the University Club, the meeting at MCPD, and finally, the remarkable turn of events at the Mellon home.

I folded one of my legs up under the other and tugged my skirt down over my knees. I sipped some water, and its coldness slid over my tongue and down my throat. Things had gone better than I'd expected; still, a preoccupation with all that had happened and was yet to happen held me in its grip.

"We still haven't been able to prove that Mr. Mellon pushed Anthony Little Eagle off the balcony," I said. "We're not done until the police charge him with murder." I paused, stared at the glass in my hand. "Poor Mrs. Mellon. Her daughter needs help, but she's so, I don't know, so inadequate."

"She's plenty pissed right now."

"What kind of man would use his own daughter like that?"

"Do you think he took pictures of her, too?"

"No. I believed Cindy when she said he didn't do it to her. But no wonder the poor girl is disturbed. Having to sleep every night in the room with those tapes, knowing what was going on upstairs and not being able to do anything about it. Do you think it was Paul Mellon's intention right from the start to use foster children for his porn business? If that's the case, I really can't believe that *no one* in my agency was suspicious. If we were all as blind about Mr. Mellon as his wife was, we might as well throw in the towel. Our agency procedures should have screened him out because of his criminal background."

I stared up at the ceiling to hold back tears. I shifted my position, placed both feet on the floor, swallowed some more water to fight off my exhaustion. It had been a long day. I looked at J. B. and found myself spiraling around his thick eyelashes, touching the hint of sadness in his brown eyes.

"We make quite the team," I said.

"Life is full of surprises," he said with a flash of that grin of his.

"You hated me at first," I said.

"I didn't trust you."

"You thought I was a white do-gooder."

"You said it, not me." He raised his palms in the air.

"Someone who lived on the reservation told me once," I said with a chuckle, "that I should just get over it, that I wasn't an Indian and never could be."

I expected J. B. to laugh along with me, but he didn't. Instead, he looked down at his hands, like he was studying them.

"I don't know what you're thinking," I said.

He lifted his head. "And you think you should?" He looked thoughtful for a few seconds, then said, "When we first met, you acted like you had a guilty conscience about something. You were overly eager to show how concerned you were."

I placed my glass on the coffee table and sat back on the couch, instinctively tucking my hands under my thighs like a guilty child. I thought about how difficult it was for me to come to terms with my place in this world, how my shame over the collective sins of white people into whose ranks I'd been born had extended beyond what was reasonable to the point where I considered myself responsible for everything, including things I didn't do and couldn't do anything about. It was my own personal struggle, not one about which I had any right to seek sympathy or understanding from J. B. My as-yet-unfinished journey, I knew, was what had compelled me to do what I was doing right now.

"Was I that obvious," I said, attempting a joke, "or were you just more astute than most?"

He shrugged. We sat together in a companionable silence.

"Sometimes I feel like I've known you all my life," I said, "but I don't know anything about you."

He lifted his shoulders up and let them down.

"Tell me about your grandfather," I said. "At least that."

He glanced around his living room. "I owe my grandpa more than just this condo," he said. "He made sure I finished high school and then paid for me to go to college. He helped me apply for an American Indian scholarship for graduate school, too, although he said it was against his principles. I wouldn't be a journalist today if it weren't for him." He took a sip of water, then placed his glass on the coffee table next to mine. "More water?"

He jumped up from his chair and headed for the kitchen without waiting for me to answer. I took a quick look around at the brick walls, the oversized windows, the wooden beams a good twenty feet above my head. I felt drained in a vague distant way as old memories returned, fragments from another time and a different place, images undoubtedly made more vivid by my fatigue. A two-room house that had once been a chicken coop...stuffed newspapers in the walls keeping the cold reservation wind at bay...

government-surplus food bags...a chipped coffee cup with a missing handle. There was a lump in my throat. Why was this coming back to me now? How could things that happened so long ago shape a life as profoundly as they had shaped mine?

J. B. returned with a pitcher of ice water and started to pour some into my glass. I glanced over his shoulder at the twinkling lights in the buildings across the street.

"Maybe there are some things you can never get over," I said, still looking out the window. "Maybe some things you never should get over. Like what happened to Anthony Little Eagle. Maybe the only thing any of us can do is try to make up in the present for what we were unable to do in the past. But do you think that's enough? Can anything ever be enough?"

I turned my face away from the window and toward J. B. He appeared to be lost in thought as he refilled his glass.

"We do some good," I continued. "We protect a lot of kids. But we make mistakes, too, sometimes deadly ones, and there's just no way to make up for those."

"Or maybe life's contradictions have a way of balancing each other out over time," he said wistfully.

"Do you have any pictures?" I asked out of the blue. "Of you when you were little?"

I expected him to give me his usual "don't go there" look, but instead he walked over to his desk and came back carrying a photo album. He opened it so it was facing me and pointed to a black-and-white picture.

"Cute. How old were you?"

He sat back down in his chair. "I got that two-wheeler when I started kindergarten, so I must have been five."

I looked closer at the picture. He was standing with one foot on the ground, the other on the pedal, squinting up at the sun, an exuberant smile on his little brown face. He looked happy. Proud of himself. I flipped to the next page, my eyes drawn to a picture taken when he was a year or two older. A woman stood behind him, her arms encircling his chest. She looked familiar. I blinked. Looked again. *My eyes are playing tricks on me.* I lifted the album up so it was closer to my face. It couldn't possibly be her...or could it?

J. B. reached for the album like he was protecting something fragile, some vulnerability at the core of his own private anguish. Suddenly there was too much air in his vast living room, too much for me to take it all in, and what I was able to suck in I wasn't able to let out fast enough.

"You look exhausted," I heard him say.

"It's late," I said.

"Come on, I'll drive you home."

I tried to stand up and slipped back onto the couch. Tried again. I was dizzy. Disoriented. I looked at J. B. and saw in his eyes a direct line to the soul wound deep inside. It was a line I couldn't cross, didn't know if I wanted to cross, wouldn't know how to cross if I wanted to. I turned away from him. With sluggish feet and a body gone limp, I walked from his condo to his car in a silence now filled with unease, with questions I dared not ask, things I dared not say. I wanted to tell him, but I didn't know how or whether I should. It wasn't what you knew or what you remembered so much as what you did with it, and I didn't know what to do with it.

And then we got into J. B.'s car, and all my confusion and everything else was immediately obliterated by the smell of alcohol. It was strong enough to get you drunk just from breathing in the fumes.

"What the..." J. B. patted the front seat and then around on the floor in the dark, searching for the source of the stench.

We both jumped and turned around at the sound of someone stirring in the back seat. An incredibly drunk man was struggling to pull himself up into an upright position behind us. I backed away from the stink of him and watched him fall backward and try again, heard the sound of empty bottles hitting each other. A couple more tries and he finally managed to prop himself up with his elbows on the back of the front seat. The dim light from the street lamp outside revealed his white dress shirt, unbuttoned at the top with a tie dangling loose around the neck.

"Hey, man, looks like you're in the wrong car." J. B. reached for the man's arms, tried to push him toward the back door.

The man struck his chin on the back of the seat. He mumbled words that were too slurred for me to understand and pulled himself up.

J. B. recoiled with disgust. "Come on, man, that' s enough, time to get out. Find yourself another bar."

The man's eyes flitted back and forth from J. B. and me. "Did ya hear me?" he said louder. "I know what ya did to my daughter. Why'd ya make her talk to the police like that?"

My mouth dropped open. "You...you're Paul Mellon?"

"How did you find my car?" J. B. asked.

Paul Mellon lurched toward us and fell backward again, pulled himself up. "I was watching. I saw you bring Linda and Cindy home. I followed you."

"You were hiding near your house?" I said.

"How do you know what your daughter said to the police?" J. B. asked.

Paul sucked in his breath, swiped at tears that were running down his cheeks. "Linda called. What'd ya do to her? Cindy's... Cindy's ga problems. You shouldn't a done that."

I clenched my teeth. I wasn't afraid. I was disgusted. And angry. It was two against one, and with Mellon unsteady to the point of being incapacitated, it would be easy to subdue him if we had to. I felt strangely sorry for him, too. He sounded genuinely concerned about his wife and daughter.

"Your daughter told the truth," I said. "You shouldn't blame her for that."

"Ya need to fix things with my wife," he said. "She'll listen to ya. She says ya care about kids. Ya can help my daughter. Ya need to make it right."

"The only way to make it right is to turn yourself in," J. B. said.

Without any warning, there was the sound of glass shattering. I screamed. The car jolted from the force of the gunshot through the driver's side window. A gust of warm air rattled the bones in my feet. I ducked and grabbed J. B.'s arm to pull him down with me. A shard of glass on the car seat pierced my finger.

J. B. sat up, his hands raised in the air. "Your daughter's okay," he said. "We saw her. She's all right."

"You better pray she is. You're gonna take me back home right now and make it right," Paul Mellon said. "Consider that a warning shot." His voice now sounded sinister, vicious.

"Okay, man. Okay." J. B. turned the key in the ignition.

"Drive. No funny stuff."

J. B. did what he was told, not looking back or to either side, his head frozen by the gun pressed against the back of his neck. I didn't dare take my eyes off the gun, Mr. Mellon's finger on the trigger. *Don't say anything,* I said to myself. *Don't breathe. Don't set him off.* I knew the car had to be moving but there was no movement.

"Turn here. In the alley."

I bit my tongue to keep myself from jumping at the unexpected sound of Mr. Mellon's voice.

"Park here. Behind the garage." He waved the gun toward the door. "Get out. Try anything and I'll shoot. Now walk."

There was a light in the kitchen window. When we reached the back door I could see Mrs. Mellon and her daughter sitting at the table, their shoulders touching, their heads down. Paul Mellon kicked in the door and pushed us in front of him. His wife screamed. His daughter's eyes widened and her body went rigid.

"Go ahead, tell 'em. Make it right. Tell 'em all I ever did was for them. Tell 'em all I wanted was to take care of them." He staggered and fell against the refrigerator but managed to hold onto the gun.

J. B. raised his hands in the air. "We can't do that, man," he said. "You know we can't."

"I said tell 'em!" He waved the gun back and forth, first at me, then at J. B., then back at me.

Mrs. Mellon leaped from her chair and slammed her hands on the table. "I told you not to come home, you bastard!" she yelled. "I only called you to tell you I never wanted to see your lying face again. I can't...I...how could you do what you did? And then use Cindy to hide the pictures like that! How could you do that to your daughter? Who are you? I don't know you." She dropped onto her knees, her arms raised and her hands pointing up to the ceiling.

"Linda, baby..." Mr. Mellon took a step toward her.

"Stay away!" She held up her palms to stop him. "Don't you dare come any closer!"

He stepped back, a look of uncertainty on his face.

"Look man, it's over." J. B. said. "The police have the DVDs. They know what you did."

"They know you killed Anthony Little Eagle, too," I said.

"No! No! Not that, too!" Mrs. Mellon's eyes became huge, but the rest of her body shrank.

Mr. Mellon glared at me. "I didn' kill that kid," he said.

"Liar!" his wife shouted.

"I'm tellin' you, Linda, I didn' hurt that boy. Okay, I took pictures. We needed the money. But you gotta believe me, Linda, baby, I didn' do anything to that boy."

Mrs. Mellon covered her face and mumbled into her hands. "Liar, liar, liar..."

Cindy Mellon pulled herself up, then. It seemed to take all of her energy. She held on to the table. "I didn't mean for him to die!" she cried out. "It was an accident. I just thought maybe if he broke his arm...like Ellie..."

I froze. The girl's head hung down, her hair falling in her eyes. What was she saying?

"Nobody wanted him to die," I said.

Mrs. Mellon's hands were still in fists, her face in rage at her husband but her eyes crying out to her daughter.

"Cindy, don't..." Mr. Mellon's voice broke. He reached out his hand, started to take a step toward her, stopped, a look of anguish on his face. "Don't, Cindy...please...don't say anything else. I can't protect you any more."

"It was you?" I blurted out. "You pushed Anthony Little Eagle off the balcony?"

"No!" Mrs. Mellon cried out. "She didn't! It wasn't her fault!"

"Cindy...*please*...don't." Mr. Mellon wiped the sweat from his forehead with his free hand.

I clenched one hand into a fist. What was going on in this house? Who were these people? I stifled an urge to lash out at

Mr. Mellon; he still had the gun in his other hand. I looked from him to Mrs. Mellon and back again.

"The two of you," I said through gritted teeth. "You, you don't deserve to..." I caught myself, bit my tongue. I squeezed my eyes tight, tried to ratchet down the anger.

"No!" Mrs. Mellon cried out. "You can't take this child, too. She's mine!"

"Why?" J. B. said to the girl in a soft, gentle voice. "Why did you do this?"

Cindy Mellon looked at him with eyes filled with tears. "How else was I supposed to stop him? He was going to take Tony upstairs." Tears were streaming down her face. "Someone had to stop him." She glared at her mother. "Someone had to do something." She looked at her mother again and then fell onto the floor sobbing, her head between her knees, her arms holding her legs. J. B. went over to her and crouched down, put his arm around her shoulder.

"Now see what you did," he said, looking up first at her father and then her mother.

"That's it," Paul Mellon yelled. "You shoulda shut up."

He waved the gun in the air. He pointed it at J. B.'s head, his face contorted with rage. There was no time to warn him.

"Jamie!" I shouted, and I lunged at Paul Mellon's hand.

There was a flash of white behind my eyes. A searing pain ripped through me. A moan, long and slow, filled my body as I fell forward and down, down, down. I rolled onto my side and drew my legs up to my chest, felt the warm air curl around me like a womb. There was a sound of sirens in the distance, the trumpets of the angels. I looked up and saw Jamie standing over me, wide-eyed, staring. Then everything went black.

THIRTY-SIX

"She's back."

I opened my eyes and blinked, blinded by the whiteness surrounding me—sheets...curtain around my bed...walls...ceiling light...nurse's uniform. I tried to pull myself up into a sitting position but fell back onto the pillow.

"Careful with that shoulder," the nurse said.

I turned my head to the side and saw J. B. sitting in a chair next to the bed. "Are you okay?" I asked.

He tipped his head up, slowly down. "Mellon dropped the gun right after you charged at him." His voice faded away, then returned. "Mellon and Boyle are both in police custody. Boyle's enraged and Mellon's a mess, carrying on about how he loves his wife and daughter so much it's almost believable. The girl's in the hospital for observation..." His voice receded, came back. "It's over. We did it. We got them."

"Mellon didn't kill Anthony," I mumbled. "I was so sure..."

They must have given me something for pain because I saw J.B.'s lips moving but his voice had disappeared. My eyes closed involuntarily and I drifted in and out of sleep.

Seven-year-old Jamie sits next to me in the county car, like a wooden soldier with his arms rigid at his sides. I back the car out of the driveway and he turns around, waves good-bye to his foster parents, trying so hard to be brave. "Don't worry," he yells out the window. "I'll be home in time for my birthday." The bright green lawns, colorful flowers and leafy maple trees get smaller and smaller until everything he has known all his life disappears. "Please, turn around," he cries. "Take me home. I don't want to go." He screams, howls, starts to choke. Hiccups swallow his sobs. My knuckles are white on the steering wheel. I press my foot on the brake and the car comes to a lurching stop on the side of the road.

I opened my eyes. My pillow was wet with tears. J. B. was still there, watching me.

"I'm sorry," I whispered.

My eyes closed again.

I fold Jamie in my arms and stroke his hair. Tick licks his face. The dog's fur is soon soaked with tears. Jamie falls into an exhausted sleep. An hour later he wakes to a world that is foreign to him—a place of dirt roads and barren land, unpainted and weathered shacks surrounded by crushed and broken glass, old tires, rusted cars, mud and weeds. A group of people stand in front of his new home. His little sister waves a sign that says, Welcome Home, Jamie. His mother and father stand arm in arm next to his brothers. Everyone moves toward the car, smiling. May Goodheart and members of the tribal council carry presents. Jamie turns away, becomes the wooden soldier again.

"Jamie," I said out loud.

J. B. coughed and I opened my eyes. "Nobody calls me that," he said. He moved to the edge of the chair like he wanted to ask me something, but then sat back with a shake of his head. There was no discernible expression on his face, no regret, resignation, anger. I pushed myself up, propped two pillows behind my back.

"I didn't know," I said. "Not until I recognized your foster mother in the picture."

"I don't remember you," he said.

"I was the reservation social worker. I was Mrs. Waters back then. That was my married name. I knew Josephine Buckley, your birth mother. I drove you back to her and your family."

"I have no memory of it," he said.

His eyes filled with moisture, and he became seven-year-old Jamie to me again, the boy I ripped from the only parents he'd ever known and returned to the parents from whom he'd been stolen at birth. The tears that flooded down his beautiful walnut-brown face then became my tears now. The sorrow that bruised my heart then bruised it still. The injustice that had suffocated me then still suffocated me now.

"I was too young to know what to do." I struggled to push myself further up on the bed with my good arm. "But I knew...I knew you should have been returned to your parents when your siblings were, when you were still a baby. It wasn't fair that you weren't. It wasn't fair to you...or your parents...or your foster parents. It wasn't fair to anyone. It was unforgivable. I am so sorry. So, so sorry."

"My foster parents told me..." His voice sounded distant, as if coming from some private space far away or deep inside. "They told me they'd come and get me, but they never did. I never knew why until..." His voice cracked and he gripped the chair's armrests.

I breathed in his pain, thought about how confusing it must

have been for him as a child. "Mary Williams loved you very much," I said.

He turned away. "She was a coward," he said.

"Your foster mother couldn't bear losing you," I said. "She wasn't as strong as you."

He looked at me then as if yearning for the answer to a question too daunting for him to ask.

"My mother never talked to me about what happened," he said.

"Someone told her you died when you were a year old," I said. "That's why she stopped coming to see you. I don't know how or why that happened because I wasn't working at the county then. But I know your mother never stopped loving you. She thought about you all the time, dreamed about you every night. When I met her she asked me to find out what happened to you, how you had died, and that's when we discovered that you were alive and had been living with Mary and Wayne Williams all your life.

"Your mother wanted nothing more than to have you back, but she loved you so much that she was willing, for your sake, to give you up. She knew how loved and happy you were with your foster parents. Though it broke her heart, she and your father decided to relinquish their parental rights so the Williamses could adopt you.

"But when they went to court, the judge said that an injustice had been done to you and your parents. And he was right, Jamie. You were robbed of your family, your community, your culture. The judge ordered me to bring you back to them, to give them back to you. He did the right thing but he did it too fast. When he ordered me to drive to you to the rez in three days, your mother was terribly worried about what that would do to you. There wasn't enough time to prepare you. She knew you didn't know her." I paused and took a deep breath. "We all worried about you."

"Then why..." His voice cracked. "Why didn't she come to get me?"

His seven-year-old face looked into my questioning eyes. "Your mother didn't come to get you? Do you mean why didn't she come to get you when your sister and brothers were returned from foster care?"

He looked away, as if considering how much he wanted to say. "I kept running away from the rez," he said. "Someone always found me before I reached the end of the road and brought me back. Everyone was nice to me and all, but I didn't belong there. When I was thirteen I ran away and no one came after me, so I hitchhiked all the way to my foster parents' house. My foster dad told me how Mom tried to kill herself after I left... after you took me...to live on the rez. She was in the hospital for a while then, but later, when she was home again, she tried again and succeeded. He called Grandpa Harold and Grandma Rose and they came over and said they wanted to take me in. I lived with them after that.

"My grandpa said if my mother, my real mother, cared about me, she would have come to get me, or she would have at least called to see if I was there and how I was doing. So I always thought..." He stared at his hands in his lap. "She never came."

I raised my arm to wipe the wetness from my cheeks and the pain in my shoulder made me wince. "Love doesn't always look like we think it should," I said. "Listen to me. I wasn't there to know what happened, Jamie, but I knew your mother. If Josie Buckley thought you kept running away from the rez because you wanted to go back to the foster home that badly, then I know she loved you enough to let you go, even if it broke her heart. And I know it had to have broken her heart. She would have always waited and hoped that you would come back. I can't believe she never called to see how you were doing or that she never tried to see you. In fact, I'd bet my life that she did."

He flinched, clenched his hands into fists. "Grandpa Harold wouldn't lie to me," he said.

"I'm not saying your grandfather didn't love you," I said. "I'm not accusing him of lying. I wasn't there. I'm just saying I know how much your mother loved you."

His eyes focused on the wall behind me. "He had a funny way of showing it," he eventually said. "But my grandpa loved me, too."

We lapsed into silence for a few minutes. I couldn't deny the care and love his foster parents and grandparents had provided. I couldn't imagine their pain when they lost Jamie, a pain deep enough to trigger Mary Williams' depression and lead her to take her life. I thought about Josie and how much she'd lost, what she'd sacrificed for her son. But mostly I thought about Jamie and what he lost, what he never had.

"Josie...your mother...put you at the center," I said.

He took in a quick breath and his eyes widened. "She always whispered that in my ear," he said. "Now I know what she meant." He leaned back in his chair, his face a bit brighter.

"Your foster mother did, too." I paused as a wave of sympathy for Mary Williams moved through me. "Both of your mothers loved you."

He was silent for a couple minutes, then he said, "Funny, I don't remember you at all."

"I ran away, too," I said. "I went to graduate school. I always felt guilty about not going back to the reservation to find out what happened to you. The truth is, I was too scared to find out."

I thought about how I'd anguished for decades about whether Jamie would ever be able to piece his cracked heart back together again. And now I knew that in spite of having so much taken from him, in spite of the unjust hand he'd been dealt in life, he had found a way to survive.

"Yet here we are," he said.

I nodded and felt my neck for the necklace May Goodheart made for me but it wasn't there. I closed my eyes and fell into my own reflections. J. B. had made himself a successful journalist and created the kind of lifestyle I'd assiduously rejected. His identity was woven more tightly into the dominant social fabric of society than was mine. We both were alienated from the cultures into which we'd been born; he had been robbed of his, and I had renounced mine. In a way, both of our lives had been fiction, and now maybe our quest for justice for Anthony Little Eagle would help us find a way to rewrite our histories.

We sat together in silence, each of us in our own space, each of us knowing that much more remained to be said.

EPILOGUE

The last of the red and yellow leaves fluttered from the tree branches like little flags in the chilly wind. I tightened the wool scarf around my neck as I made my way to the front door of the American Indian Community Center. The scant warmth left in the sun's rays signaled the end of autumn and foreshadowed the months of below-zero windchill temperatures and icy sidewalks soon to come.

Peter Minter hadn't explained why he wanted to meet today. I wondered what could be so important that it couldn't wait until next week, when I would see him at the meeting of the Governor's Foster Care Reform Task Force. He'd been appointed as the Indian Child Welfare representative and I'd been appointed to represent the Human Services and Public Health Department. Only now, well, I guess I represented myself, since I no longer worked there.

Peter was at a table in the back of the Red Fox Den Café, strands of his shoulder-length gray hair lightly touching his black-framed glasses. Sam Chasa, wearing his grease-spotted chef's vest, as always, sat across from him. I was surprised to see J. B., decked out in a dark blue double-breasted suit and blue striped shirt that must have cost a fortune, sitting next to Peter. "Whatever this is about must be newsworthy," I said with a smile as I approached the table.

Sam and Peter both stood up to shake hands with me. J. B. remained seated. Our eyes met. I shifted my weight from one foot to the other like a silly schoolgirl. It would have been strange and insufficient to shake hands with him, yet presumptuous to do what I really wanted to do, which was to hug him. I gave him a little wave and quickly sat down on the other side of the table.

"So," Sam Chasa said, "what's it like to be retired?"

"It's better this way," I said.

Sam, like a lot of other people, preferred to think that I'd retired, and I didn't correct him. It was too complicated and personal to explain why I'd resigned, too fraught with the risk of misunderstandings, either positive or negative. Some of my social workers, based on what I'd heard from Lynn Winters, believed I'd been forced to resign. Betsy Chambers had threatened to fire me at first, when I told her everything J. B. and I had done, but later she was as sickened and appalled by what had been going on in the Mellon home as I was.

Inez Koreskovsky was fired on the spot when the missing pages from the case file, and Paul Mellon's criminal record, were discovered in her cubicle. She wouldn't say why she never shredded them but I figured she'd finally been trapped by her own arrogance and laziness. No one shed a tear to see her go, but there were a few tears at my going-away party, and Betsy had pulled me aside to tell me she was no longer angry at me and that she accepted my amends.

"Thanks to Sylvia here," Peter said with a warm smile, "it looks like we're finally getting the state to make some changes in the foster care system."

"Thanks to *both* of us," I said. "You and I have been pushing for these reforms for years."

"So are we here to talk about the lawsuit that was filed on behalf of Anthony Little Eagle's parents against the state?" J. B. pulled his pen from his pocket. "Is there news?"

"I'm afraid justice for the Little Eagles will take a while," Peter said. "I think the state will eventually settle, pay the family, and institute some policy changes. But these cases can take years."

"The lawyers took my deposition well over a month ago," I said in agreement, "and I haven't heard anything since." I paused, thought about how at least now I could speak freely and without any conflict of interest to both the governor's task force and the Little Eagle litigation team, could tell the truth about how the foster care system had failed.

"Congratulations, J. B., on your series in the *Tribune*," Peter said.

"Your exposé nailed it," Sam said. "That's what forced the governor to act."

"That," Peter added, "and the recommendations made by the child death review panel."

"The story's not over yet," J. B. said.

"That's right," I added. "Not until Paul Mellon and Adin Boyle are locked away for a long time."

"Boyle's got the best lawyers money can buy, but Bradley Finch..." J. B. looked at Sam and Peter to explain. "Finch is the cop who covered up the death of that baby in the Mellon home..." He turned back to me and continued. "Finch is singing like a bird, so his testimony will be critical."

I turned to J. B. as if it were just the two of us in the café. "At least Cindy Mellon wasn't responsible for that baby dying," I said. "But who knows what's going to happen to her, how long she'll be institutionalized for treatment. There is good news about Ellie Moon, though. Lynn Winters tells me she's responding well in therapy and her adoption will be finalized soon."

"I hear you two came close to getting knocked off," Sam said.

"Yet here we are," J. B. said, with that grin of his that had always made my heart melt into one massive puddle.

I don't know why, but I started laughing then. That got J. B. laughing, which made me laugh all the harder. Soon I was laughing so hard I had to keep wiping the tears from my eyes. The contagion spread to Sam and Peter, and they joined in, only with puzzled expressions on their faces. Finally, we wore ourselves out.

"So," I said, as I wiped my eyes one more time. "Why are we here? What is this meeting about?"

"Just getting to that," Sam said with a nod to Peter.

"The community center board has an annual awards banquet," Peter said. "They voted unanimously to give an outstanding journalism award this year. To you, J. B."

"Yes!" I clapped my hands. I was thrilled about the award, and about the shift in Sam and Peter's perceptions of J. B. that it confirmed.

"The banquet is next month," Sam added.

J. B. smiled. He looked pleased.

"I guess that means you accept." Peter reached out and shook hands with J. B.

"Here." Sam pushed a pad of paper and pencil across the table. "Write down the names of the people in your family and any others you want us to invite to the banquet. That way we'll know how many places to reserve at the head table. Oh, and you'll need to let us know what name you want on the plaque, too."

"J. B. Harrell."

"Okay. Makes sense to use your pen name, since it's a journalism award," Sam said. "Just wanted to give you the choice."

J. B. stared at me. I shook my head. "I didn't..."

Sam interrupted me with a raise of his hand. "Here in Indian country, we make a point of knowing who's who," he said. "Your brother Jay stops by whenever he's in town. He always asks about you. Says your mother wants to know how you're doing."

"I haven't..." J. B. started to say something, in a voice just shy of too low to be heard. His eyes were moist.

"The past isn't past when the present is caught up in it," Peter said, his eyes soft with compassion.

J. B. picked up the pencil and printed the words *GUEST LIST* in capital letters on top of the page. He wrote the name Josephine Buckley down first, followed by John Buckley, his father. After that he wrote his brother Jay's name, then the names of his other siblings. He paused, glanced over at me, and then added my name to the list.

"My mother is sure going to be surprised when she gets the invitation." He slid the pencil and pad of paper across the table to Sam.

"She'll be thrilled to see you," I said.

"She'll be shocked that we know each other," he said. "She'll never believe we solved a murder together."

We both fell silent then. He looked down at his manicured fingernails, studying them as if they held the promise of hope for the future. I closed my eyes and listened to the steady humming of the refrigerator in the kitchen, fully aware that the universe had just given each of us a second chance.

Acknowledgements

My deepest gratitude goes to the children and families whose life stories inspired and informed *At the Center*. I have been assiduous in protecting their anonymity in the specifics while aiming to capture the essence of their real-life experiences: *At the Center* is a work of fiction and all persons, geographic locations, agencies, and community organizations are entirely the creation of my imagination.

Writing this book has been a team effort. I am indebted to two outstanding writers, editors, and teachers who were critical to the team. Hal Zina Bennett coached me through the first draft many years ago, and the wizardry of Max Regan helped me transform *At the Center* into the novel you now hold in your hands. Thank you to my writing group members, Mary Kabrich and Roger Roffman, who provided wise feedback at every stage of development. A special thank you to readers of different drafts of the manuscript: Janis Avery, Rex Browning, Charlie Cooper, Pauline Erera, Nancy Johnston, Nocona Pewewardy, and Dorothy Sturdevant. For the final stages of production I am grateful to Kyra Freestar for her outstanding copyediting and to Kevin Atticks and the Apprentice House publishing team. As always, my deepest appreciation goes to my wife, Susan, whose constant support makes it all possible.

At the Center: A Book Club and Readers' Guide

Book Club Questions and Topics

1. What is the significance of the novel's title, *At the Center*? Discuss possible meanings and why you think the author selected this title.

2. With which characters did you feel the most sympathy and connection? Why? How did your opinions and feelings about them change as the story unfolded?

3. Both Sylvia Jensen and Mary Williams seem driven, to the point of compulsiveness and even self-deception. What is it that motivates them?

4. How would you characterize the relationship between Sylvia Jensen and J. B. Harrell? How does it change as the story progresses? How would you characterize it at the end?

5. What are your feelings about Jamie Buckley? How do they change as the story unfolds?

6. Each of the main characters in *At the Center* make choices or take actions that have moral and ethical implications. Which decisions would you have made? Which would you have made differently? Why? Did your notion about what was best or right shift in the course of your reading?

7. Were you surprised by the plot? Was the ending satisfying? If so, why? If not, why not? How would you change it?

8. What main ideas and issues does the author explore? What do you think was the main theme?

Discussion Questions for Graduate and Undergraduate Students and Helping Professionals

1. Early in their relationship, Sylvia asks J. B., "Why don't you want to be an Indian?" and he responds, "Why do you want to be one?" In 1972, Mary Williams confronts the school principal's stereotypes about Jamie by insisting that he's "just like any other little boy." Discuss different ways that the concepts of racial identity development and cultural competence are played out in *At the Center.*

2. What are the similarities and differences between the two time periods in the story, 1972 and 2005, particularly in regard to the relationship between white Americans and American Indians?

3. What were some of the failings in the child welfare system in regard to Anthony Little Eagle's death? How might an agency respond in a positive way when there is a tragedy like this one? How can administrators help social workers and supervisors? What supports and training should be put in place? What support is needed by foster families in regard to accidents and deaths?

4. Jamie Buckley was placed in foster care in 1972, before the Indian Child Welfare Act was passed. Anthony Little Eagle was placed in foster care in 2005, after the law had been in place for seventeen years. Discuss the intent of the ICWA and how it might have helped the two boys. What cultural issues need to be understood and addressed before children are placed in foster

homes? How have other foster care and child welfare laws, policies, and procedures changed from 1972 to 2005? What changes are needed now?

5. In what ways did Sylvia Jensen (2005) and Mrs. Waters (1972) uphold and/or violate the values and ethics of the social work profession? Do you think any of their actions were justified, and, if so, why? Discuss the conflicts faced by the social workers in *At the Center.* How do you think they handled these conflicts? How do you think they should have handled them?

Further Resources

Child Welfare/Foster Care
Child Welfare League of America
  http://www.cwla.org/
Children's Rights
  www.childrensrights.org
National Indian Child Welfare Association
  www.nicwa.org
The Indian Child Welfare Act of 1978
  http://www.nicwa.org/Indian_Child_Welfare_Act/

—

Racial Identity Development/Cultural Competence
A summary of racial identity models from Jeff Mio, professor of psychology at California State Polytechnic University, Pomona
  www.cpp.edu/jsmio/325/powerpoints/identity.html
A cultural competence continuum, by Terry Cross, MSW
  http://nysccc.org/family-supports/transracial-transcultural/
  voices-of-professionals/cultural-competence-continuum/

—

DiAngelo, Robin. *What Does It Mean to Be White? Developing White Racial Literacy.* New York: Peter Lang Publishing, 2012. A useful book for whites who want to be more than well-intentioned.

Duran, Eduardo and Bonnie Duran. *Native American Postcolonial Psychology.* State University of New York Press, 1995. A book that shows the necessity of understanding intergenerational trauma and internalized oppression in order to understand Native Americans today.

Helms, Janet E. *A Race Is a Nice Thing to Have: A Guide to Living as a White Person or Understanding the White Persons in Your Life.* 2nd ed. Framingham, MA: Microtraining Associates, 2007.

Horse, Perry G. "Twenty-First Century Native American Consciousness: A Thematic Model of Indian Identity." In *New Perspectives on Racial Identity Development: Integrating Emerging Frameworks*, edited by Charmaine L. Wijeyesinghe and Bailey W. Jackson. 2nd ed. New York University Press, 2012.

About The Author

Dorothy Van Soest is a writer, social worker, political and community activist, and retired professor and university dean. She holds an undergraduate degree in English literature and a master's degree and PhD in social work. She is currently professor emeritus at the University of Washington with a research-based publication record of ten books and over fifty journal articles, essays, and book chapters that tackle complex and controversial issues related to violence, oppression, and injustice. Her debut novel, *Just Mercy*, published in 2014, was informed by her widely acclaimed investigation into the lives of thirty-seven men who were executed by Texas in 1997, and inspired by victim-offender restorative justice dialogue programs. *At the Center* grew out of her experiences with the child welfare system. Dorothy Van Soest lives in Seattle, Washington, where she is currently working on her next novel, a story based on her experiences with the New York City public school system during the 1968 teachers' strike. Her website is http://dorothyvansoest.com/.

Apprentice House is the country's only campus-based, student-staffed book publishing company. Directed by professors and industry professionals, it is a nonprofit activity of the Communication Department at Loyola University Maryland.

Using state-of-the-art technology and an experiential learning model of education, Apprentice House publishes books in untraditional ways. This dual responsibility as publishers and educators creates an unprecedented collaborative environment among faculty and students, while teaching tomorrow's editors, designers, and marketers.

Outside of class, progress on book projects is carried forth by the AH Book Publishing Club, a co-curricular campus organization supported by Loyola University Maryland's Office of Student Activities.

Eclectic and provocative, Apprentice House titles intend to entertain as well as spark dialogue on a variety of topics. Financial contributions to sustain the press's work are welcomed. Contributions are tax deductible to the fullest extent allowed by the IRS.

To learn more about Apprentice House books or to obtain submission guidelines, please visit www.apprenticehouse.com.

Apprentice House
Communication Department
Loyola University Maryland
4501 N. Charles Street
Baltimore, MD 21210
Ph: 410-617-5265 • Fax: 410-617-2198
info@apprenticehouse.com • www.apprenticehouse.com

"..."

"..."

"..."

"..."

The first time Jamie disappeared it to his ...

... days ago. It was the day of the court hearing, after ...

... me decided to appeal the judge's decision instead of an

... ewer. If it had been an ordinary day, Jamie would have come

home from school to the smells of dinner and the sound of

voices gossiping on the radio about people getting married, giv-

ing birth, dying of natural causes. She would have given him a

snack while he chattered about his day. Then he would have time

off to play with Tommy until dinner.

But it hadn't been an ordinary day. As soon as Jamie got

home, she and Wayne had ordered him into a room they had

... him that his parents ... he would him that ...

... home. His parents were ... to care for him but they

were better now and he would be going to stay with them for

a while. They emphasized that it wouldn't be for long, and that

they would come to get him and bring him back home as soon

as they could.

... rid of him ... refused to talk to Officer ...

... phone ... Jamie had disappeared in so

... it was impossible for anyone to reach him.

CPSIA information can be obtained
at www.ICGtesting.com
Printed in the USA
FFOW02n0732191015
17748FF